7/28/09

WITHDRAWN

the MORGUE and ME

JOHN C. FORD

VIKING

VIKING
Published by Penguin Group
Penguin Group (USA) Inc., 345 Hudson Street, New York, New York 10014, U.S.A.
Penguin Group (Canada), 90 Eglinton Avenue East, Suite 700, Toronto, Ontario, Canada M4P 2Y3
(a division of Pearson Penguin Canada Inc.)
Penguin Books Ltd, 80 Strand, London WC2R 0RL, England
Penguin Ireland, 25 St Stephen's Green, Dublin 2, Ireland (a division of Penguin Books Ltd)
Penguin Group (Australia), 250 Camberwell Road, Camberwell, Victoria 3124, Australia
(a division of Pearson Australia Group Pty Ltd)
Penguin Books India Pvt Ltd, 11 Community Centre, Panchsheel Park, New Delhi – 110 017, India
Penguin Group (NZ), 67 Apollo Drive, Rosedale, North Shore 0632, New Zealand
(a division of Pearson New Zealand Ltd)
Penguin Books (South Africa) (Pty) Ltd, 24 Sturdee Avenue, Rosebank, Johannesburg 2196, South Africa

Penguin Books Ltd, Registered Offices: 80 Strand, London WC2R 0RL, England

First published in the U.S.A. by Viking, a member of Penguin Group (USA) Inc., 2009

1 3 5 7 9 10 8 6 4 2

LIBRARY OF CONGRESS CATALOGING-IN-PUBLICATION DATA
Ford, John C. (John Christopher), 1971–
The morgue and me / by John C. Ford.
p. cm.
Summary: Eighteen-year-old Christopher, who plans to be a spy, learns of a murder
cover-up through his summer job as a morgue assistant and teams up with Tina,
a gorgeous newspaper reporter, to investigate, despite great danger.
ISBN 978-0-670-01096-7 (hardcover)
[1. Criminal investigation—Fiction. 2. Murder—Fiction. 3. Extortion—Fiction. 4. Journalists—Fiction.
5. Photography—Fiction. 6. Family life—Michigan—Fiction. 7. Michigan—Fiction.] I. Title.
PZ7.F75315Mor 2009
[Fic]—dc22
2009001956

Printed in U.S.A. • Set in Minion • Book design by Sam Kim

To Mom, Dad, and Joe

the MORGUE and ME

AUTHOR'S NOTE

Petoskey, Michigan, is an actual city in northern Michigan which bears almost no resemblance to the version portrayed in this book. Go see for yourself. You'll like it. And give my apologies to the medical examiner.

Prologue

When you're eighteen years old and you shoot somebody in a public place at two in the morning, of
course you expect some attention. Especially when it's the person I
shot, and especially when you're found right there on the scene with
that person at your feet, gasping away in a pool of blood that seeps
around your shoes. Still, I find it really embarrassing.

It's strange to be in the paper every single day. In the first story,
under the giant headline, they ran a blown-up version of my high-
school graduation photo. The cap looked ridiculous, not to mention
my blotchy face or the magenta robe, four sizes too big. Over the next
week, they used three different pictures of me in a parade of humiliating poses: fake smile, half-closed eyes, *in my pajamas.* I don't know
where they dug them up, but they must have run out, because yesterday they called the house and asked for more. My mom called them
"vultures" and hung up.

Reporters from the *Courier* have interviewed half the town about me. And it isn't just them—television vans from Grand Rapids and Detroit are sitting on the street outside, hoping to catch a glimpse of me. It's a waste of time for everybody; my parents have forbidden me to leave the house, and I'm in no mood to break that particular rule just now.

If you ever get famous (maybe I should say *notorious*) you'll notice something. People say things about you that are just plain lies. They pick up on something about you, and then they repeat it over and over until they think it explains all your actions. In my case, they say I'm a loner. In today's paper, this guy I barely know said, "Chris always kept 'way off to himself. He would sit alone in the cafeteria at lunch, reading books about astrology and stuff. It was pretty weird." First of all, it's *astronomy*. Second of all, having intellectual pursuits and eating by yourself doesn't make you some kind of terrorist, which is what the guy was saying.

When this happens to a group of people, it's called *stereotyping*. When it happens to an individual, it's called *in-depth reporting*.

My parents hired a psychiatrist for me. Our sessions take place on the back porch, over glasses of lemonade and my mom's oatmeal cookies. He says that I'm "disassociating" from my traumatic experience, which is why I talk about the shooting so lightly. My "levity problem," he calls it. I say my parents are paying that guy too much. Cops and soldiers use humor to get them through, and no psychiatrist beats them up about it. If I'm going to be a cop myself—actually, a spy—shouldn't I start adapting now?

Then again, maybe the shrink has a point. Maybe I'm a little screwed up right now.

My name is Christopher Newell. Classes start in a few weeks at Northwestern Michigan University. I'll be a freshman. Not to brag, but I was valedictorian of Petoskey High, and I won the Regents Scholarship—and no matter what anybody is saying, I intend to start college on time.

Some crazy things happened in Petoskey this summer, things that some people wouldn't believe. I guess that makes sense; I have a way of getting caught up in my own fantasies. But everything that happened to me was real—and I won't apologize for anything I did about it.

PART I

THE MORGUE
AND ME

or

PORTRAIT OF A CORPSE

1

It was the job at the morgue that started this whole thing.

It wasn't my top choice, mind you. I had planned to work in the NWMU astronomy department over the summer. My parents are both professors at the university, and I figured they could pull the appropriate strings. That was the idea back in May, anyway, before I got arrested during an unauthorized visit to the university's new $75 million planetarium.

It happened on a Saturday. Prom night, to be exact. I didn't go. I couldn't see myself dressing up in a tux and going to parties with people I didn't know very well and acting like a clod on the dance floor all night, just because you're supposed to. It's not that I'm anti-social, exactly. I'm just more the observing type, and stars are my favorite thing to observe, so I decided to check out the planetarium.

What else was I going to do—sit in my room thinking about Julia Spencer all night?

They hadn't quite finished construction on the planetarium, so they didn't have the alarm all geared up yet. I had just seen this Bruce Willis flick where he did a trick with his credit card to pry open the lock on a bad guy's apartment door. I couldn't believe it when it worked on the south entrance. The whole thing was a bust, though— they had me in plastic handcuffs within about five minutes.

The campus security officer said he didn't care how many moons of Jupiter were visible, it was still breaking and entering. He loaded me in the back of his car and carted me off to the campus police station, where I had a very unpleasant chat with the sheriff before my parents used their pull to get the charges dropped. Still, I wasn't going to be getting any job offers from the astronomy department.

My mom cried a little bit over the planetarium affair. She taught in the biology department and told me she could arrange an internship there. Her tone suggested that I should be very thankful and accept immediately. My dad said they always could use researchers in classics, too.

Around that time, though, the *Courier* ran a classified ad for a job at the morgue. It went like this:

MEDICAL EXAMINER seeks janitorial help.
Min. Qual. Flex. Sched. $8.50/hr. 15 hrs/week.

Naturally I hopped right on it.

"Naturally," I say, because my life's goal is to become a spy, or at least a spyish-type figure. Based on my preliminary research (namely, rentals from the "Cloak and Dagger" section of University Video),

I'm thinking seriously about the National Security Agency. Working at the morgue might teach me something about forensic pathology that could come in handy later, I figured. It's not like I had better alternatives; they don't train you in fingerprinting at the knickknack shops in town.

"Oh my Lord," is what my mom said when I told her that I was going to call about the job. She was making vegetarian lasagna at the time.

We were in the kitchen, where my dad was reading Chaucer. He lowered his book. "That's positively macabre," he said. That's how he talks. "Sometimes I think you would have enjoyed living in the Middle Ages."

My mom peered at the advertisement. "It's just fifteen hours a week."

"I don't need that much money," I said.

It was true, too. I had already won my full-ride scholarship to NWMU. It came with a housing allowance, which was like free money since I had decided to live at home. A part-time job was perfect—it'd leave me plenty of time to practice photography.

I put together a slapdash résumé that filled just under half a page, including a line for interests ("Astronomy, Comic Books of the 1940s, Edgar Allan Poe, Photography") and faxed it over. To my surprise, they called me in for an interview the very next day.

The morgue isn't far from our house; nothing in Petoskey is. The sign on Route 14 says, WELCOME TO PETOSKEY: WHERE NATURE SMILES FOR SEVEN MILES, but every single word of that sign is a lie. For one thing,

Petoskey is six miles long at best. It sits on Lake Michigan—the West Arm Bay, to be precise—an hour's drive from the Upper Peninsula and, if you care to go farther, Canada. Tourists come up in the summer, when you could say that Nature winks at Petoskey. For the other nine months, it blows a harsh wind off the lake that freezes nose hairs and stunts tree growth. And snows in heaping portions.

The morgue sits in the basement of Petoskey General Hospital, a beige building that looks like the world's most unimaginative sand castle. My boss there, aka Dr. Nathan Mobley, aka the medical examiner for Emmet County, was a piece of work. He had pale, blemished skin—imagine a thin layer of cottage cheese and you won't be far off—and bulky shoulders that did a kind of roly-poly thing when he tottered around on his black cane. Basically, he was like an old, abandoned home creaking on its hinges.

I had my five-minute interview with Dr. Mobley in his office, where he sat behind a wooden desk about the size of the *Titanic*. Everything in the office seemed to be at least a hundred years old, including Dr. Mobley's faded gray suit and the sorry-looking briefcase at the side of his desk. He wheezed into his handkerchief and perused my résumé with narrowed eyes. The whites of them were yellowish, like his hair and his skin and his fingernails. We didn't have much of a Q-and-A session. He just asked me if I wanted the job ("yes, sir") and then grumbled about his office being a public trust and its importance to civilized society, or something along those lines.

After that he led me on a tour of the autopsy room. It had a tile floor with a black drain in the middle—for bodily fluids, I supposed—

and was trimmed with low-tech silver gadgetry. As Mobley explained it, my job was simple. I cleaned the dull green tiles and the grout between them. I cleaned the stainless-steel table bolted to the floor, the collection of different-sized bowls, the outsides of the body coolers. I cleaned the large, square windows that looked out onto the hallway and into Dr. Mobley's office. I cleaned the scale they used to weigh organs, and a bunch of other instruments, including the pair of pruning shears that had been made for hedges but apparently played some useful role in opening a cadaver.

When the tour ended, Dr. Mobley took me back to his office and explained the filing system. "The chores shouldn't take that long. Do them three times a week, I don't care when. If I need you for something particular, I'll call you in."

With that, he sat down again and fixated on a stack of documents lying on his desk. I sensed a conclusion to the interview.

"Look forward to working with you," I said.

I wasn't really looking forward to that; actually, I'd already decided to try to limit my contact with Dr. Mobley. It was quite easy to do, since he rarely came to work—at least, to his office in the basement. He also worked as a pediatrician on the second floor, but I tried not to think about Dr. Mobley tending to small children.

Another doctor—Dr. Sutter—kept a set of keys to the morgue. He was the one who let me in when I showed up. It may have been his only actual responsibility. Dr. Sutter had to be eighty years old, and as far as I could tell he spend most of his day doodling on a yellow pad.

"Ah, young Christopher!" he said with his customary good cheer when I showed up one Saturday in the middle of June. "Can't let you down there today, they're busy. Doc Mobley says come back tomorrow if you can. If not, just come around next week."

On the one hand, with Dr. Mobley down there, I was more than happy to leave. But the way that Dr. Sutter said he was "busy" got me thinking that there might be an autopsy going on, which I couldn't miss.

I nodded, told Dr. Sutter good-bye, and then headed straight down to the morgue.

Don't get me wrong. I'm no freak. Like I said, I had a vocational interest in seeing an autopsy. Plus, I was five weeks into the job and hadn't seen as much as a kidney stone—it was hard not to be a little jazzed.

The door leading to the morgue has frosted glass on top that says MEDICAL EXAMINER in black letters. Normally it's dark, but a yellow light was glowing against the window. It was cold in the basement, and the doorknob chilled my hand. Muffled sounds came from inside. A symphony of nerves started playing along my spine.

Act casual, I told myself. *You're just coming over to do your job. Whistle if you need to.* I waited for my breath to slow and turned the knob.

Dr. Mobley and a police officer stood in the autopsy room with their backs to me, looming over a body laid out on the stainless-steel table. A body bag lay on the floor, crumpled and looking like it might blow away any minute. I stood in the hallway, unnoticed, watching through the glass partition.

I couldn't see Mitch Blaylock very well. I didn't know his name then, of course. He was just the unlucky guy who phoned in dead that morning and whose body had ended up in the Office of the Medical Examiner of Emmet County.

The policeman, though—I recognized him right away. The broad back, the cropped red hair, the cocky way he had his hands on his hips. Sheriff Harmon. I hadn't seen him since the planetarium incident.

Dr. Mobley maneuvered a swinging lamp over the body; it threw a gruesome sheen on the man's waxy skin. I was rooted in place, absorbed by the sight and trying to calm my stomach, when Dr. Mobley looked my way. He clutched his handkerchief to his mouth and uttered something. The sheriff took the cue. He strode out into the hallway and closed the door behind him.

He had heavy cheeks with dark eyes pressed into them like chocolate chips lost in cookie dough. A smell of sweat, greasy food, and pure animal aggression radiated off the sheriff's uniform. He eyeballed me and grunted.

"Doc says you should go on home," he said.

Part of me wanted to run, but I was too curious to go away that easy.

"I left something in the office last week," I said. "I'll just grab it and go."

"Make it quick," he said, and I felt his eyes linger on me as I walked down the hall.

When I got to the office and looked back in through the window, the sheriff had returned to Dr. Mobley's side, their attention fixed on the body. The doctor pointed to something on the dead man's chest. The sheriff was blocking my view, but I had lost my enthusiasm for the project. What was I going to see, really? It wasn't like they had his chest cracked open or anything good like that.

Just get going before they kick you out.

I figured I'd just bang around the desk a little, pretend to do a search, and then scamper out. I lifted a few papers off the desk and then opened the top drawer with the pens and scissors and Dr. Mobley's nasal spray. The desk had large drawers on the sides, which I knew that Dr. Mobley never used.

I pulled one open, all ready to shut it again, when a glinting light caught my eye. It came from the clasp on Dr. Mobley's briefcase, which wobbled inside the drawer when I pulled it out. The briefcase shouldn't have been there—Dr. Mobley always kept it at the side of his desk, out in the open. It had been in that spot every time I came in, a little eyesore of cracked brown leather with Mobley's initials branded into the side: NHM.

It was a doctor's bag, the kind that pries open at the top. The clasp on the briefcase wasn't sealed, and the mouth of it was open wide enough for me to see an envelope lying at the bottom.

I checked the window. Dr. Mobley and Sheriff Harmon talked casually across the dead body. Quickly, I knelt down out of view.

The dull sounds of their conversation drifted in as I considered the envelope. Why would he hide his briefcase in the drawer? And what was that rectangular shape inside the envelope? The air in the office turned hot and close.

The sheriff is going to check on you in a minute. Get this over with.

The envelope crinkled against my fingers when I pulled it out. The flap, unsealed, pulled away easily. The mass inside was a few inches thick.

There were three stacks of bills bound in coarse brown paper bands.

They were hundreds.

2

I counted the first stack as fast as I could, kneeling out of view, wetting my thumb four times before making it through the fifty bills. That was $5,000. The other stacks were the same size—another $10,000.

Fifteen thousand dollars in cash.

It was the kind of money you don't see unless it's written on an oversized check, with maybe some showgirls standing in the wings. But it was right there. In my hands. Something about this was wrong, but I had no time to wrap my mind around it because footsteps were coming down the hall.

I stuffed the cash back in the envelope, pitched it into the bag, and shut the drawer. Sweat broke across my forehead as I dove over to the sofa, where I had just lifted a cushion and assumed a puzzled face when the sheriff strode into the office.

"What'd you lose—loose change?"

"Ha! No, my library card." I threw the cushion back and lifted the next one. "Thought it might have slipped under the cushions when I was filing the other day."

"Come back later, when the doctor isn't so busy."

My heart jackhammered against my ribs as the sheriff's tiny dark eyes bored into me. They looked disturbed, like I was a joke he wasn't getting. "Oh sure," I said. "Sure. It's probably in my bedroom or some—"

"You're the Newell kid," the sheriff said suddenly. His head leaned and his eyes burned hot with memory. The memory of me, the kid with the professor parents who got off the hook that night at the planetarium.

"Uh, yeah. I guess you remember we've actually met. Under slightly less pleasant circumstances. Not that an autopsy is a pleasant—"

"Just come back later."

"Righto," I said, and took off.

I drove home in a haze. Past the cutesy stores on Taylor Road, the library, the freaky cemetery at Hart Square with weathered tombstones slanting from the ground like an old man's teeth. I didn't register any of it until I reached the end of our driveway and returned from the fog.

I looked up and cringed.

On our front porch, my father posed in an awkward stance: shirtless, eyes closed, thin arms spread-eagled. His bony legs quivered as he tilted himself into a human Leaning Tower of Pisa. Daniel, my precocious oddball of a ten-year-old brother, sat cross-legged on a wool blanket with his hands on his knees. Music floated from Daniel's stereo, playing a tune that might have been called "Triumph of the Miniature Wind Instruments."

This disturbing activity had been going on for a month or two. My dad and Daniel called it "Yoga Night."

I checked up and down Admiral Street for witnesses, but thankfully it was empty.

"Dancer's Pose," Daniel called with crisp, Buddha-like command.

My dad launched into a complicated reorganization of his body parts. The pose should have been called Irregular Pretzel. "How was work?" he said with faltering breath.

"Fine." This wasn't the time to bring up the money—not on the street, in the middle of Dancer's Pose.

My dad got himself balanced. Daniel returned his hands to his knees. Their serenity unnerved me.

We ate on the screened back porch, where Daniel set the table every night with an absurd, military precision. He's quite a nefarious character, but my parents have no idea because he does such a good job of playing the perfect child. He sat ramrod straight, looking at pictures on my camera with his usual frown.

It's a nice camera, a Nikon D50 SLR, which Daniel likes to swipe from my bedroom so he can flip through the pictures on the back screen, criticizing my technique. Lately I've been trying to take artistic shots of Lake Michigan at night. Sounds easy, but it's not. Daniel shook his head, thoroughly disappointed. His antics would have bothered me more just then if I wasn't busy trying to figure out why

Dr. Mobley would have $15,000 cash lying around his office. I hadn't come up with anything yet, except the notion that I should probably tell my parents about it.

I'd have to minimize the snooping-into-Dr.-Mobley's-things element, although that did play a sizable role. My mom passed around some bok choy while I considered how to finesse the issue.

"More gloom and doom," Daniel said, displaying the screen to my parents, who hummed their agreement.

"They're a work in progress," I said.

My mom took the camera from Daniel and stuck it on a side table, next to a brochure about Coeur d'Alene, Idaho, where she and my dad were going on vacation. They were leaving Daniel and me alone, together, for the first time.

"Why don't you ever take a picture during the day?" Daniel said.

"I like night scenes."

Daniel took a dainty sip of milk. "Yeah, and I like to be able to tell what I'm looking at."

"Now, Christopher," my mom interjected, "your father is going to talk to you this evening about what you'll have to do while we're gone. Right, dear?"

"Sure, we'll talk it over. He can handle it." My dad shot Daniel a smile. "What I want to know is, who's going to look after whom?"

"I'm looking after myself," Daniel said, happily forking a green bean into his face. "I don't know about him." My parents broke into distressingly hearty guffaws at that, until finally it died down and my dad asked me again about my day at the morgue.

"Yeah, well—"

"Do we have to talk about dead people while we're eating?" Daniel said.

"Actually, they did have a body in there today."

Daniel shivered. "Gross. Did you touch it?"

"Oh!" my mom said before I could get back on track. "Before I forget. You'll never guess who won the Regents Scholarship this year."

She was looking at me in a meaningful way, and I knew precisely the meaning behind that look.

"Julia Spencer," I said.

"How did you know? Have you two been in touch? Do you see her?"

My blood rose with each of her breathless questions.

"No, we don't talk, Mom. And we won't be in touch the next time you ask, either."

"That's a depressing thing to say," my dad said.

"He works with corpses," Daniel reminded the table.

"Well," my mom said, "I thought you might be interested or, God forbid, happy for Julia doing so well. And the two of you, winning the same scholarship . . ." She trailed off in sorrow over my obtuseness.

The Spencers used to live next door to us. Julia is one grade below me, and we were friends until my junior year. And then, abruptly, we weren't. My mom had no idea what had happened between us, which is why she still brought Julia up all the time.

"What?" she said, when she caught me rolling my eyes.

My dad reached an arm across to her. "Dear, the referenda on Miss Spencer . . ."

"Couldn't have said it better myself, Dad."

My mom placed her napkin on her lap. "It wasn't anything like that. It's just that, well, at the very least you're going to have to see her at the scholarship ceremony. After that, I won't mention her name in your presence, if that's what you want."

She sighed and focused on her beets.

I couldn't concentrate on anything for the rest of dinner— anything, that is, besides how it had felt to walk away from Julia's locker a year and a half ago. I'd thought about that a lot. I'd constructed a vivid memory full of colors (the green Homecoming banner), sounds ("Christopher, please . . ."), and smells (kiwi lip gloss), but it happened so long ago I couldn't say how much of it was real anymore.

The sting was real, I knew that much.

I felt it all over again and never managed to bring up Dr. Mobley.

The next day, the *Courier* ran the story on the bottom half of page A7, between the Word Jumble and an advertisement for Dirty Dan's Landscaping and Snow Removal. I don't normally read past the front page, but I wanted to see if the morgue's latest guest had made the paper. He had, but it wasn't much of a story:

LOCAL MAN EXPIRES IN MOTEL
Art Bradford, Senior Reporter

Mitchell Blaylock, 26, was found dead yesterday morning at approximately 2:30 a.m. in the Lighthouse Motel on Route 14.

Blaylock attended Petoskey High School, where he played safety for the 2001 Falcon football team.

He later spent three years with the Oscoda Cadets of
the semi-professional Erie League.

Sheriff Dale Harmon reported that the cause of
death is unknown.

At least I knew the guy's name, Mitchell Blaylock.

I tore the article from the paper and called my best friend, Mike
Maske.

Mike lives in a wooded area at the edge of town, in a house that's
basically a glass rectangle and gets photographed for design maga-
zines about every other week. His parents are rich, hot tempered,
and about to get divorced. On the rare occasion they're home, Mike's
usually eager to escape. He bounded out as soon as I pulled up
behind his mom's silver Porsche Boxster.

He was wearing his customary summer garb: Tevas, long-sleeved
T-shirt, and a pair of glimmering basketball shorts. His aviator sunglasses reflected the sun as he drank from a cup with pink sludge in
it. His latest concoction.

"Calling it Strawberry Fields," Mike said as he folded his lanky
body into the passenger seat. "Wanna taste?"

I declined. Mike's been on a smoothie kick lately. He wants to start
a chain of smoothie stores with drinks named after popular songs.
It's about the hundredth business idea he's had since we bonded over
his plan to sell digital baseball cards on the Internet back in sixth
grade. I thought for sure he'd be Forbes's Businessman of the Year,
but the only scheme he's followed through on is becoming a small-
time bookie for college students at NWMU, which, according to
Mike, he does pretty well at.

Anyway, I figured Mike had learned a thing or two about keeping cash from watchful eyes, so I was eager to get his take on Dr. Mobley's hidden stash.

I gave him the basics as we drove toward the harbor. They have food stands and pleasure boats down by the docks there. If you're lucky, maybe a few girls in bikinis. It's sort of our default destination, but I had something else in mind.

Mike had his head back and his knees up on the dash—more interested, it seemed, in savoring the subtle flavors of Strawberry Fields than Dr. Mobley's $15,000. I had to prod him when I finished: "So, c'mon, what do you think?"

"I guess it's weird," Mike said lazily, "but I don't know."

"Help me think. Why would anybody carry around so much money? Maybe you'd take a big wad of cash to an auction?"

"An auction? For what? Farm equipment?" Mike shook his head, downed his drink, and tossed the cup into the backseat (which, to be fair, has a kitchen-sink aura of untidiness). "The guy had a bunch of cash; we'll never know why. Mysteries of the universe, man, they're all around us. Go with it."

It was time to pull out my big gun—the theory I'd hit on that morning. "All right, listen to this. He's not just the medical examiner, he's a pediatrician, too. I think he's selling Ritalin or something. Maybe Xanax. Illegal prescriptions, you know. It's big business."

"I could see that," Mike said. "A fine conspiracy theory you've got there. Now drive on, Jeeves." He tilted his seat back, catching rays, his hair floating in the wind.

I should have expected as much. Mike thought I read too many spy novels. Last year, he said more girls would be into me if I "got out of my head" every once in a while. I asked him if he got his psychological insights from dating shows. *No*, he'd said, *Julia Spencer*. It's the only time I've ever wanted to punch him.

Mike had fallen half-asleep by the time I parked the car. We were across the street from the hospital parking lot. The dashboard clock said 11:55—about the time that Dr. Mobley left work on Mondays.

Mike's head swiveled in confusion as he put his seat upright.

"Uhhhh, what the hell are we doing here?"

"We're going to tail him."

3

Dr. Mobley didn't leave until 12:20.

It was just a theory, but I figured that if we followed him around for a bit, we might find something out about his (hypothetical) secret life that somehow involved carrying large amounts of cash. I have to give Mike credit—he was being pretty cool about going along with my plan.

"Hallelujah," he said when Dr. Mobley's rusted red Buick finally turned out of the exit. I pulled onto Mercury Drive, a few hundred yards in back of Dr. Mobley's beater.

A mile down, Dr. Mobley turned in to a strip mall and headed for Dino's, a pricey restaurant where parents take their NWMU-student kids when they come up to visit.

I found a spot in the back of the lot. "Slink down," I told Mike, but we didn't need to bother—Dr. Mobley was oblivious. He took forever to dock his boat in a handicapped spot, and then another half hour to teeter inside. He almost lost his balance on the way; he had to steady himself on a motorcycle parked near the entrance.

It was a red racing-style motorcycle, and for a second I thought Dr. Mobley and the bike were going to topple over together. Finally, he made it up the steps, and the restaurant door closed behind him.

Within two minutes Mike was shifting about in his seat. He was like the rookie cop in a bad stakeout flick. That would make me the wizened professional investigator—the one who always explains to the young buck that police work isn't as glamorous as they make out in the academy. I'd hand him a coffee, maybe some pistachios, and tell him to settle in for a long night. The steam from my cup would shroud my face as I kept watch, brooding on my marriage that'd been wrenched apart by long hours on the job. My marriage to a girl named Julia—

"Dude, it's going to take that guy all day to eat," Mike said. "I mean, this is a blast and everything, but . . . oh no."

His eyes had snagged on something in front of a clothing store. An athletic girl held blue shopping bags in her hands like barbells, scowling into the sun. Her thick blonde hair swished as she scanned for her car . . . and found us instead.

"Ohhh no," I said.

Dana Ruby. The mayor's daughter and, more importantly, Mike's on-and-off girlfriend. Mike takes most of life in stride, but the two of them made a volatile mix. A lot of people at Petoskey High claimed to hate her, but they would've died to be friends with her. It was something about her ego—magnetic, repulsive, and roughly the size of Lake Michigan.

She was prancing toward us like a runway model: high knees and wounded lips and "dare me" eyes. She had the looks to pull it off.

"So, uhhh, there's something I didn't tell you," Mike said.

"You're back together?"

By then she was almost to the Escort, spreading her bag-laden hands in a *wtf?* kind of way. She leaned inside the car and gave Mike a Euro-peck.

"Hey, Newell." She was the only one in the world who called me by my last name. "So, what might you boys be doing? There's something kinda pervy about two guys just sitting in a car together in the middle of the day, you know. Just FYI."

I thought we were going to have to explain ourselves, but then her face brightened with a thought. "Hey, did you tell him about my party? Newell, you're totally invited."

"Umm, no, not yet," Mike said, and she slapped the side of his head. It was playful, but it brought back a memory. I had watched her play volleyball once, and when she spiked the ball, there was something scary about it. I remember thinking: *anger issues.*

Mike glanced at me. "Yeah, he'll come."

"Righto. I'm there." I'm not the biggest fan of parties, but Mike is unusually vulnerable when it comes to all Dana-related matters, so I couldn't let him down.

"So let's do something," Dana said. "Unless this parking lot is more exciting."

It was just the excuse Mike needed. He was halfway out of the car before she even finished. "Sorry, dude, but I'm gone."

"No problem."

"Come with, Newell," Dana said, but I made some grumblings about needing to put some hours in at work, which was actually true.

They said good-bye and drove away in Dana's Jetta, with the Top 40 station blasting into the wind. After that, it felt pretty ridiculous to just sit there alone.

Things at the morgue were back to normal. With Dr. Mobley at lunch I could have searched the whole place, but there was nothing to look through other than his trench coat (pockets empty) and an old pair of winter boots (also empty). The brown briefcase was gone. The desk had no new infusions of cash. Dr. Mobley had left some documents for filing, but that was about it.

The only item I noticed was in the top drawer—an empty plastic case for a Vista View digital photo memory card. I could hardly imagine Dr. Mobley using a digital camera, but it made sense that he would buy the cheapest brand. I tried a Vista View card once, and my pictures reeked.

I had planned to save the best part of the day—taking another look at the dead guy—for last. Work first and all that. But my curiosity got the best of me and I headed to the autopsy room.

I had no idea how long a dead body stayed at the morgue, but Mitchell Blaylock had come in just yesterday. I tried the body coolers one by one. The first two were locked, but the third one opened at my pull. The drawer glided open until the whole body, covered in a white sheet, slid out into the stark light and bumped to a stop.

I covered my nose against the sweetish smell coming off him. The sheet ended at the ankles, where a pair of bony feet stuck out. He had a tag on his toe—it looked like a luggage claim—with his name written in green ink: *Mitchell A. Blaylock, No. 09-341.*

Squiggles of shiny black hair peeked out from the top of the sheet. The guy had been dead for more than a day and still could have starred in a Pantene ad. I grabbed the edge of the sheet and thought for a good three seconds about whether I was being disrespectful. With a breath, I drew it away from his face.

There's no way around it: Mitch Blaylock was an ugly guy. His nose was too long and his eyes were set too far apart and he had wispy little eyelashes. A scar ran through his lip. Worry lines spiked his forehead and a smudged blue tattoo colored his chest. He had puffy muscles in his upper body, the kind you get doing construction instead of at the gym.

His body told a story I would never know. It made me slightly sad, and then disgusted with myself for disturbing his peace. I returned the sheet over him and slid him back, dazed and eager to get done with my work.

I filed Dr. Mobley's papers: correspondence with the medical examiner in Washtenaw County, copies of a budget proposal, and some reports from the state. At the bottom was a death certificate for Mitchell Blaylock. Original death certificates got filed with the county, a copy went to Lansing. We held our own copy in the office, and after a while it would be sent to storage somewhere and then forgotten about, like the bodies themselves.

The certificate, one page long, had even less information than the *Courier* article—just his name, dates of birth and death, not much more. The surprising item was typed at the bottom, not far above Dr. Mobley's narrow, chicken-scratched signature. This is what it said:

"Cause of death: Deceased shot self."

I turned right around, returned to the autopsy room, and pulled Mitch out again.

"Me again," I said apologetically as I checked for evidence of the suicide. He hadn't shot himself in the mouth, or the temple. Or anywhere else I could see. I held my breath and nudged his head just a little, to check the back. Nothing there.

Consumed with a morbid curiosity, I pulled the sheet down to his knees. For a minute, I had trouble processing what I saw.

The five bullet wounds made a raggedy circle on his torso. They were tidy and small—polite looking, you could say. I counted the five entry points again. One of the bullets had probably entered his heart. One of them, perhaps, his liver. My stomach revolved on itself.

There was a conspiracy after all, and I had just found it.

4

This called for the police.

Dr. Mobley was covering up a murder. I mean, it was obvious. A guy can't shoot himself five times in the chest. Think about it.

I *would* have gone to the police, too, but then I realized I couldn't.

Sheriff Harmon—he'd been there the whole time. He had stood right there in the autopsy room, right next to Dr. Mobley, looking at Mitch Blaylock's body. He had chased me out of the morgue. Whatever had happened to Mitch Blaylock, the sheriff was deeply involved.

For all I knew, he was the one who paid off Dr. Mobley to rule Mitch's death a suicide. For all I knew, Sheriff Harmon had put those bullets in Mitch's midsection.

I don't know what other people would do when faced with this situation, but my natural instinct was to take a bunch of pictures.

If the "Cop Dramas" section of University Video has taught me nothing else, it's that a murdered body is technically a crime scene, and you have to preserve any evidence of it that you can. Failure to respect this principle usually gets you yelled at by a grizzled detective with an alcohol problem and/or an acne-riddled forensic technician eating Chinese food over a Petri dish, so you're wise to obey. Anyway, they'd be putting Mitch in the ground any day now, and those bullet wounds might be the only proof of his murder.

Lucky for Mitch, I had my camera in the car. Nobody in the hospital batted an eye when I scurried out to the Escort and returned moments later, hiding my Nikon under my shirt as best I could. I went with the portrait setting and fired off forty pictures of Mitch's body (this was no time to be skimping), trying to capture the evidence just right. I drew the sheet over him and pushed him back into place, my heart still ticking with the fear of being caught and the strange, illicit thrill of uncovering a major crime.

Back in the Escort, I was too keyed up to think. I headed out onto Mercury Drive with no destination in mind.

There *was* one policeman I could have gone to—a guy I could trust. Tim Spencer. He graduated Petoskey High four years ahead of me, when the Spencers still lived next door to us. He had once been a towering figure in my life, back when I was seven and he taught me how to throw a curve with a Wiffle ball. A few years later he starred as running back for the Petoskey Falcons; he ran for 2,000 yards and scored 24 touchdowns the year they won the Class D state championship. I went to every game just to watch Tim. But he was Julia's brother, and we hadn't talked since things went sour. Something in me seized up at the thought of approaching him now.

The article that I had torn from the paper that morning swirled around the dashboard, blown by the wind. I trapped it with my hand, pulled to the side of the road, and read it again. The name of the reporter was Art Bradford.

I was in no mood to go home just yet, and it was barely past noon. Maybe Art Bradford could shed some light on the subject. Maybe Art and I would become crime-fighters together.

I pulled a U-turn on Mercury and headed to the *Courier*. Where things would lead after that, I didn't know. Maybe Art and I would buy capes.

5

The newsroom of the *Petoskey Courier* reeked of microwave popcorn.

Newspaper minions were marching documents back and forth to the beat of ringing phones and a stereo set on Petoskey's Lite Rock 95. The room had a big wooden table, perfect for heated editorial meetings on the affairs of the day, and a patchwork of flimsy cubicles behind it. Maybe a quarter of the cubicles had bodies in them. Most of those were male, thin of hair, dressed in business shirts rolled to the elbow. Many of them had phones to their ears.

Nobody noticed me, which I took as an invitation to nose around. Halfway through my self-guided tour I found a nameplate on one of the perimeter offices: "Art Bradford, Senior Reporter."

Unfortunately, the office was empty. It didn't look like Art was in crime-fighting shape, to judge from the seaside photo of himself and a woman occupying the better part of their mammoth beach towels.

I took a pen from his WORLD'S BEST FISHERMAN mug and jotted a note on his pink memo pad:

> Dear Mr. Bradford,
>   Please call me whenever convenient. This regards your story from June 14 about Mitchell Blaylock.
>   Sincerely,
>   Christopher Newell
>   (231) 555-9713

I placed the note near his computer. Art had furnished his office with a clock radio playing nature sounds ("Brazilian Rains," according to the display), which blocked out the busy atmosphere quite nicely. I was just standing there, soaking up the smooth vibe in Art's island of calm when I met her for the first time.

"Screw you, Art!"

I spun toward the voice, coming at me from just outside the office.

"Screw! You!"

She held a page with lots of red ink on it in her hand. She was wagging it in my general direction as she burst in. "Whoops, sorry," she said, looking me up and down with a not-actually-that-apologetic look on her face. "You from China Palace?"

"Uhhh . . . China Palace?"

"I'm seriously going to murder someone if my egg rolls don't get here soon. Seriously."

"Egg rolls?"

I was having trouble forming thoughts.

She had damaged hair and fishnet hose. Her fingernails had chipped blue paint on them, chewed down to nothing. She wore a leather bracelet with spiky things on it, and it wouldn't have surprised me to learn she'd just come from a bar fight. And still . . . she was insanely hot.

I can't really explain it. Torn jeans can look better than new ones, and scars can be sexy—that's about the best I can do.

There wasn't much room in the office; we were standing a foot apart. I tried to clear out of the way and whacked my knee against the chair, hitting a funny bone in my leg that I didn't realize existed until that moment. The chair wobbled as I clutched my knee, and by that time she was full-on cackling at me.

I stood up and blood rushed to my head, making me woozy.

"Got you good, eh?" she said.

"Uh, yeah. Thanks." I have no idea why I thanked her.

She removed a sparkly purple pen from behind her ear and started toying with it in her hands. I got the impression that I was amusing her, the way a helpless victim amuses a villain in a James Bond movie. In a second she would laugh darkly and pull a lever, and the floor would open beneath me to a pool of man-eating sharks.

"So, who are you?" she said.

"Umm, I was just looking for Art Bradford."

"Makes two of us." She waved the red-marked page again. "Guess

I can't help you. Sorry about the knee." Then she shrugged and wandered away, and suddenly the office felt horribly empty.

I scurried out with my head down, feeling a need to escape quickly and without further incident. I heard something on my way out to the parking lot—the voice of the insanely hot woman, yelling "Hey!"—but I figured she wasn't calling for me, and even if she was, it would only lead to more embarrassment.

The Escort was hot from sitting in the sun. I bathed in the sauna conditions with my head against the steering wheel, picturing her face, trying to think of suave lines I might have said to hold her attention. I couldn't come up with anything.

"Hold still," my mom said, adjusting my tie.

Daniel and my dad had been waiting in the car for ten minutes. My mom was wearing a dress and pearls, one of her few nice outfits. I could never get used to seeing her in them. She taught, and did most everything else, in denim and flannel. Now she smelled of perfume and wore lipstick that looked bright and awkward on her face. Beads of sweat had broken out on her brow as she worked my collar; she always got unduly nervous for formal events.

Satisfied with the knot, she patted my chest and said, "There, let's go."

We headed for the east side of town, where Mayor Julian Ruby Jr. lived. He hosted the annual ceremony at which the NWMU Regents bestowed their scholarship upon its lucky recipient. Those Regents are pretty crafty—they give it to you before your senior year, so that you'll get lazy and won't even bother applying to other schools. It worked on me last year. The Regents encouraged previous winners to attend the ceremony, and as much as I wanted to disappoint them, my parents would hardly let that happen. I stared out at the A-frame houses and a swath of unpurchased vacation properties on the ride over, preoccupied with thoughts of Mitch Blaylock. In the background, Daniel was expounding some kind of theory about Euclidian math for my parents' evaluation and comment. The time for telling them about the money and the body already seemed long past.

The Rubys' front lawn rose elegantly up to their fieldstone house, which loomed high over the street. Behind it, white tents sprang up from a lush backyard greener than a traffic light. Chemicals, no doubt.

The mayor was handing out programs by double doors as thick as unabridged dictionaries. His glasses sat high on his chipmunk cheeks, shining with fake cheer.

"Aha, the Newell family," he said as if we were all old chums. "Place cards are in the living room. Enjoy a drink before we head outside."

He was so stiff and nerdy, the polar opposite of Dana. She used to complain about him in school, telling Mike and anyone else who'd listen about the fights they got into over money, her curfew, whatever. In Dana's stories, the mayor always came off as strict and vaguely jealous of the fabulous life that Dana was destined to have after getting out from under his thumb. It struck me as mean back then, but I shouldn't have judged her; five seconds of the guy was more than I could take.

I followed in my parents' wake to a sunken living room cleared of furniture. A wagon-wheel lighting fixture illuminated the assembled mix of town and gown, which was pimpled with University Regents in red jackets with crests on the pocket.

A photographer from the *Courier* stood in the middle of it all. He was shooting pictures for the society page with a Canon EOS 30D that made me envious of him, beer gut and all. I considered asking if he knew anything about Mitch Blaylock but discarded the thought when I saw the indiscreet way in which he ate a miniature spinach turnover.

Daniel dragged me over to the table with the place cards, where a Regent with red Brillo-pad hair was chatting up a blonde who qualified as glamorous by Petoskey standards. She held an empty cup in her hand, her eyes wandering about for a drink tray as she lolled at the Regent's side.

My dad broke off from a collection of professors at the fireplace to give me a clap on the back. "Christopher, get your mother and me a glass of red wine, would you?"

"Sure."

Daniel proudly presented him with our place cards and followed me, wide-eyed and hip level to the crowd, to the bar. "Two red wines, please," I told the bartender.

He poured them and handed me two plastic wineglasses. "For your folks, right?"

"No. The little guy."

Daniel beamed at the bartender. "And two fingers of Cuervo, please."

The bartender laughed and told Daniel to scram. Just then the blonde woman sidled up beside him. Her hair fell in a lustrous curtain to her shoulders. She winked at the bartender as she poured a drink for herself. "I'm doing your work for you," she said.

He leered back at her. "Guess I owe you a tip, then."

From across the room, the mayor gave them a cold stare.

"Let's go," Daniel said. He led us back through the chattering crowd where, at points, I had to turn my shoulders to get through.

Halfway across the room, a finger tapped at my shoulder.

"Hey, I was hoping to see you here." The guest of honor, Julia Spencer.

Bright, sparkling eyes. Chipper as ever. Like nothing had ever happened between us.

I went numb for a second. The only thing I felt was a warm buzzing across my skin, the faint residue of humiliation.

Julia was wearing a turquoise dress, with her nails done in immaculate pink polish. Her hands played at a drawstring around her waist, while her extra-white teeth glistened in the light. The fact that I hadn't yet managed a response, I could see from her frozen smile, was getting weirder and weirder by the second.

Daniel tugged at my pant leg. From across the room, my mom gave me a tender look. The nervous energy built until I resigned myself to the fact that this conversation was actually going to happen. I entrusted the glasses to Daniel.

"Later, Lothario," he said, and took off.

Julia eyed me cautiously.

"So, congratulations on the scholarship and all," I said finally.

She dipped her head. "Oh, thanks. This is weird, huh? All these people."

"You get used to the fame after a while."

She paused for a second, then laughed nervously. "Still funny, I see."

She played at her belt some more, a twitchy smile flashing on her lips. The jostling crowd forced us uncomfortably close.

A Regent bumped into Julia and she turned a little pirouette. "Ugh. This is annoying. Come on." She grabbed my hand and pulled me through the milling bodies toward the front of the house.

People at school thought she was just vanilla—a good girl so shy she blended into the wall. I'd been around her long enough to know it was only a shell. Underneath was something bolder, something headstrong and fearless and fun.

Her hands were pale and cool and soft, like they'd been the night I'd held them for the first time, when she convinced me to go night-swimming in the lake. We'd been hanging out most of the summer. She pulled me along and we ran off the dock together, and by the time we hit the cold, dark water, I was halfway in love with her. I thought that night meant something. But when I asked her to Homecoming two weeks later (abandoning, for once, my well-advised anti-school dance policy), she'd looked at me as if I was a curiosity. "Christopher, please . . ." She'd looked sad about something, which didn't make sense to me. So I asked her again.

"No, Christopher. Just . . . no." That's an exact quote: the words are seared into my head.

Turns out, she was already going with some knob from the soccer team. I'd been imagining things. I'd avoided her ever since.

I followed her to the foyer, where the Regent with the red hair was standing by himself, looking forlorn. Apparently he had been ditched for good.

"So look," Julia said. "I've wanted to ask you . . ." She trailed off, struggling with something, and I wasn't about to throw her a line. "How come you never called me? You know, back then."

It was a ridiculous question, really. Julia had left me a few messages after the Homecoming debacle, saying she hoped that we could still hang out and blah, blah, something, something. It was nice of her, I guess, like it was nice of the United States to give Japan aid after we dropped the bomb on them. But I had no desire to soak in my own humiliation—of course I didn't call.

"Well . . . ?" she said.

Was she serious? *Well, see, you were the only girl I'd ever liked, and then you rejected me, and my soul has been in a state of repair ever since.* I probably should have said that—ask a stupid question and all—but I didn't.

Maybe I just wanted to avoid the conversation, but my mind went to Mitch Blaylock. Now that I'd had to face Julia, I might as well talk to Tim. He was the only policeman I could trust. The one person who might help me get to the bottom of things.

"So, hey, is your brother here?"

Her head reared back a little. "Christopher . . . I'm trying to talk to you."

"Yeah, right, but I need to ask Tim something."

Julia pinned a curl behind her ear, like she was frustrated but being all patient about it. I didn't get it: I was the one who'd been frustrated.

We didn't get any further, because a buzzing came through the windows. The lonely man with the Brillo-pad hair looked up from his drink for the first time in minutes. A throbbing, mechanical, gargling sound grew until the panes shimmied a little. Just like that, it shut off.

"Well," Julia said in a deflated sort of way, "here's your chance."

"What do you mean?"

She stepped to a window and peeled back the curtain. A guy was getting off a motorcycle in the driveway. "Tim's here."

He was headed for the front door, scrubbing his thick brown hair back to life after it being under his helmet. I'd never seen Tim on a motorcycle before—he must have bought it in the last year.

"Oh my God." My voice cracked.

Julia didn't hear me. She pulled the door open for her brother.

Tim bounded inside, bigger than I remembered. "Heya, Christopher Newell! Long time."

Heya—his signature greeting. I'd forgotten about that. He had big arms, and when he clapped me on the back I felt it all the way through my chest.

Then he was giving Julia a hug. I stood there awkwardly, forcing myself to smile. Forcing myself to make eye contact and act as normal as possible.

"Hey—are you all right?" Tim said.

He and Julia were inspecting me. I guess they saw it on my face.

"Oh, sure." *Keep your voice level,* I told myself.

Keep your eyes on them.

Don't look at the motorcycle.

Tim's motorcycle: it was a red, racing-style job.

The exact same one from Dr. Mobley's lunch.

6

In the backyard, paper lanterns glowed against the underside of the white tent. The NWMU orchestra played (poorly), and eventually the mayor took the platform. During his speech, the last three scholarship winners—*moi* included—had to stand behind him looking stupid. Daniel made faces at me the whole time. Finally the mayor stopped talking and awarded Julia her framed certificate. I have the exact same one; it's under my bed. Everybody cheered. Julia turned bright red.

The whole evening, the glamorous blonde sat at the head table with a stony look on her face. Tim was out there, too, but I tried not to look at him. My mind was racing to conclusions. Conclusions like: Tim and Dr. Mobley were eating lunch together, so Tim knew all about Mitch Blaylock, so he probably did the guy in. I was halfway tempted to call him a murderer and perform a citizen's arrest on the spot.

By the time the caterers swept the dessert plates away, it was almost dark. We walked over the grass to our car, and my parents shouted good-byes to friends through the thickening twilight. My mom linked her arm in mine and asked me in her best casual voice what Julia and I had talked about. "Our favorite sexual positions," I said.

My mom said she got the point. She chuckled and put her arm around me. It would have been a nice kind of moment if my mind wasn't going crazy thinking about that motorcycle, and the morgue, and the holes in Mitch Blaylock's body.

I needed to bounce this off someone. I needed to find out more.

I needed to call Mike.

I did it the instant we got home, and our conversation was pretty disappointing.

"Even if they were at the restaurant together, which you don't even know, it doesn't mean anything." Mike let out a breath on the end of the line, like he had just collapsed onto his bed, exhausted by another one of my conspiracy theories.

I wanted to write it off, too—Tim had been my hero—but I couldn't. I was pacing my room semifrantically just to release some energy. "Come on, Mike. It's weird. I don't want to think that Tim killed anybody, but this whole thing is bizarre. And the police are obviously in on it."

"Umm, not to boge your high, but it's not really that obvious to me. And think of it this way: what if it is Tim? Do you really want to find that out?"

"Somebody got *murdered*, Mike."

"Says you."

"If you saw these pictures I took of him, you'd be saying it, too."

There was a background noise on Mike's line. He laughed awkwardly and put the phone close to his mouth, talking low. "So look, Dana's hanging out tonight."

"Oh, she's there now?"

"Yeah, just walked in," he said, and then Dana must have grabbed the phone from him. Her voice came loud through the line—"*What up, Newell?*"—and then it was Mike again, laughing in my ear.

"Guess I'll leave you to it," I said.

He was going to be no use.

The next morning, I woke up to a *thwack-thwack-thwack*ing sound from outside my window.

A week ago, Daniel and my dad had started making an elaborate bird feeder. They're always doing stuff like that, for the sheer enjoyment of educating themselves in random and vaguely useless disciplines: in this case, carpentry and bird-watching. They planned to log the birds who ate at the feeder after they installed it on the birch tree. I gave up trying to ignore Daniel's precision hammering and rolled out of bed.

Mitch Blaylock must have been gnawing at me in my dreams, because I was thinking of him the minute I got up. Before I even showered, I stuck my memory card in my laptop for a look at the pictures. I had just brought them up on the screen when I heard a pattering in the hall.

"Christopher?"

"Just a sec, Mom, getting dressed."

Good God. In a word, the pictures were sickening. It struck me that I had taken an undue number of close-ups of the bullet wounds against Mitch Blaylock's pale skin. If my parents happened to waltz in and see them, I would be wearing a straitjacket within the hour.

"You had a phone call this morning," my mom called through the door. "From Julia Spencer!" A dramatic silence. "I bet you could still get her at home!"

"Mmmmm . . . okay . . . thanks." I was madly shutting down screens.

I could sense my mom biting her tongue, and then I heard her feet on the stairs. I checked about fifty times to make sure I hadn't saved the picture files to my computer and stuck the card safely back in my camera.

My mom was unloading sacks of organic produce when I got downstairs. The *Courier* had a huge headline about some judge who'd gotten in trouble for accepting bribes. I checked through the paper for stories by Art Bradford, but no dice. I flopped it down, helped unload some kale and bags of unidentifiable grains that didn't look entirely edible, and considered my duty done. It was time to get going.

"And where are you off to?" my mom said.

I had my camera strapped around my shoulder—after looking at those pics, I would have secured it with a deadbolt if that were physically possible—so I just said the first thing that came to mind. "Thought I'd take some pictures downtown."

A distant cheer went up in the backyard, which no doubt signaled completion of the finest bird feeder northern Michigan would ever know.

"See ya," I said, and gave my mom a peck on the cheek.

As I left, I knew it was killing her not to mention that I hadn't called Julia back.

Mitch Blaylock died here, I thought when I parked the Escort at the Lighthouse Motel. It was 10:53 by the dashboard clock, and the morning light didn't flatter the place. Before me, the motel rooms framed an outdoor pool in a U shape. The doors were painted robin's-egg blue; the sun hit them head-on, revealing grimy streaks of dirt. A rust-stained waterslide drooled into the pool, where leaves gathered in the gutters. A single jet on the waterslide sent a wayward arc of water throbbing onto the deck, a sad little fountain of hope.

The hotel office stood at one end of the U. A man in a wife-beater and cutoff shorts held a garden hose in one hand. He had tree-trunk legs, and he was drenching flowers at the base of a sign. It flashed the word *Vacancy* over and over. The man didn't seem to care about me one way or the other. He went to the side of the building, turned a squeaky knob, and left the hose lying in the grass when he returned to the office.

I wasn't sure what I was doing there. Mike was right, I wasn't eager to discover that Tim Spencer had killed Mitch Blaylock. But (a) maybe Tim didn't, and (b) I couldn't leave it alone anyway. They tell us to follow our dreams, and my dream was to catch people doing bad things. This was a golden opportunity.

The Lighthouse Motel has been around forever, but I'd never inspected it up close. It would have fit perfectly into a spy novel: *The Lighthouse Motel sat on a lazy bend in Route 14, the main artery into Petoskey. Citizens found it an unsightly building, but mostly they had forgotten it, like a stain on a kitchen counter not quite ugly enough to bother eradicating. After a while they just stopped seeing it. A man had been murdered in that motel—*

Someone was knocking on my window. Loudly.

It was the insanely hot woman from the *Courier*, which made me wonder if maybe I was still fantasizing. Or maybe, better, she was stalking me. I rolled down the window to find out.

"You again," she said. "You're popping up all over."

"Yeah, me again. Hi."

"So listen . . ." She stopped to fish for something in her bag and came up with the memo I had left for Art Bradford, Senior Reporter. Apparently, she had decided to intercept it. Hmm. Her eyes found what she needed and looked back at me. ". . . Chris. We need to talk."

I almost said something. I make everyone call me Christopher. It fits the savvy NSA operative I hope to be someday. "Chris" feels neutered, like the professors who ride bikes around campus with straps around their pant legs. But something about the woman turned me to jelly, and I made my first-ever exception to the name rule.

"Umm, okay. About what?"

"What do you think? C'mon, we're going to lunch." She walked over to her car, not bothering to check if I was following her. On the way, she pulled out a cell phone and tossed the gum she'd been smacking into some bushes.

The car was a black Trans Am. It had a T-top roof and a gold falcon painted on the hood.

It fit her perfectly.

Five minutes later, I still didn't know her name. She had simultaneously lit a cigarette and dialed on her cell before we left the Lighthouse parking lot, precluding any introductions. Without checking for traffic, she raced out of the lot and headed toward town on a stretch of Route 14 that she treated like the autobahn. The Trans Am's hood started rumbling when the needle hit seventy. She paid no mind to that, or to the dark hair swirling across her aviator sunglasses. I had no idea where she was taking us, and I didn't care.

Her face was a cross between a china doll's and a vamp's. The china doll was in her sapphire eyes and her porcelain cheeks. The vamp was in everything else. She gripped the steering wheel with one hand set at twelve o'clock, oozing confidence. She had the fishnet hose on. I was never going to associate those things with the chunky Goth chicks from Petoskey High again.

I pegged her at twenty-six, but I was hoping she was younger. She had to yell over the wind to be heard on the phone. From what I gathered, she was calling the *Detroit News*, and she kept getting transferred from one person who said they didn't have her résumé to a second person who said the first one had it. With each new transfer, she slammed the steering wheel and cursed.

It felt weirdly intimate to be in the car as she went about her daily business, which from my brief experience seemed to involve a fair amount of drama and shouting matches. Not that I minded. I was nervous being so close to her, though. A cold sweat was spreading from my palms to my chest to my forehead, when I noticed the laws of inertia thrusting my body forward at a distressingly powerful rate. The vamp had angled off the road and jammed on the brakes. I wasn't wearing a seat belt, and I had to brace myself against the dashboard. The Trans Am skidded for fifteen yards across a dirt parking lot, into one of the four spaces provided for customers of Ray's Beef Burgers.

Dead center. Very cool.

I was still clinging to the dash with white knuckles when she said, "Screw this," and ended her call.

"Sorry about that," she said. "That's rude as hell, I know, talking on the phone with you right there. Anyway . . . Tina McIntyre. Let's get some grub. I know it's early, but I'm starved." And then she grabbed a bag from the backseat and was out of the car.

Inside Ray's, she plunked down in a booth with her back against the wall and her spiked-heel boots up on the plastic.

"So, when's your birthday, Chris?" she said.

"Uh . . . September twenty-fourth."

"Libra. Hmm. Very nice." She pointed to herself. "Taurus, like you couldn't tell."

We weren't the only ones in the place, but it was close. In a far booth, two old men drank coffee and shot bull with the cashier. When a waitress came, her eyes darted between us as if to confirm the age difference and speculate as to the nature of our liaison.

Tina ordered two house specials (beef burgers) and an outrageous amount of other stuff. Luckily I had left the house without breakfast that morning, so I joined in. The waitress gave us a final questioning look and scurried away on toothpick legs.

A crusted ketchup dispenser and two paper-thin napkins sat on the speckled table. Tina reached into her bag. It was black with a white skull and crossbones painted on its side. Her hand emerged holding a file folder with newspaper clippings sticking out from the edges. She blew some hair away from her face, took off her sunglasses, and gave me the once-over.

"So tell me why you're interested in Mitch Blaylock," she said.

"Oh, I was just curious."

"You were just curious?"

I hadn't decided on how much to tell her, and I may have been a little flustered by all the hotness. Taking it slow seemed like the right approach. Somewhere, raw hamburger sizzled against the grill.

"Well, I'm a sports fan and the article said he played professional football, so, well, I don't know . . ."

She was twirling her sunglasses on the table, staring at me with bored eyes.

"How about this? I'll pay for your lunch if you stop being an asshole."

"An asshole?" So no, I wasn't sweeping her off her feet.

"Don't take it personal or anything. I'm just saying, the guy played *semi*-pro football. That's like Little League, only you get minimum wage and a kegger after the games. It's nothing special. You're lying."

"Yeah, maybe," I said, trying to manage the butterflies in my stomach. The whole encounter had been such a whirlwind that it didn't fully hit me until that second that Tina might have some useful information about Mitch's murder.

"You know something about him," I said.

She shrugged, noncommittal, as the waitress labored over with our food. I felt slightly emasculated as she plunked a cherry Coke, a vanilla milk shake, and most of everything else in front of Tina. The waitress left and Tina munched her chili fries, staring out the window.

"This was probably a mistake," she said, and I was filled with an intense panic that I would never see her again.

It was time to dive in. I breathed deep. "Okay, you're right. I know something about Mitch, too, and you're gonna want to hear it. But you've got to be straight with me. We need to pool our information if we're going to get anywhere." She was chewing her burger at the moment, so I added, as definitively as possible, "You go first."

I actually sounded pretty tough. It was the most assertive speech I'd ever given, and I'd delivered it to the most attractive woman on the planet. I thought I might puke.

Tina leaned back against the booth, produced a Marlboro Red from her pocket, and struck her lighter.

"You don't mind, right?" Smoke came floating out with her words.

"Uh, no."

"Forgot how crappy this food is." She tapped at the foil ashtray and contemplated me for a long moment.

"Something tells me you're all right," she said.

I let the smile bubble up to my face and told her to fire away.

"Okay, all I know is, that Mitch Blaylock story should have been mine. I answered the call about it, from the sheriff himself. That's kind of unusual." My heart did a little up-tick at her mention of the sheriff. I was clinging to the hope that he was more involved than

Tim Spencer, and this was good news: he definitely knew about the body before it ended up in the morgue. "The sheriff asked for Art specifically. Art's been at the paper longer than dirt, and the two of them are pretty tight."

"How tight?"

"I'm gettin' to that. Anyway, when Art told me why the sheriff called, I figured he was going to send me out to write it up. It's a nothing story. 'Man Croaks at Local Dump.' Sure, it's tragic, blah. But big deal. You can't do much with it."

She was right—the food was terrible. I pushed my plate away. From across the dining room, the old guys were checking Tina out.

"That's exactly the kind of crap assignment Art loves to give me," she said. "We have a personality conflict, you could say. Or you could just say he's an ass."

The waitress appeared again. She seemed hurt that we hadn't enjoyed Ray's handiwork. "Anything else?"

Tina ashed on the remains of her burger. "Nope."

The waitress slapped our bill down and left in a huff.

"But instead of sending you, Art went himself?" I said.

"Exactly." Tina jumped up in her seat a little, all enthusiastic about my brilliant deduction. "See, you're getting it."

I wasn't actually getting it. I was glad the sheriff was the one who'd called the paper, but it didn't sound like any big deal to me. If Tina wasn't insanely hot, the whole lunch might have been a waste of time.

"And then, when I told Art that Blaylock had just gotten out of jail, he didn't blink."

I looked up from my shake. "What?"

"He just said it'd be more respectful to keep it out of the story, him being dead and all. I knew something was up then. Art would *never* care about being respectful."

"Mitch Blaylock had been in jail?"

"I know, right? You see what I'm saying."

She reached into her file and splayed out two clippings from the *Courier*. One story was three years old, about a robbery at the Pit Stop on Route 7. It said that an unidentified man had assaulted the attendant and gotten away with $155.52 from the gas station's cash register. The other story—a week later—reported on the arrest of Mitch Blaylock for the crime. Apparently, police had traced it back to him through his license-plate number, which they got off a tape from the Pit Stop's surveillance camera.

Tina gave me approximately a second to digest the stories and said, "He spent sixteen months in Jackson on the robbery and assault charges—he had priors for drunk driving and possession. Got paroled, came up here a month ago. And now he's dead. Now, if you were writing a story about that guy, don't you think you would have mentioned that?"

I started to agree, but Tina waved the question aside like it was unfair to ask of someone without professional credentials.

"I know I would," she said. "Screw the quote-unquote respect."

"You think the sheriff told him to keep that out of the story?"

A smile broke across her face, and for a moment my heart was too enraptured to beat. "Yeah, smarty. I think the sheriff wanted something kept quiet. Which Art would do in a second. He'll do anything to stay in their good graces. The prick."

She fished a dill pickle from her plate. "So, that's what I know," she said as the waitress collected our plates. She was still giving Tina the hairy eyeball.

"No tip for her," Tina said. "Anyway, your turn now—better be good."

As I considered my options, two things happened. First, I realized that she had never asked me how old I was. I liked her for that. Second, Tina stripped off her long-sleeved t-shirt. There was another, regular T-shirt underneath it, which read, KISS ME, I'M CHESTY.

"What I tell you," I said with a voice that may or may not have quivered, "you can't print in the paper. At least until I tell you it's okay."

She raised her hand. "I would go to jail before revealing a confidential source."

I had a feeling that I was her first, but I didn't press it.

Instead, I told her everything I knew.

"Damn," Tina said.

I had told her about everything: the bullet holes in Mitch's body, Dr. Mobley's bogus death certificate, the money in his briefcase, and his secret rendezvous with Tim Spencer. When I finished, Tina crushed out the last cigarette in her pack—the foil tray had taken about all it could.

She picked the check up off the table. "Guess I owe you lunch for not being an asshole."

She paid and we carried our shakes to the parking lot, where Tina perched on the Trans Am's back bumper and watched the trucks whiz by on Route 14, stirring the weeds. The air smelled of grease, but it didn't matter. I could have stayed there all day.

"Did you write the story about that judge who took the bribes?"

"Don't I wish. Guess you heard on the way over, I'm trying to get a job with the *Detroit News* or the *Free Press*. Cracking a story like this would help a lot." She lowered her shades to get a clear look at me. "So tell me, are you some kind of a brain?"

"I'm not dumb."

"Yeah, you're a brain, I can tell. So how do you figure this thing?"

"The obvious. Somebody paid Dr. Mobley off to conclude that Mitch committed suicide."

"Sure, but who? The sheriff?"

"Probably," I said, but I wasn't sure I believed that. If the sheriff was the only one involved, it wouldn't explain Mobley's meeting with Tim Spencer. "Maybe it was some kind of botched arrest or something."

She nodded, and we just sat there, enjoying a strangely comfortable silence, until finally Tina stretched and grabbed her keys. It was a wrapping-up movement, and it gripped me with a kind of horror. I had known her for about an hour, but the prospect of a Tina-less summer filled me with mortal dread.

"So, what do we do now?" I said.

She opened the door to her car. "I'm going to write a story about this, if I can find out what happened."

"Look," I blurted, "I didn't come to the paper just to tell somebody what I knew."

"Oh?"

"I want to find out what happened, too. If you try to investigate this, you're going to have to do it on the sly, without Art finding out. You could use me. You know it."

"Easy, tiger."

"Sorry."

"No, I like the energy." Tina jammed her straw around inside her shake. She was watching me closely.

"What we need to do," I said to fill the silence, as my heart did gymnastics over the prospect of joining forces with her in a Clark Kent–Lois Lane kind of way, "is find out who killed Mitch Blaylock. That'll answer the question of where the money came from, and how Mobley is connected to this whole thing."

"C'mon," Tina said, and hopped into the Trans Am. When I got in beside her, she shot me a grin.

"You aren't going to puss out on me halfway through?"

"No way."

She fired up the engine. "Better not. Let's get the hell out of here."

PART II

NO EXPERIENCE NECESSARY

or

SUNKEN BLUFFS

7

We hit eighty-five on the way back to the Lighthouse Motel.

Tina sighed heavily as we turned into the motel's dreary lot. "Too bad you didn't just swipe that fifteen grand, huh? I know I would have."

I didn't know what to say to that, so I let it go. Tina burst out laughing.

"I'm *kidding*, gullible. We'll work on that."

"Uh . . . I guess I should go," I said.

"Not so fast." Tina turned in her seat. "We need to move on this. First stop, right here. Lighthouse Motel. Get everything—what they know, who found the body, any details you can. Make sure to get exact quotes and the spellings of any names." Tina produced a reporter's notebook from her bag. "Here. It's on me."

"You want me to do this?"

"Good, you've got ears. I'm late for something else. You'll do a great job. And oh . . . do you have a camera?"

I couldn't believe it; she was into photography. This was a common interest, something to build on. "Yeah, a Nikon D50," I said a little excitedly, "with a 50-200 millimeter—"

"I don't give a crap about the *specs*, Ansel Adams. Just get a picture of that stiff if you can. It'd be great to have."

I relaxed for the first time in an hour. "Beat you to it," I said. "Got forty of them, suitable for framing."

"Hot damn!" Tina scratched my head. *Good dog.* "All right, can you meet me at the paper, noon tomorrow? With a report on what you found out?"

"Noon," I said.

"See ya, sexy."

I climbed out of the car in a bit of a daze.

An electronic bell chimed when I entered the office, a tiny space overloaded with a stand of vacation brochures and a water cooler dripping slowly onto the Astroturf carpet. I was actually doing this.

The man who had been watering the flowers gave me a sleepy look from the counter. He had dark hair that went past his shoulders and needed combing. Behind him, a full set of keys hung from the pegboard. The lazy eyes, apparently, were all the greeting I was going to receive.

"Hi there. Christopher Newell, special assignment reporter from the *Courier*." It just came out, but I liked the ring of it.

He groaned. "You aren't here about those ads? I paid for them two weeks ago. Really brought in the business, too." This, I detected, was sarcasm.

"Oh, it's not about that. I'm here about the guest who died, Mitch Blaylock."

"What about him?"

"Well, I'm just running down a follow-up piece. Nothing special. You might see it in the Sunday rag, B section, if you keep your eyes peeled."

"I'll have my scissors ready."

I may have been getting carried away with my role. "Getting to it then," I said, and produced the reporter's notebook for effect, "did you happen to be on duty the night it happened?"

"No, matter of fact. It was all over by the time I got back. Out with the boys."

"Excellent. So, who was on duty?"

He nodded to an Employee of the Month sign that had last been updated two years and three months ago. The frame had cheerful, sparkly decorations, but the picture inside was yellowing and sad—a dreary woman with stringy hair who couldn't be bothered to smile. It looked like a Christmas card from prison.

"And who's that?"

"Abby."

"Last name?"

"Shales."

"Shales—perfect, great." I wrote it down. The guy wasn't too chatty, but I was determined to win him over. "So, Mitch Blaylock. Did he stay here for a long time?"

"'Bout a month. I usually don't let people stay that long without paying. I did with him, though. He talked so damn fast, always promising to pay up the next couple days or so. I was getting pretty fed up. Fact, I was about to kick his ass out when he died." The man shook his head a little. "Never did get paid."

"That's quite a shame," I said, although I don't think he noted my irony. "Could I get a look at his bill possibly, to see if he made any calls while he was here?"

He looked at me with new skepticism and swept hair out of his face in a wide-arcing maneuver. It fell on the back of his Kid Rock concert T-shirt. "I don't know about that."

I decided to leave it for the moment. "What about visitors—did Mitch have many?"

"Nah," the manager said, settling his elbows on the counter, comfortable again. "I felt sorry for the guy, kinda. Maybe that's why I kept giving him a break on the bill. Who wants to talk to an ex-con, you know? Said he came here straight from prison. I believed him, too, the way he went on about how great it was to shower, and eat some real food, and how it was weird to see new faces all the time, every day, and all that. Guy was a real talker."

"Okay, great, I think that might do it." Behind the counter, a door opened to a room that appeared to be his living quarters. A TV tray with a pizza box on it sat in front of a couch. An episode of *Jeopardy!* played into the emptiness. It felt lonely.

I closed my notebook and took a half step away from the desk. Tina wouldn't mind being used like this. "The reason I ask about the phone numbers—well, you might have noticed the woman I came here with?"

His eyes sparked to life. "The one out there? With the body?"

"That's the one," I said. "Renee works in the mailroom. As it happens, she's half sister to Mitch, but she didn't even know he was back in town. Really broken up about it. Sad, really, she's so . . . vulnerable. Anyway, she wanted me to find out if Mitch had tried to call her from the motel. Ease the pain, I guess." I let it sit for a second.

"Renee?" the guy said.

"Yeah, Renee Hottington. She wanted to ask herself, but she couldn't manage it today. Too emotional. I'm sure she'd be extremely thankful if, you know, you could do it."

He spent a moment finding a printout on his desk, which I guessed was Mitch's bill. "Well, what's her number?"

He clicked a pen, ready to take it down. I had to give him credit. I walked over and gave him a fake number. He wrote it down, which gave me enough time to look at the entries for three local calls that Mitch had made, all to the same number. I closed my eyes and repeated it in my head for safekeeping.

The guy shook his head. "Looks like he didn't call her."

"Well, like I say, I'm sure her thanks will be plentiful."

"Tell her to come over any time," the guy said as I walked out the door.

Daniel and my dad were listening to the second bill of a Tigers doubleheader. The radio on the table was an ugly, scuffed thing that Daniel had built himself from scraps he found at the city dump; it had won him the second-grade science fair in a walk. The announcer's voice came through clear enough to tell that a Minnesota Twin had just brought in two runs with a double up the gap.

"That's right," my dad said, "for a double you draw half a diamond."

Daniel marked a score sheet with his Detroit Tigers pencil. I had to hand it to him; nobody bothered learning how to score a baseball game anymore. Soon, Daniel would be the sole master of civilization's lost arts.

"And do you plan on spending a lot of time with this woman?"

We were all in the kitchen, and my mom was into her twentieth question about Tina McIntyre, whom, I'll admit, I'd been a little evasive about. I'd let it slip that I'd eaten lunch with a reporter from the *Courier,* but telling my mom that I was spending my summer investigating a murder with her wouldn't have flown.

"I don't know yet. I guess I'm kind of doing an internship."

"And are they paying you?"

"No."

My mom fussed at the tempeh burgers on the stove. She had impeccable radar and seemed convinced there was something she didn't like about my new friend. "Well . . . I'm sure that your father and I would like to meet this Tina before we leave for vacation. If you're going to be working with her, or whatever it is."

My dad threw me a helpless glance.

"Fine, Mom," I said.

"And I don't suppose you've called Julia back?"

I gave in after dinner. Crickets called to each other as I sat out on the back porch, portable phone in my hand, dreading the call to Julia. The wicker lounge chair was making my butt ache. What this was all about, I had no clue.

The kitchen curtains separated and my dad peered out at me.

"There you are," he said when he reappeared on the porch. "Keep this in a safe place." He handed over a printed page with flight numbers for my parents' trip, times of departure and arrival, phone numbers for the airlines, the hotels they were staying at, the hotels' phone numbers, street and e-mail addresses, fax numbers, and their rent-a-car reservation number.

"You forgot the state tree of Idaho," I said.

He smiled. "Whatcha doing?"

"Calling Julia Spencer. Don't tell Mom. She'll want a transcript."

"Nonsense. She'll just pick up the other line."

"How about you go man it for me?"

"Aye-aye, Captain." He saluted, then gave me an awkward man-punch on the shoulder. I shifted myself upright and dialed, hoping to get voice mail. Julia answered on the first ring.

"Hey, Julia. I heard you called."

"Yeah. Wow, you called back."

Not this again. Julia obviously had developed a deranged obsession with my calling patterns, but I didn't feel like talking about it any more than I had at the mayor's.

"So, I forgot to ask you something the other night," she said. "Well, I didn't really forget, you just seemed a little weirded out."

"Yeah, I guess I was."

"I mean, I don't blame you. It was a little bizarre for me, too. Anyway, so I saw Mike and Dana downtown a few days ago."

Julia knew Mike pretty well, but I had no clue why she'd want to call me about a run-in with him and Dana. A pit was forming in my stomach.

"Mike and Dana?"

"Yeah. So, Mike told me about the party at Dana's house. I mean, I don't even think she likes me, but Mike said I should definitely come. I haven't been hanging out with a lot of people from school, so I was kind of tempted."

Julia was getting revved up. Words were tumbling out of her mouth like they did when she got nervous. It used to happen when she'd read lines from a play. I helped her prepare for an audition once—one of those stupid things that I'd thought was just an excuse for us to hang out, like playing tennis or night-swimming in the lake.

The play was *The Crucible*, and Julia was a pretty terrible actress. The nerves colored her cheeks and mangled her words and flattened her voice to a monotone. If you thought about it, it took a lot of bravery to act so badly in front of someone else. I sat in her room back then, listening to her practice, and I thought: *I couldn't do this.* We went over and over the soliloquy, and she butchered it every time, and I might have fallen in love with her a little bit then, too.

She got cast as Bewitched Girl Number 3, but I never saw her perform. Opening night was just after Homecoming.

Her voice paused, and I could hear the crickets again as she hesitated on some kind of verbal cliff. "I thought maybe you'd want to come along to the party?"

"Like, go with you?"

A rushed laugh came over the phone. "I mean, not like a date or anything."

"No," I said. "Obviously."

"Christopher, c'mon." Her voice was whiny, like I'd offended her. "I just want some company, you know? Dana's going to have a million friends there. So what do you say?"

I didn't want to go, but I couldn't back out on Mike, either. "Well, actually, Mike already told me about it."

"Oh, great," Julia chimed. "So we're on?"

"Ummm, yeah I gu—"

"Awesome. I'll pick you up."

I hung up the phone, more confused about Julia than ever.

8

The suffocating popcorn smell was gone, but other than that, the *Courier*'s office felt the same as it had before. I stood at the entrance, proudly clutching the phone number I'd gotten from the guy at the Lighthouse Motel. I followed the rough-edged sound of Tina's voice to a cubicle with pictures of NASCAR drivers tacked to the walls and Dr Pepper cans strewn about the desk. She hung up the phone midsentence when she saw me.

"Look who's here," she said, and snatched the scrap of paper out of my hand. "Whaddaya got?"

"A phone number Mitch called three times from his room."

Tina nodded slowly. "Nice work, genius. What's it for, the country club?"

"The country club?"

"Yeah." She rummaged through a teetering pile of books on her shelf and pulled out an old Petoskey High yearbook she'd gotten from somewhere. She turned to a flagged page with a picture of Mitch sporting a ridiculous-looking mustache. "Says here he caddied at the country club back in high school. That's the only thing I've been able to find out about him, except that we missed his funeral. They had it yesterday."

"Oh."

Tina had learned more about Mitch Blaylock in half a day than I had in three. "I just called around to the cemeteries, took about five minutes. But this is a real start," she said, flicking at the phone number. "So c'mon . . . who was he calling?"

"I figured we'd look in a reverse directory."

If you've seen enough movies with crusading journalists, you learn that newspapers have these phone books ordered by phone numbers instead of names. Tina didn't seem impressed by my knowledge.

"Hmmm. Yeah, we could do that. Or how about this?" She picked up the phone and dialed the number. "Sometimes you just gotta get your hands dirty, Chris."

"Oh, okay." I stared at a picture of Tony Stewart spraying beer at his crew, feeling pretty useless, while Tina waited for someone to pick up. The hypnotic tones of Petoskey's light rock wafted through the newsroom.

"Five bucks says it's a chick," Tina said, then gave me a shushing motion. She listened for a second and hung up the phone.

"Warne and Lovell," she said to me. "Ever heard of it?"

I had. "They're lawyers."

"Shysters," Tina said grimly. "Wouldn't you know it."

⚘ ⚘ ⚘

Warne & Lovell had a prime location. The offices were on the second floor of Petoskey's most "historic" building, above a restaurant called Tellers that had been converted from a bank. My mom and dad went there for anniversary dinners.

Tina blared a playlist of "Angry Songs" on the way over while I told her what I knew about Warne & Lovell. It wasn't much. It was the town's first law firm, and Mayor Ruby had been a big shot there before he left to become a judge, and then on to politics. I figured Tina would know more about the place than I did, being a reporter and all, but she told me she'd just moved to Petoskey six months ago and was still catching up on everything.

We parked on Main Street—it took my ears a minute to adjust to the calm after the radio died out. Tina threw her gum into a gutter on the way to the entrance, which had a sign noting that the firm had been established in 1937. We took the elevator to the second-floor office.

"What exactly are we going to say to them?" I asked. "'We know Mitch Blaylock was murdered and were just wondering if you might have done it?'"

Tina snapped her sunglasses together as the elevator door opened. "We'll think of something. C'mon."

The office had blood-red carpeting and smelled of flowers. A woman sat at the reception desk, wearing a headset. She addressed us in a whisper: "Can I help you?"

"Hopefully," Tina said. "Somebody in your office was in touch with a man named Mitch Blaylock in the past week or so. Do you know who that might be?"

"I'm sorry, there's no Mitchell . . . whoever here."

"Yes, we know—"

The phone was ringing. The receptionist gave us a saccharine smile and raised a finger, begging patience. She eventually patched the call through, then made a showy effort to re-engage with us, as if getting back to a nettlesome problem of advanced trigonometry.

Tina had lost patience with her already. She slapped her reporter's notebook on the counter and said, "How about this—is Warne around? Or maybe Lovell?"

"Mr. Lovell is no longer with the firm," the woman said, basking in superior knowledge. She dialed a number, swiveled, and mumbled something about "Mitch Blayless" into her headset. "Ms. Warne will see you in a minute," she said finally, with a sour look on her face.

We headed to the guest chairs. "Bitch," Tina muttered.

I recognized Kate Warne immediately. She appeared at the edge of the reception area in a short-short skirt, the light shining off her blonde hair the same way it had at the mayor's party.

She nodded a greeting, looking us over carefully. Tina had lost her leather bracelet, which probably helped us pass muster. Also helpful, she didn't have a lewd T-shirt on. Kate Warne didn't seem to remember me from the mayor's party, which made sense—she'd been far too occupied with the bartender.

"Why don't we talk in my office?" she said, and strutted back down the hall she had emerged from. We passed a half-furnished office with cardboard boxes and flat spots in the carpeting from the legs of bygone chairs. We ended up in a corner office with a view of

Main Street. The walls were bare except for some crisp black-and-white photographs. No curtains on the windows.

Kate Warne introduced herself as she poured a glass of water from a pitcher with lemon slices floating inside like lily pads. Her legs were long strings of muscle, and you could see almost all of them in that skirt. She sat straight at her desk, her head high.

"So. You were asking about a Mitchell Blaylock, is that right?"

Her husky voice was the one touch of grit that hadn't been buffed clean like the rest of her. Suddenly I could see her eating macaroni and cheese in front of a wrestling broadcast, and I liked her more.

"Yes—" Tina started.

"I can't help you very much on that—don't know him. He may have been calling for Lawrence."

"Is he a lawyer here?" Tina said.

"Formerly," Kate Warne said. "May I ask what this is about?"

For a split second, I could almost see the wheels spinning in Tina's brain before her face settled into a theatric grimace. "It's a bit of a sad story," she said, and crossed her hands on her lap. "He died a couple of days ago. Very young."

Kate Warne's face softened, the frosty veneer gone in an instant. "Oh, I'm so sorry."

"Thank you. Actually, I didn't know him very well. I'm just a reporter. Mitch grew up in Petoskey and played professional football, you see. The *Courier* may do a little piece on his career. And Christopher"—Tina threw sympathetic eyes on me and tilted her head, isn't-he-cute style—"he's an intern with us. And he was Mitch's greatest fan." Tina was making out the article like some kind of

Make-a-Wish project for my benefit, which was making me feel slimy. But Warne was gobbling it up.

"We think that Mitch may have been in contact with someone at your firm before his death," Tina said.

"Yes, I see," she said, now giving me the too-cute look as well. "Unfortunately, I think Lawrence is probably the only one who can help you with that. Lawrence Lovell."

"Nobody else here who might have talked to him?" Tina asked.

"I doubt it. We have a small staff. Lawrence and I are the only lawyers." She stopped and took a sorrowful breath. "*Were* the only lawyers. He just resigned."

"Does he have a contact number?" I said.

Kate Warne picked up a fountain pen and marked the back of a business card. She handed it over to me. "His cell. Mine's on the front, just in case."

"Thank you," Tina said, shaking her hand. Kate Warne gave me a buck-up nod as we departed. My eyes swept across the modern office one last time before leaving, and stopped halfway.

In one of her black-and-white pictures, Kate Warne stood next to the sheriff, smiling brightly.

9

Tina had seen the picture, too.

She whipped out her cell as soon as we left the office. "Friend of mine at the paper," she explained to me, cupping the receiver. "She wrote those stories about the dirty judge. She knows everything." Her friend must have come on the line then, because Tina started asking about a connection between the sheriff and Kate Warne.

We hopped into the Trans Am and I shut off Tina's stereo before it could blow out her friend's eardrums. Tina listened eagerly.

"You rock," she said into the phone, then clapped it shut.

"What's the deal?"

"They're brother and sister," Tina said. "How about that?"

The sheriff's fingerprints were turning up everywhere. He'd called the story in to Art Bradford at the paper, which Tina said was unusual. He'd been there for the bogus autopsy. And now, it turned out Mitch Blaylock had been calling his sister's law firm.

"He's got to be the key to all this," I said. "But it doesn't mean anything yet."

If Kate Warne had told us the truth, Mitch wasn't even calling for her. We needed to talk to her partner. From him we could find out Mitch's real link to Warne & Lovell, and whether it would lead back to the sheriff like everything else.

"Get what's-his-face on the horn," Tina said.

She was talking about Lawrence Lovell, and I wondered if the fact that I knew it meant we were soul mates.

I fished Warne's card out of my pocket and called the number on the back. It rang four times before a honey-glazed voice told me I had reached Lawrence Lovell and that he regretted the fact that he couldn't speak to me. I found him hard to believe. Tina spit her number out for me and I left it in a message.

"Buzzkill," Tina said, and I knew what she meant. We'd just started getting somewhere, and now we'd have to wait for the guy to call back. Tina sulked, revving the engine at a traffic light. I tried to think of other leads and only came up with one.

"Got time for a trip to the country club?" I said.

Tina nodded, smiling. "Good call. Why the hell not?"

The light turned green. She blasted the "Angry Songs" mix and floored it.

A huge sign saying NEW PETOSKEY RESORT AND SPA marked the entrance to the country-club complex. Tina pulled in and we followed a snaking road to an intersection with little wooden signs pointing the way to the spa complex, tennis courts, and the cardio theater. The signs were affixed to a pole at odd angles, like those ones in the middle of nowhere pointing to TIMBUKTU, 607 MILES in one direction and CAIRO, 1,290 MILES in another. I think they were supposed to be cute. Tina kept on until we reached another blizzard of signs: INDOOR/OUTDOOR POOL, WHITEFISH RESORT, LAKE VIEW CONDOMINIUMS, GOLF ACADEMY, and the OLD CLUBHOUSE.

She stopped in the middle of the intersection, reading intently. "Christ, you need MapQuest to find your way around here. You know your way around this place?"

"Nope."

I'd been here a long time ago, when it was just a regular little golf course. But I'd never actually set foot in the New Petoskey Resort and Spa, which was kind of weird. Weird because there'd been a huge scandal when it opened a few years ago, and it was all anybody in Petoskey talked about. I'd heard so much about it I felt like I knew the place, but now I was seeing it for the first time. The fairways on either side of us were carpeted with electric-green grass, bare of trees, and silent as a church. A worker in a white jumpsuit mowed a stretch of grass that already looked perfect. He glanced over at us and frowned, pegging us as riffraff. He probably wanted to come over and straighten our collars.

"If Mitch was a caddy, maybe we should try the clubhouse first," I said.

Tina nodded and followed the sign until we arrived at a black asphalt parking lot the size of a football field. The clubhouse in front of us looked like a winter lodge. Golfers gathered to the side of it, taking lazy practice swings and scrubbing golf balls in a red machine. Tina shaded her eyes and looked off to our left, where we could see the resort's signature building—a fourteen-story glass tower of luxury hotel rooms with built-in Jacuzzis.

I knew about the Jacuzzis because of my parents. I knew a lot of details like that; the golf course was all they'd talked about for a long time. I knew the hotel had 160 rooms, I knew they'd built three new golf courses, I knew the names of the chemicals they used to make the grass green, I knew that the place we were standing used to be a cherry orchard. The country-club property stretched for about a mile ahead of us, where there used to be a forest.

Tina sighed as she took in the glaring tower.

"You know why I moved here?" Tina said. "I saw a picture of the bluffs. I applied to the *Courier* the next day."

We both laughed.

Petoskey Bluffs had been the town's claim to fame. They were pictured on the town seal, the *Courier's* masthead, and all the old travel posters ever made. They were pretty cool, those bluffs. At their highest point, they formed a 340-foot coastal wall that dropped down to the edge of the lake. People used to set up lawn chairs at sunset, just to watch them turn a bloodstained orange. It was the kind of thing that Julia and I would have done together in high school, if the bluffs hadn't disappeared by then.

The developers wanted to make their new golf courses look like the ones in England, which don't have trees on them, so they clear-cut the forest. But as it turned out, the forest had been playing a vital role for Mother Nature, absorbing rain and sheltering the bluffs from storms on the lake. When the spring rains came, the bluffs crumbled right down. It was the worst environmental disaster in the history of Michigan. The entire twelfth fairway—the part on the town seal— slid into Lake Michigan. Just like that, Petoskey's natural wonder had become a mudslide.

That was four years ago, so the bluffs were wiped out before Tina even applied to the paper. I guess research wasn't her strong suit.

In the clubhouse, lacquered wooden benches circled a huge fireplace in the center of the lofted room. To the side, newspapers hung from wooden racks near a cluster of stuffed chairs. The place would have felt pretty cozy except for the dead animal heads peering down from the walls.

We wandered down a hallway to the management office, which had a glass door with the names of club officials stenciled onto it. Inside, a beefy man with a tattoo on his neck manned an antique reception desk that cramped his giant body. Behind him was an oil portrait of a slick man in a power tie, gazing importantly into the distance.

The guy at the desk was reading something with a pencil at ninety degrees to his temple, about like you'd do with a gun if you were highly depressed. Maybe the job was getting to him.

Tina groaned.

"What?"

"Guy I dated," she said. "Perfect."

She inhaled deeply and charged ahead. Up close, I could see the receptionist's tattoo (a dagger) and the thing he was reading (*Pro*

Paintball Monthly). I wondered how things had ended between him and Tina and braced myself for fireworks.

"Hey, Tina," he said with surprising tenderness.

"Hi, Bob. Guess I'm the last person you expected to see walk through that door."

He shrugged boyishly. "You could say that."

"Well, good to see you." Tina grabbed my shoulder, breaking the mood. "Anyway, I decided to start robbing cradles, so say hi to Chris."

Bob chuckled and shook my hand with something that felt like a Thanksgiving ham.

"Any bigwigs available?" Tina asked, thumbing back to the names on the door.

"You need an appointment," Bob said apologetically. "They aren't around anyway, though."

"Can we schedule something?" I said.

"Sorry, you'd need to call their secretaries." Bob motioned to the slick guy in the painting, "That's the president, Alexander Corbett. If it's something important, you probably want to talk to him. Whaddaya need, anyway?" He looked down at his magazine as soon as the question escaped his mouth. "Not to be nosy."

"Don't sweat it," Tina said. "We'll call ahead sometime."

She gave him a smile, which he seemed to like, and then we left Bob, the tender tattooed muscleman, to his paintball. As we left, the oil image of Alexander Corbett watched over him like a father giving him an inferiority complex.

"Get me a drink," Tina said outside the office. "Quick."

10

She pulled me back through the lodge area with the huge fireplace, where we spotted a bar and grill on the far side of the room. The place was called Putters, with tables covered in green linen and paintings of fox hunts. Tina made a beeline for the bar, tended by a chubby black guy who was clearing the empty glasses of a sporty young couple.

Tina ordered a Bloody Mary. I got a Coke and asked her what the deal was with Bob.

She waved it off. "Nothing really. He's a nice guy. Too nice, but I should have been happy with him—usually I'm an asshole magnet."

Our drinks came then. Tina thanked the bartender and crunched into her celery stalk. The guy to the side of us was getting up. He wore sunglasses and one of those hats worn by paperboys about a hundred years ago. And old men in Italy. And American guys who think they should be Polo models. His date/wife/fellow-Polo-model was putting her purse on her shoulder while they debated the matter of who had their car keys.

When the bartender circled back to check on us, Tina pointed her celery stalk at him. "You ever hear of a guy named Mitch Blaylock?"

He wiped his hands on a pristine white towel hanging at his waist. "No, don't think so."

Tina got her bag out. She reached into her Mitch Blaylock file and retrieved a photocopied picture of Mitch from his high-school year-book. "This is him. Think he worked here, a long time ago. Before the redevelopment."

The bartender held the picture for a long minute. He was old and brought it close to his glasses. The Polo-model dude held out his check, but the bartender paid him no mind. His date coughed.

The bartender slapped the picture down. "Nope. Sorry." He took the check and punched the couple's bill up on the old-school register, which whirred and dinged ferociously.

Polo model turned the picture around. "I've seen him," he said.

"You have?" Tina asked.

"Sure. I remember that guy. He was around here last week, Friday, talking up a storm. Kinda drunk, too."

The guy's date stuffed their change in her purse. "Sweetie, let's go," she said.

"Just a sec, doll."

They used their sweet talk like knives on each other. The woman gave up and tore for the lobby. The red puff-balls on her socks bobbed up and down on her way out.

"Yeah, he got kicked out," the guy said. "That's why I remember."

"He got thrown out?" I said.

"Yeah. It's usually a mellow crowd, but this guy was pretty sloppy. The lady with him looked embarrassed."

"Lady?" I said. "Who?"

"Hell if I know. Kinda young. The guy put up a little fight when they threw him out, but he went quiet in the end. He was all, 'Hey, can't a guy have a drink?' And then he left."

Tina bit off another chunk of celery. "With the girl?"

The man chewed his gum aggressively and removed his sunglasses for a better view of Tina. "Don't remember. I could give you a call if something comes to me."

"Thanks a lot," Tina said. "We don't want to hold you up any longer." She nodded toward the lobby, where his date was tapping her toe like they'd be late getting out to the yacht.

He laughed. "Forget it. Maybe I'll see you up here. I come with my friends. Sometimes alone." His smile lingered on Tina as he parted.

"See what I mean?" Tina said. "Asshole magnet."

She polished off her Bloody Mary and *oomph*ed in appreciation. "But that guy"—she pointed to the bartender—"he's the real deal. He better watch out."

The bartender threw his head back. His cackle echoed through the open room.

Tina said the Bloody Mary had hit her pretty hard and that we'd better eat lunch before she hit the road. "Not that I'm normally this responsible," she said. "I guess you're a good influence or something."

We stayed and made friends with the gray-haired bartender, whose name was Buddy. A few golfers stopped at the bar while we ate, and after a while they started sticking. They had half pencils stuck behind their ears, and they kept snatching their score cards from each other. They would point at them and bark things and burst out in baritone laughs.

My eyes kept returning to the fox hunters on the wall, elegant in their tight red jackets with gold buttons, blowing pretty horns on their way to the kill. Julia would've hated the place—she was big on animal rights and had gone vegetarian in seventh grade. It's one of many reasons my parents liked her so much.

"My mom and dad tried to stop them from building this place," I told Tina.

She turned to me sharply. "Really?"

I nodded. "It was back before the disaster happened." My parents just wanted to preserve the beauty of the bluffs. They thought the hotel would be ugly, and they were against the chemicals and tree cutting to build the country club's three golf courses, and the spa, and all the rest of it. Memories started flooding through me: our street lined with cars every other Wednesday; packed meetings of the Ad Hoc Committee to Preserve Petoskey's Beautiful Spaces on our back porch; the green yard-signs: DON'T BLIGHT THE BLUFFS.

"What'd they do?"

"Everything they could, pretty much. They had protests. They tried to launch a boycott."

"It didn't work?"

"No. Everybody in town hated them."

The developers said Petoskey would be a new golf mecca: people would flock from Detroit to play their three English-style links golf courses, right in Northern Michigan. The people in town believed them—they wanted the tourism business badly. They thought my parents were freaks.

The only people who supported my parents were their friends from NWMU. And Julia, who spent a lot of weekends working on the cause. I didn't do much to help.

After the bluffs slid away, the earth collected in the lake and blackened a mile-long section of Lake Michigan's blue waters. Because it came from a golf course, the earth had been soaked in chemicals that poisoned every fish within twenty-five miles. It was a long time before they stopped washing up dead.

Afterward, a lot of people claimed that they had been with my parents all along.

Tina put some money down on the bar and told me lunch was on her. "It's cool that your parents tried to stop this place," she said. "I wish I'd gotten to see those bluffs, just once."

I nodded, feeling ashamed that I hadn't helped try to stop the resort, when Buddy the bartender saw us getting up. He left the crowd of golfers singing the University of Michigan fight song and came over. He wiped his hands on his towel, now dirty from a day of work, and leaned in.

"Look, there's something you should know. About Blaylock."

11

"**I** knew him from way back," Buddy said. "He caddied here years ago, when it was just the one golf course." Buddy waved his arms out toward the golf courses and the rest of the resort.

"Did something happen back then?" I said.

"No, not then. I mean, Mitch was a character. I think he was selling some pot to the other caddies, little stuff like that. He had a big mouth, thought he was going places, but he was pretty harmless."

"So what is it?" Tina said.

"The night he was in here. The night he got kicked out?"

"Yeah?" Tina and I said together, scooting forward on our stools.

"That was the same night he died." Buddy let it sink in, then tapped a copy of the *Courier* sitting on the bar. We'd been helping him with the crossword earlier. "I saw it in the paper."

Tina got out a pen. "Was that guy right—was he here with a girl?"

"Yep. I don't know her, though. Heard him talking to her about some big score he had coming."

"What was it?" Tina was practically jumping over the bar.

Buddy shrugged. "Don't know. Mitch always talked like that. Always had some fortune coming down the pike, usually something illegal. You stop listening after a while."

"Can't you remember anything? Was it drugs or what?"

"Nah, I don't know. He wasn't exactly getting into specifics, not when I heard him, anyway. Not even Mitch was that stupid. I figured he was just talking to impress her anyway—it looked like he'd just picked her up that night."

"Did she leave with him?" I asked.

"Yeah," Buddy said. "Had his arm around her when they walked out. She was young, too, like the man said. But that's all I know."

Tina scribbled down some notes. She looked up and smirked. "Why'd you hold out on us, Buddy? You looked right at that picture and said you didn't remember him, with a straight face."

Buddy chuckled. "You hadn't worked your charm on me yet. No, I'd never forget Mitch."

Back at home, I lay on my bed with an absurd sense of accomplishment. I broke out my reporter's notebook and copied down the facts that Buddy had told us, then studied my collection of business cards: one from Kate Warne and one of Tina's that I had taken from her cubicle.

I liked having those cards. Perhaps a Rolodex was in my future. A Rolodex and a fedora and snappy banter for the dames, like in movies from the "Gumshoe" section of University Video. I'd be quick-witted and streetwise, a man of honor in a dirty world. *Femmes fatales* could tempt me with their gams, powerful men could offer bribes, but it wouldn't matter: I'd be incorruptible.

Daniel's familiar noises floated through the wall. He was conducting some kind of science experiment in his room, and I drifted off to the *tink-tink* of his Young Scientist beaker set.

It was dark when he woke me by jumping up and down on my bed. I half expected news of cold fusion.

Instead, he had Mike on the phone.

"I'm taking you to the Hideaway," Mike said. "And I'm really bored, so don't say no. Pick me up in ten minutes."

The Hideaway was Mike's bar of choice, a grimy joint ten miles outside Petoskey on the road to High Point, a town that nobody much cared about. Some of Mike's NWMU clients drank there because they didn't check IDs, which was the place's biggest attraction. I tried to stay away from it, but I wanted to hear about the Dana situation, so I gave in.

On the way, I filled Mike in on the investigation. We hadn't actually found out very much, but we knew that: (a) there was a girl involved, and (b) Mitch was planning a crime of some sort. How those things might connect the dots to the sheriff and/or Tim Spencer, I wasn't quite sure. On the plus side, Mike was finally showing some interest.

"So who was the girl with Mitch?" Mike asked when I'd finished.

"They didn't know," I said as we pulled into the parking lot with brown smoke flying up around the Escort. I couldn't imagine a girl Mitch picked up at the bar being the key to the crime, so I wasn't too worried about that part. "I just hope that Lovell guy returns my call."

"Even if it leads back to Tim Spencer?" Mike asked as we walked toward the Hideaway's red-painted door. We'd been through this already. I shrugged the question away, but Mike grabbed my shoulder and stopped me. "Think about that, man. Would you *really* want to find that out?"

"Tim couldn't murder anybody," I said. But then, I had seen his motorcycle in front of the restaurant. When he showed up at the mayor's house, I'd been convinced Tim was in on it. I had even wondered if Julia knew what her brother had done and was just being nice to me to find out what I knew. It was a crazy thought, but also the best explanation I'd come up with for her weird friendliness.

Mike waited for a better answer. Mosquitoes orbited around the lights in the awning like a million tiny tetherballs.

"I want to find out what happened, Mike."

He stared me down for a long time, like he wanted to argue about the stupidity of my conspiracy theories again. But I wasn't going to give it up now. He knew it, and his shoulders slumped in resignation. "Yeah, okay," he said with a nod. The moment had passed; we were cool again. "So, Tina . . . is she hot?"

"Insanely."

Mike clapped me on the back and we went inside.

In the dim corners of the Hideaway, people played pool and threw darts at an electronic board with flashing red lights. Plastic Red Wings pennants dipped from the ceiling, celebrating a Stanley Cup win from ten years ago. A somber mood hung in the air like smoke.

Mike nudged me toward some open stools and ordered two Buds

from a woman behind the bar. I wasn't much of a drinker, but Mike was always hopeful. He rested his elbows on the bar, hunting for girls.

"See anything?"

There wasn't a lot to choose from, but I made out a girl in a far booth. "How about her?"

"Who? Chernobyl?" Mike scoffed.

I tried not to laugh, but it took some work. He was talking about her fake tan, which did, in fact, look much too orange. She must have been a regular—he couldn't have come up with the name on the spot.

"So, what's the deal with you and Dana?" I said.

"Ehh, who knows? She called me out of the blue and we just sort of picked up again. Judging from past experience, it may not last forever."

"Out of the blue?"

Mike nodded and swigged his beer, but he couldn't keep his straight face for long. "Okay fine, I called her. Happy, Dick Tracy?"

He didn't wait for a reply. His eyes were following a girl in a scarlet sports jersey who breezed in and wafted to the stool next to him. She must have been another regular; within a minute, the bartender plunked a cocktail with a sorry-looking cherry in front of her.

Mike gave me a wink and turned to her. "Excuse me," he said, "I seem to have misplaced my Congressional Medal of Honor. You don't happen to see it over there, do you?"

"No," the woman said, cracking a smile. "Should I get my bullshit detector out and look for it?"

"That's okay, I still have my other two at home." Mike offered his hand. "Pleased to meet you. Mike Maske, man of your dreams."

She smiled broadly and told him her name was Bailey. How he got people to fall for this stuff, I'd never know. "Sorry, I have a policy against dating guys who wear sunglasses indoors. I just came to say hi to a friend, anyway."

"Bring her over." Pointing at me, Mike stage-whispered, "Maybe we can lose the third wheel."

Bailey gave a little wave to her friend. "Abby's married—she's not interested."

I tightened at the name and followed the path of Bailey's eyes. It was hard to believe I hadn't seen it before.

I clutched Mike's arm.

"What is it?" he said.

"Chernobyl's the one who found Mitch Blaylock's body."

Abigail Shales had the body of a twelve-year-old and the face of a forty-year-old. It looked the same as it had in the Employee of the Month picture at the Lighthouse Motel, except for the dirty orange color.

She and her snaggletoothed husband drank tall boys, sitting opposite each other in a booth. They looked like chess players, only there was no board between them and there probably never would be. I pulled up a chair. The detective at work.

Snaggletooth had a flowing mane of feathered black hair. He pushed his sleeves up his forearms. "What's up?" he said in a mildly challenging way.

"Friend of Bailey's." I had brought over my Bud bottle for credibility with my subjects. I might have brought Bailey, too, but Mike was trying to make inroads. I set it on the table and looked at Abigail Shales. "I heard you found some stiff at the Lighthouse Motel."

Abigail did a lazy shrug. Snaggletooth leaned back and said, "She sure as hell did. Gave her a pretty good scare."

"Did not," Abigail said.

"Well, I had to come over when I heard about it," I said. "Hope you don't mind."

"Nah." Snaggletooth leaned back, basking in their celebrity status.

"I've never seen a dead body before. What'd it look like?"

"Dead," Abigail said. She crushed out a cigarette like it was a reenactment.

"Yeah, but, I mean, was he, like, sitting on the can like Elvis—"

Snaggletooth chuckled. "On the can like Elvis, that's good."

". . . or you know, bleeding all over the place, or what?"

Abigail sneered. "It looked alive, only not."

"That's actually kind of deep," I said.

She clasped her beer in her hands. "The guy was facedown; I don't remember about blood. Sorry I didn't take pictures for you."

"Well, next time then," I said. I was cracking Snaggletooth up.

"Shut up," Abigail said to him.

They treated each other like wayward dogs in need of training. I backed away slightly. "Well, I didn't mean to bother you," I said.

"Sit down man, she'll tell you about it," Snaggletooth said. "Don't be rude, baby. The guy's just asking."

"There ain't nothing else to tell," Abigail said.

"Oh, come on." I think Snaggletooth wanted to hear about it more than I did. Abigail didn't speak.

"It's no big deal," I said.

"No, you asked nice, she can tell you nice."

"The hell I can," Abigail said.

Snaggletooth pointed at her. "Watch out. I'm serious."

She diverted her eyes to me. "He was a messy guy, okay? His room smelled like b.o. You happy now?"

"Why do you have to be such a bitch?" Snaggletooth said.

Abigail considered the question while she poured her beer. The head frothed down the sides. She finished pouring and slung it into Snaggletooth's face. It splashed into his eyes and dribbled onto his shirt, at which point I concluded Abigail Shales wasn't going to be any help.

Snaggletooth shot out of the booth, looked at her like he was trying very hard to restrain himself, and dripped out the front door.

When I dropped Mike off, the Escort's clock read 12:40. My parents would be wondering where I was. I turned on the brights and watched for deer in the evergreens.

It was the best kind of night: total blackness, clear and still, full of mystery. I cut the radio and let the cool air wash over my cheeks.

I don't know where he started following me.

I was shooting down Sheridan Road, passing the sign for Moby the Motorboat Salesman, when I first noticed the headlights behind me. A red light stopped me at a Shell station that had been out of business for years. Cracks in the shattered cashier's window glistened in the streetlight like a spiderweb. The traffic signal hung low on the cross wires. It stayed red while the car drew up behind me. I flipped the mirror to ease the glare.

The shoreline provided the fastest route home. I turned onto Lakeside Drive and passed the harbor where Mike and I hung out, with fishing boats covered up in tarps for the night. The lighthouse stood at the end of the jetty, far ahead of me. At the intersection with Main Street, a flashing yellow traffic light reflected off the huge anchor decorating the plaza square. Raindrops started thumping against the windshield.

The car had been following me a hundred yards back the whole way. It didn't feel right. I turned left toward the coast guard headquarters to test him. He followed me, and then followed me again through two more turns on a pointless, circular route back to Lakeside. I tightened my grip on the steering wheel and inched forward. The rain misted the pavement between us.

The car held back when we reached another red light at Washington, too far behind me to read the license plate. His brights were blinding me anyway; I couldn't make out anything except the silver paint job. The signal clicked green. I jammed my foot on the gas.

The Escort accelerated toward a tricky part of road I'd ridden on my bike a thousand times before. Ahead of me, Lakeside Drive made a half circle around an outcropping of rock, veering right and then turning back left. I swung with it to the right and for a split second the Escort slipped loose of the road. My muscles tightened in fear, but then the tires caught again and hurled me forward.

I raced to get to the other side of the curve, where the silver car would lose sight of me with enough distance between us. On the far side of the rocks, I checked the mirror and didn't see him. I braked and swept a hard left turn onto an unmarked street. The Escort barely missed the white-painted stones marking the road.

I cut my headlights. The road climbed steeply before splitting off in two directions, one of them toward Tina's neighborhood. The Escort rambled up the hill, dropping gears for traction. I kept the accelerator to the floor, hoping the silver car hadn't spotted me when it swung around the bend.

I chose the right fork, then made arbitrary turns until finally it felt safe to stop the car. My heart drummed as heavily as the rain against the hood, but I didn't see any sign of the silver car. I couldn't stand being in the Escort anymore. I got out and headed to Tina's address—which, I admit, I had looked up in the phone book out of curiosity.

She answered the door in a long gray T-shirt that said I WISH THESE WERE BRAINS. Her voice got scared when she saw me.

"Christopher?"

"Can I come in?"

"God, yeah, what are you doing here?"

She set me down in her living room. My adrenaline escaped and I fell slack against the sofa.

"You're shaking," she said, rubbing my arms. Her jet-black hair, tousled with sleep, smelled of cigarettes. "What happened to you?"

"Somebody followed me. I lost him at the bottom of the hill."

"Followed you?"

"Yeah. I went out with Mike. I was on my way home, and this car followed me."

My Nikes had holes in them, and the wet grass had soaked through my socks. I took them off before I realized what I was doing. I shouldn't have been that comfortable around her already.

Tina tossed aside my shoes. "Yeah, that's good. Okay, I'm not exactly great at this hostess crap, but let me see what I can do," she said, and went down the hall.

I lay down under a thin blanket piled on the back of the sofa. Petoskey had a thousand homes like Tina's, matchbook-sized places with exteriors painted in bright pastels to attract summer renters. Hers was *Miami Vice* blue. She had a window open, and the lake air swept through like a tonic. My eyelids fell.

Tina's voice called in from somewhere: "Tell me everything! Start at the beginning!" The strain of the night was hitting me, and I heard myself emit a feeble sound.

A towel and an AC/DC T-shirt landed on my face. "Hey!" Tina said, retreating to the kitchen. "You just woke me up at one in the morning, and I'm making you hot chocolate. Spill it."

"Yeah, okay." I toweled off, put the dry shirt on, and told her: about going to the Hideaway and talking to Abby, the way she bickered with her husband, and then finding the silver car on my tail. A television rigged with a homemade antenna was sitting on the counter between us, dividing the rooms. The cord hung uselessly a foot above the shag carpet.

Tina emerged with two mugs of hot chocolate and sat cross-legged on the floor. I tried not to stare at her shirt.

"Too bad you didn't get that license plate," she said, slurping her drink. "Are you really sure you were being followed?"

"Yeah. I did a U at the coast guard center, and he followed me the whole way."

"All right. But I mean, why? What do you think they wanted?"

"I assume it has something to do with Mitch Blaylock."

Tina leaned back on her elbows. "Well c'mon, genius, who do you think it is?"

I had no answer. Any number of people could have known we were looking into Mitch's death—Kate Warne, the sheriff, Dr. Mobley, even the hotel manager—but what any of them would get out of tailing me, I had no clue. The chase was making less and less sense.

"Are you sure it wasn't that Abby chick? Or her husband?"

"No, they're probably still at each other's throats."

We turned it around in our heads for a while. I set my mug down on the coffee table, wedging it around Oreo crumbs and scattered DVDs and a bottle of Maker's Mark. An oversized concert poster of The Clash hung raggedly on the far wall. A huge tropical plant sat in the corner of the room, between a stereo system and a bass guitar with a broken string. I felt warm under the blanket.

Tina got up and turned off the kitchen light. A lamp in the corner had a T-shirt slung over it, casting a red glow over the shadows. Tina looked down at me with dangling black hair. Her cheeks caught the scarlet light as she smiled and bent her knee into my stomach. "Slide, Clyde."

She slunk down onto the cushions. "Don't worry, I'm not going to try anything," she said.

It was a deep sofa and there was room for both of us. But there she was, next to me, and I could almost feel the heat of her body.

Her breathing became regular, and I carefully propped up on an elbow, wired and taking it in. A postcard from San Francisco sat on the table, next to a ticket from a motocross event. It was frozen in a splotch of green candle wax. Beside it was a picture of Tina and a friend in front of Comerica stadium in Detroit, wearing dark sunglasses and smiles, an open blue sky behind them.

I focused on the image of Tina and held it in my eyes. I closed them and went to sleep.

I woke up at seven o'clock. It took me a second to remember where I was, and why. Tina's face was right in front of mine, her eyes closed peacefully, her unpainted lips pink and thin. The night came back in a rush, and then the realization that I had never called home.

Tina didn't move as I placed the blanket over her and got to my feet. It took me ten minutes and five drafts to write her the following note: *Thanks for the hot chocolate. Later, Christopher.*

12

ou have *got* to tell us if you aren't coming home at night."

"I'm sorry."

"I know you aren't in high school anymore, but that's one thing you've just *got* to do."

"I know."

"That's not a lot to ask."

"I know, Mom."

"That's just courtesy. Your father and I don't want to be up all night worrying about you. That's a burden on us."

"I'm sorry."

"We treat you like an adult now. You don't have to tell us where you are every second. But if you're going to live here, you have to tell us if you're going to be out all night."

"Mom, I'm sorry, I know." She *was* treating me like an adult—she hadn't even asked me where I had been. A knife of guilt twisted in my stomach.

She sighed and laid her hands on her thighs. We hadn't moved from the kitchen, where she'd been sitting in her robe when I got in. A quarter inch of coffee sat in the pot she had made sometime during the night. She sniffed, rubbed her eyes, and disappeared into the refrigerator.

The morning sun came hot through the kitchen window. It felt like the worst had passed, until my dad slipped into the kitchen, bleary-eyed. He trained an evil eye on me as he poured the last of the coffee. "Would you like to tell us where you spent last night?"

Ugh.

Buckle up.

"I stopped by Tina's. She's the person from the *Courier* I told you about. That's where I was."

My dad sniffled away his morning grogginess. "This is the young lady you just met?"

"Yes."

His eyes darted to my mom. In a split-second look they communicated volumes of unspoken fears, disappointments, general bafflement, reconsideration of their parenting techniques, conjectures on my future (tattoo parlors? rehab? reality TV?), and musings on the extent of their son's sexual corruption and/or perversity. "We'd like to know when you're going to be out all night."

"Yeah. I know."

"This woman Tina," he said, "how old is she?"

"I have no idea."

"Is something . . . going on with the two of you?"

"We talk to each other. Verbal communication is going on with the two of us. The occasional car ride."

"And sleeping over," my dad said.

"Not on purpose. Well, I don't know . . . touché, I guess."

"Okay, that's that then," my mom said, calling off the dogs. She turned from the stove, where some French toast had just started to sizzle. My favorite. It stabbed me in the heart.

Breakfast went well until I took the plates to the sink. My mom leaned over my shoulder as I was rinsing them.

"Gail tells me you're going to a party tonight with Julia?" she said.

I slept the morning away and headed for the morgue around two. I hadn't been there for three days, since finding the death certificate and getting a close look at Mitch's bullet wounds. The morgue was cold, as always. It had the same ammonia smell and the normal paperwork in Dr. Mobley's tray. The everyday details unnerved me: a man had been killed, and life at the hospital just rolled on. Soon enough, Mitch's murder would be lost in an unremembered past.

The morgue was a good place to think through the case—there was mindless work to do and a blank white silence in the air. I was cleaning underneath the autopsy table they had laid Mitch out on, reviewing what little we knew about him, when an electronic jangling sliced through the room and scared me half to death. My cell phone. Tina.

"Get over here," she said. "The shyster called back."

❦   ❦   ❦

Lawrence Lovell was staring into Tina's eyes. He was shaking her hand, holding on to it for a few seconds too long. The guy rubbed me wrong already.

"Like I said, I've only got a few minutes." His voice was even silkier in person.

Lawrence Lovell was a pretty man, maybe forty years old, obviously doing anything he could to preserve his looks: dyed hair, manicured nails, an expensive pink shirt.

His office was the half-empty one I had noticed before on our way down the hall to Kate Warne's. There were framed pictures on his desk, ready to be packed away. In one of them, Lovell stood at the stern of a sailboat, staring dramatically into the wind while his unbuttoned shirt flapped wildly against his body. He must have had no idea how cheesy it looked. There were other pictures—on lakes, in log cabins, and one with a jagged mountain peak in the distance. With apple cheeks and a sun-blocked nose, Lovell pointed triumphantly to the summit. All of the pictures looked recent. The sheriff wasn't in any of them.

Lovell knelt down by a pile of legal books, athletic in his khaki shorts and leather moccasins, and folded together a moving box. He gave Tina a smile. "So what's all this about?"

Tina gave him a vague line about doing some background on Mitch Blaylock for a piece in the paper, and how we were talking to all of Mitch's contacts.

Lovell looked at me for the first time. "No child labor laws at the *Courier*?"

"I'm an intern," I said.

"Hey, just kidding, sport."

Tina gave me a warning look. Maybe I had said it a little harshly. Lovell didn't care; he fixed the sides of the box into place and rose heavily to his feet.

"Mitchell Blaylock. I was his lawyer a few years ago." He looked up at the ceiling, his face glowing with fond memories as he continued. "That guy, he was a character. I had only been practicing for two years . . . I went to law school in my thirties, you see."

"Enterprising of you," Tina said. She was buttering him up.

"Well, thank you. My grandfather started the firm. With Kate's grandfather, actually." He reached for a black-and-white picture, a yellowed shot of the original Warne & Lovell out on Main Street. Tina drew over for a look, standing quite close to Lovell. "After Kate got divorced, she decided to carry on her grandfather's firm. Her maternal grandfather. She took on the Warne name and went to law school."

That explained why Kate and the sheriff didn't have the same last name, even though they were brother and sister. Tina didn't seem to care—her eyes had gone a little hazy as she stared at Lovell. She didn't move away when he put down the picture.

"I came a couple of years later," Lovell continued. "I never planned to be part of the legacy myself, but plans change sometimes."

"Hmmm," Tina said.

"Anyway, I was just cutting my teeth then, picking up any criminal assignments I could from the court. Poor Mitch, he got picked up on some two-year-old rap for a gas-station robbery."

"Right, I heard about that," Tina said.

She didn't need to prod him, though. Lovell was relishing the chance to be helpful to Tina. He set his phasers to charm and continued. "The evidence was solid. Mitch wouldn't take the plea the state offered, even though I begged him to." Lovell's fingertips bounced softly on the desk. It was like a casting director had called out: *All right, Lovell, now show me wistful!*

"He would call me at two in the morning, saying, 'Hey, why don't we say this,' or 'Hey, let's invent this alibi.' It would always be some insane idea," Lovell said. "Not to mention illegal, usually. I told him I'd do my best, but I wouldn't cross the line. And he never pushed me on it."

"Ethical of you," Tina said.

He shrugged. *Awww, shucks.*

That's when I started to wonder: *Is she actually . . . flirting? With this guy?*

"What a character Mitch was," Lovell said. "I remember sitting there waiting for the jury to get back. I'm sweating bullets. Mitch is facing three years in prison. We're at the counsel table, waiting there for the judge to come in, and he turns to me and says, 'That suit looks great on you, Lawrence.' I mean, what a thing to say. Broke my heart. I felt so bad for him when the jury came back."

"What kind of suit?" Tina said. Her eyes were all over his body—putting him in different outfits, taking them off. I had to stop this train, and quick.

"Were you in touch with Mitch after he got out of prison?" I said.

Lovell looked at me like I had just beamed in from Pluto.

"As a matter of fact, I was," he said. "Mitch called a few times, asked me if I knew about any jobs. I think he just wanted somebody to talk to. It was really hard not to like the guy, even though you knew he was up to no good. So yeah, we talked a few times."

I'd been hoping for a lie, but his story fit the phone records from the hotel perfectly.

A knock sounded at the door—Kate Warne, standing at the edge of Lovell's office, giving Tina and me a smile as tight as her skirt. "I see you've found him," she said. "We'll talk later?"

"Sure," Lovell told her.

She disappeared, and Lovell amped things up another notch for Tina. "Mitch looked up to me, I guess. He used to say things about how smart I was, things like that. It could get kind of embarrassing." So embarrassing that he'd repeat them to hot girls, hoping to impress them. "But, you know, Mitch just wanted a connection with somebody."

"Everybody wants that," Tina said, with far too much subtext.

I cleared my throat. "What did you talk about with him?"

"Not much. Jobs, but I didn't know of any. I offered to help him find a place."

I left him a silence to fill, but Lovell had nothing else to say. He checked his watch. "I can't imagine any of this is important. What's this—"

"No, you're right," Tina said, "it's probably not. But . . . do you know how Mitch was planning to make money? Anything he might have been planning? Maybe something illegal?"

"Another robbery?" Lovell said with a start. "No, he was trying to find a real job this time. I mean, Mitch always had a scheme in the back of his mind, usually involving money. But I don't know anything about that. Anyway, I may have given you too much information already, as Mitch's former attorney. Our discussions were privileged, of course."

"So, if Mitch was waiting on some kind of score," I said, "you don't know anything about it?"

Lovell laughed at me. "I know a few things about Mitch Blaylock, but that's not one of them."

"Well, you've been very helpful," Tina said.

Maybe he had. What he'd told us felt like the truth, but it meant that we couldn't tie Mitch to the sheriff or Kate Warne. We had just faced a major setback, but Tina was beaming. At Lovell.

He shied from her intense look. The world adored Lawrence Lovell, and he could hardly stand it. *I* could hardly stand it.

Tina handed him a card. "Here's my number."

"A pleasure."

"Was that an act?" I said by the elevators. "Please tell me that was an act."

Tina shushed me. The doors opened and she pressed the button. On the way down, a shiver ran through her body.

"What a fox," she said.

13

I avoided the topic of Lawrence Lovell on the way back.

When I got home, my mom was cooking about fifteen different items on the stove. They were meals for Daniel and me to eat while they were gone. Every once in a while my dad would come downstairs and hold up an item of clothing. My mom would either look at him like he was an alien or say, "Yes, pack that."

The hubbub over their trip preparations was getting a little much, so I took my camera out to the lake and snapped some pictures of the lighthouse. I needed a filter I'd left in my room, and the pictures looked washed out and uninspiring. Daniel would be merciless.

My heart wasn't in it, anyway. I was thinking about Mitch Blaylock. I set up under a tree in Duncan Woods and glanced through the gruesome pictures of his body on my camera, just to remind myself that he'd really been murdered. It hardly seemed possible out in the sunlight with little kids playing in the grass and dashing under picnic tables, making their parents laugh.

The tree had warmed in the sun—it felt soft and improbably comfortable, and my mind was slipping away to a dreamy place, when crunching sounds came from the gravel lot at the entrance to Duncan Woods. A police car. Driven by Sheriff Harmon. He parked, lurched out into the sunlight, and masked his black-pebble eyes behind a pair of cop sunglasses.

He sized up the crowd, thumbs hooked in his belt. I half expected the little kids to start crying and run to their parents. At the picnic benches, the sheriff folded his arms and scouted the grassy area like he was protecting us all from snipers. He probably acted like that all the time—he probably made doughnut runs feel like a matter of national security. I can't say I was surprised when his sunglasses stopped on me and stuck. He gave me the death-stare for a full minute before he took his first lazy step in my direction.

The tree started scratching at my back. I was trying to remember what I could about search-and-seizure law from all the cop movies I'd watched—I had those pictures of Mitch right on my camera, and if the sheriff saw them, I'd be toast.

He didn't stop until he was just a foot away, standing tall above me. I could barely see his face past the bulge of stomach hanging over his cinched waist. He waited to speak. I pulled the camera to my side.

"Havin' a good summer?"

A fake smile flashed on his face and disappeared just as quick.

"Lovely, thank you." The guy brought something out in me. He didn't seem to like it.

"How's your work?"

Is he trying to say something?

Is he trying to send a message?

"Tremendously instructive, I'd say."

He nodded very slowly. He continued nodding. He kept it up until I thought his neck might give and his head would roll off toward the monkey bars. My hand was getting sweaty against the camera strap.

Finally, he said, "Well, be careful." And then he walked away.

I guess he thought he'd proved something. But something in me hardened as he sauntered back to his car. I wasn't going to listen to Mike, or my parents, or anyone else who told me to give it up—I wanted to know everything that had happened to Mitch.

I'd cut my work short when Tina beckoned me to Lovell's office, and now the whole afternoon had slipped away. I drove to the morgue, wishing I could be like those B-list stars on bad TV crime shows who commune with the dead through their psychic powers and/or female intuition. They had one about a girl who worked in a morgue, and the dead people told her all their special secrets. Maybe Mitch would talk to me like that through the pictures on my camera. Maybe he'd tell me what the sheriff had done to him.

It was getting late by the time I got to the paperwork and checked Dr. Mobley's things for clues. There was nothing of note in the desk. The plastic casing for the Vista View memory card sat in the same place, starting to collect dust. Maybe I could do a good deed and point Dr. Mobley toward a better brand, I thought, as I organized the last of the papers and shut the filing cabinet.

On my way out, a shadow was outlined on the frosted glass of the entrance. A thin, feminine figure. Knocking lightly on the door.

I was hoping it was Tina and not a hospital nurse with some

question I wouldn't be able to answer, when I opened the door and found Julia.

"Surprise," she said.

Big surprise.

"Uhhh, yeah. Hi?"

She peered down the hallway behind me. "You alone?"

"Uhhh, yeah."

"Oh, good. I stopped by your house. Your mom said you might be over here, so . . . well, I took a chance. You mind?" I was too flustered to stop her. She edged past me into the hallway, staring wide-eyed into the autopsy room. "So creepy. Can I go in there?"

She didn't wait for an answer. She opened the door and walked inside, which probably violated some kind of code. I locked the front door, prayed no one would stop by, and followed her.

She had bright barrettes in her hair and a plastic bag from Mac-Gruder's Market in her hand. Setting it reverently on the table for autopsies, she took a 360 look around the room. Her dress twirled as she took it in.

"Julia. I, uhhh, what are you doing here?"

The cold metal instruments held her interest for another few seconds before she turned to me. "Don't be mad, okay? We didn't get to talk at the mayor's, and Dana's party might be crazy. I just wanted to see you and talk like normal for once in, like, ten years." She shrugged her shoulders and raised the bag jauntily, suddenly teasing. "So I figured . . . why not a picnic dinner in the morgue?"

"Oh, perfect. 'Cause you can really work up a hunger here, you know."

It just slipped out of me. She laughed, relieved that we were joking.

That wasn't supposed to happen.

I wasn't supposed to be playing along with her. I still didn't know where Julia's sudden friendliness came from, and there were serious questions to be answered before we reestablished diplomatic relations: *Don't you realize that you put my heart through a paper shredder? Do you expect me to just swallow my pride and be pals with you again? And do you know that I suspect your brother of murder?*

"I knew you'd like the idea," Julia said, oblivious as she took a salad and a pasty out of the bag.

Pasties are a kind of food they have up here. They're sandwich-like thingies that copper miners used to eat, made of dough wrapped around warm meat or chicken or whatever. They're like the original Hot Pocket. It's a point of pride in these parts.

The salad was for her, the pasty for me. The salad would have lots of black olives; the pasty would be chicken. We used to get lunch at MacGruder's all the time.

The familiar smells sent a jolt of good sensations through me, but I still didn't understand it. Julia was living in some alternate universe in which she'd never rejected me. Junior year had never happened, and we were just friends—great friends who liked hanging out in the library and gossiping about people at school, with chemistry so thick you could swim in it. Chemistry like a lake you could dive into at night, holding hands, and it would catch you.

I liked it in that universe. It didn't really exist, but it tugged at me. And I guess I couldn't resist it, because I swallowed my questions as

Julia laid out the food, picnic-style, on the table. She was still into the joke.

"I forgot the blanket," she said. "Do you mind?"

"That's okay. Hope you brought your sunscreen, though—it's pretty bright."

"Oh yeah, you're right." Julia shielded her eyes and looked up at a bar of fluorescent lights, squinting like it was the sun. Her acting was much better when she was joking around.

She smiled at me and I let it feel good. We were back there—some place where Homecoming had never happened.

I hopped up on the table and took the pasty when she offered it. She broke out her salad, and we lost ourselves in the mindless comfort of eating together. It was nice, like we'd just survived a tough day of work together and didn't need to talk. The hospital had gone to sleep and the morgue became a cocoon, still and soothing.

Julia was hunting through croutons with her fork when her chest started to shake. She was doing a bad job of holding back a laugh.

"What?"

"I'm sorry. It's just so bizarre, Christopher. I mean, you work in a *morgue.*"

I couldn't really argue the point. An explanation would involve getting into my master plan to become a spy (which she already knew about), and how the morgue had seemed to fit into that. It would sound stupid if I said it out loud.

She touched me on the arm. "But no, I mean it's good. You shouldn't be selling T-shirts or whatever. You're more interesting than that."

She got up and did a slow waltz around the room—inspecting the scales, the temperature controls on the body coolers, all the stuff that had fascinated me at the beginning of the summer. She lingered at the window into Dr. Mobley's office for a long time, then propped herself next to me on the table. It was as close as we'd been to each other in a very long time. I slipped a last bite of pasty into my mouth casually, as if there weren't huge magnetic waves bouncing between our bodies.

"Good as you remember?" she said.

I nodded. "The very same."

She held my eyes a little too long, and then lay down on the autopsy table with a sigh. She pulled the swinging lamp over herself. "I'm just going to sun myself here for a while, if you don't mind."

She was stealing looks at me, expecting me to laugh, but it reminded me too much of Mitch Blaylock. The image of him hit me like a truck. We were eating a pleasant meal with happy memories on the cold, steel table where his dead body had lain. Where his murder had been covered up. If I'd still been eating, I might have gagged.

I said I wanted to do something about his murder; I had told myself I'd find out who did it. But was there really any chance of that? Tina and I didn't know what we were doing, and Mitch wasn't going to magically reach me from the beyond.

"Can a girl get a lemonade?" Julia said. She was still lying there, insulting Mitch without knowing it.

"We shouldn't be here," I said. "Let's go."

She felt the change and roused herself as I collected the wrappers and napkins. I did it in a rush, quick-stepping to the trash and waiting for her by the door. Julia stayed put on the table, making a point of it. She hugged her knees to her chest and looked at me strangely. At the moment, I didn't really care.

"Just . . . wait a sec," she said firmly. She held my eyes until I took my hand off the door.

"Christopher, I'm here because I miss you." She talked slowly, even-toned. I could see it meant a lot to her, but she was staying in control, looking me in the eye. It was like she'd watched an instruction video from Dr. Phil. "I know things got screwed up with us, and I don't know what you think of me or why you're freaking out now. But look: I still like you a lot, and I just really want to be your friend again."

I waited a second, to let her know I'd listened.

"Thanks," I said. "But it's really not about that."

14

he didn't buy it. She didn't move from the table.

"What's it about, then?"

"I can't really say."

Her eyes got darker as she stared me down, trying to figure me out.

It was nice that she wanted to hang out, it really was. And maybe she was right—maybe the memory of Mitch's body wasn't the only reason I wanted to get out of the morgue as soon as possible.

I knew how things went when Julia and I became friends. They went magnificently. And then I got hungry for more, and her friendship turned into a tease, and it ended in heartbreak by a locker door or some other horrible place, smelling of kiwi lip gloss.

"Thanks for coming," I said. "It was cool of you. But I'm going to drive separately to Dana's tomorrow night."

That did the trick.

"Okay," she murmured, as she lifted herself to the ground. Her feet landed lightly on the tile and we left the hospital in silence, not really together at all.

It rained hard the next day, like the clouds had something to prove. I was eager to do something about Mitch, but our leads had dried up and Tina was busy. Art had her on a deadline, she said when I called.

Without her company, I did the next best thing and checked for any stories she had written in the paper. It was kind of pathetic.

The lead story was a glorified press release telling of a golf tournament at the New Petoskey Resort, written by none other than Art Bradford. They had secured some "celebrities" from downstate to participate—a fifteen-year-old Grand Rapids girl with a hit tune from a Disney movie was singing the national anthem. She'd been caught with a bag of cocaine on her last trip to L.A., but Art had only praise. Typical.

The picture showed the girl smiling beside Alexander Corbett, the club president, in front of the glass tower of hotel rooms. It was terrible composition, really—I could have done better in my sleep, and that's not bragging—but I recognized Corbett immediately from the oil painting at the country club. He really chewed up the camera with his toothy smile. The article was full of his quotes about how having the stars there would "spotlight the world-class status of our great resort."

At the bottom of the front page was a follow-up article about the judge suspected of taking bribes. They had a picture of him, too. It was the guy with the Brillo-pad hair from the scholarship ceremony.

No wonder no one wanted to talk to him—the guy was a known criminal. The article said the full extent of the bribery problem in the Petoskey court system had yet to be discovered, and that's when I stopped reading. The *Courier* could really get you depressed if you let it.

I camped out in the living room and watched a Bond marathon, with the rain spattering the windows. Daniel and my dad had taken to the study for chess. In the kitchen, my mom was making massive lists for their trip: "Trails to Hike," "Organic Restaurants: Idaho," stuff like that. Every fifteen minutes my dad would emerge from the study with a bewildered look, rub his face, and call back in, "One more game."

The rain was tapering and *Casino Royale* had just come on, when my cell phone rang. From the porch, silverware clanked as Daniel set the dinner table.

"Don't even think about bailing," Mike said on the phone. Dana's party—I'd almost forgotten.

"Too late."

"Dude . . ."

He didn't need to say any more. I'd promised.

A bright yellow glow poured from the windows of the Rubys' house, showering down over the lawn still sparkling from the rain. Here and there, shadows skirted against the first-floor curtains. I'd waited as long as I dared and now it was ten thirty. I hated these things.

Walking into a party can be the loneliest feeling in the world. I edged through cars bunched tight in the driveway and dragged myself up to the imposing front doors. Maybe you were supposed to walk right in. Mike would know. I knocked, doubting they could hear me over the music throbbing from inside. It felt like a heartbeat when I put my hand to the door.

Some guy I didn't know opened it. Sweat-marks pocked his T-shirt and his beer swished around in his plastic cup like he'd been hurrying. He must have been expecting somebody, because his smile fell when he saw me. He gave me an awkward "hey" and retreated quickly, like I might be contagious.

"Hey," I said back to nobody. A girl-band tune screamed from the speakers into the empty living room. I walked through, feeling like an invader.

In the kitchen, I could hear the voices coming up from the basement. Everyone was gathered there, being loud and happy. It sounded like a lion's den. I should have headed down, but I got a shot of nerves and saw an intriguing piece of opened mail on the Rubys' granite counter. They were oversized photographs from the ceremony, clipped to an envelope sent by the guy from the *Courier* with the nice camera. It felt like eons ago. The mayor handing Julia her certificate. The crowd milling under the white tent. A violinist straining with concentration against a background of white lights and shiny faces. The guy was good.

My solitude was broken when a girl bounded up the stairs, her cheeks flushed with alcohol and her ponytail flopping about. She saw me and stiffened. Her name was Sophie Hamilton—she was a year ahead of me and we'd taken physics together. She wrote left-handed in huge, bubbly letters and missed the soccer playoffs with a sprained ankle. All the girls on the team painted her number (26) on their cheeks for the game.

She had no idea who I was, of course. It happened to me all the time—the fate of the observer, I guess. She gave me an obligatory quarter smile and poured a glass of water at the fridge. I played out the awkwardness, acting all consumed by the pictures, wanting to go back home.

The mayor shaking hands with a Regent. Kate Warne having a cocktail with some professors. They looked extra-frumpy by comparison. I wondered if there would be a picture of the corrupt Brillo-pad-haired judge, the one who had traipsed around the house all alone, just like me.

Feet sounded against the steps. I hoped it was Sophie going back downstairs but then I heard Dana's voice: "Hey, Newell, just root through my crap, why don't you?"

She glowered at me from five feet away.

"Oh, sorry." I blush easily, and I could feel my cheeks going neon. Sophie was standing behind Dana, interested now, giggling that I'd been caught.

Dana broke into a laugh and put her arm around me. "Just messing, Newell, relax. I don't care."

Smelling pleasantly of rum, she grabbed the pictures out of my hand and stared. Her head wavered as she focused on the top picture, determined to say something profound. "My aunt's a complete hottie. Don't you think?"

She leaned in for my opinion. Her breast pushed softly into my ribs.

I pointed to Kate Warne. "That's your aunt?"

"Not for real. She and my dad worked together, so she was always around, growing up. Aunt Kate—she's friggin' awesome. Don't you think she's totally hot?"

"Hey, do you know anything about her partner? That guy Lovell?"

Dana's lip curled. "Why?"

"Well, actually, I'm working at the *Courier.* I'm doing a little thing about their firm."

"What the hell, Newell? We're at a party and you want to talk about *work*?"

I decided to give up, but Sophie had left and there was no one else for Dana to talk to. "All I know is, my aunt Kate rocks. That Lovell guy is like a degenerate gambler or something. He's always down at Black Bear. Plus, he hit on me once."

Black Bear was a Native American casino a few hours south of Petoskey. Dana was putting more of her weight on me as she talked—if anybody saw this, they were going to get the wrong idea.

"That's why she's kicking him out," Dana continued.

"Because he hit on you?"

"No, because he's a degenerate gambler and never comes to work."

"Right," I said, nonchalant, furiously taking mental notes. It couldn't hurt to have some dirt on Lovell, the object of Tina's misplaced affection. "So she's making him leave the firm."

"Basically." Dana's eyes fell closed as she nodded. "Newell, are we done with this yet?"

"Yeah, let's go," I said, pretty sure I wasn't going to get any more details.

Dana grabbed fast to the banister and led the way to a hot basement full mostly of guys who'd already graduated from Petoskey High. Dana had always hung out with people in classes ahead of her. Almost always male. It was a key part of her allure, I think.

I expected Mike to be holding court, but he was shrunken in the corner with some burnouts I barely remembered. His eyes tracked Dana as she floated ahead to group of freakishly tall dudes in paper-thin T-shirts that put their biceps on strategic display. I think they'd been football players, or maybe Nordic gods. Dana nuzzled next to one of them like she'd done with me in the kitchen. He was getting the enhanced version. Without missing a beat, the guy slung his arm around her waist. I understood the lost look in Mike's eye: it must have been like this all night.

Before I could get over to him, I caught a glimpse of Julia through the crowd. She was leaning against the wall, listening to some babble from a stray Nordic god/football player with a peeling suntan. Julia had a beer in her hand that the guy must have given her, and that she probably hadn't touched. Her nail polish was gone and her hair was down—she looked sort of stunning in an effortless, hippie-child kind of way. The guy was working overtime to entertain her. I almost felt sorry for him.

He rambled on, oblivious when Julia's eyes met mine and held for a moment—both of us checking, I think, to see how things were sitting after last night. Something hopeful spoke from Julia's look. I'd been trying to protect myself in the morgue, but now I found myself wanting to talk again, to pick up the jokes, to go with the magnetic pull coming from her spot against the wall. I did a tiny nod toward the man-god standing next to her and rolled my eyes just a hair. The barest smile twitched on Julia's face.

Before anything else could happen, a hand descended on my shoulder. "Took you long enough," Mike said.

"Yeah, sorry."

"We're out of here. Like, ten minutes ago."

15

Twenty minutes later, Mike and I pulled into the Hideaway's dirt parking lot. Mike parked his Porsche between a red Ford Ranger and a blue Ford Ranger.

Time didn't seem to move in the Hideaway. Mike ordered us two Buds again and the same bartender brought them to us. The Red Wings pennants still hung from the beams, the same smell of chicken wings and carpet mold suffused the air. Maybe it wasn't the best atmosphere, but I was glad he'd stolen me away from the party. Strange thoughts about Julia had started congealing in my mind back there—like maybe it could happen this time, maybe she'd like me enough. I'd been on the verge of a colossal mistake, and Mike had saved me without even knowing it.

"So who was he, anyway?" I said, knowing Mike would be incapable of talking about anything but Dana.

"Some guy from the pool," he said.

Dana worked at the public swimming pool, which none of the tourists knew about and which was actually pretty nice. Mike and I had gone there just about every day two years ago, when he and Dana were a more definite thing. My mom took Daniel swimming there once a week.

"Have you ever seen them together there?" I said.

"I haven't gone there since we used to." He shook his head in deep dismay. "They've probably been at it all summer."

Maybe it was true, but I couldn't say I cared. Dana fed off drama like cupcakes. In eighth grade a rumor had started about her and the twenty-five-year-old swim coach, this guy who played in a band and had good hair that the girls could never stop talking about. The rumor swept through the school like wildfire. When Dana didn't exactly deny it, the details grew into a richly embroidered legend. (Supposedly it happened backstage at one of his shows, with body shots of tequila, a canister of whipped cream, and other stuff I forget.)

Finally the principal brought the coach in to question him, and there was talk that he'd be fired—that's when Dana cracked and admitted she'd started the rumor herself. She'd made the whole thing up, just to put a spotlight on herself.

It made me think: maybe Lawrence Lovell hadn't hit on her after all. It could have been just another one of her stories, something that made her seem interesting and wanted. Maybe Lovell wasn't even a gambler, and Kate Warne wanted him out of the firm for some other reason entirely, one that involved Mitch Blaylock. Maybe she was protecting her brother, the sheriff.

Dana had probably invited the pool guy to the party just to start a fight between him and Mike—a spectacle for people to talk about for the rest of the summer, with her at the center. Whatever. I was glad I didn't have to worry about it; I was glad I didn't have to worry about Julia.

I waited out Mike's doldrums awhile, then dragged him over to the dartboard. His game was off, but the competition brought him out of his dark hole. Eventually he put an old White Stripes song on the jukebox and took an interest in the Tigers game playing on the bar TV. After the Tigers shut down the White Sox in the ninth, Mike checked his betting slips and came up beaming. "I just made three hundred bucks."

"Cheers," I said, glad to have him back again.

Mike waved for the bill. "I got it, bro," he said, watching his hand peel bills from his money clip like he was a third party to the action. He flicked some jagged tens onto the bar. It was too much money, but Mike didn't care—his dramatic streak was coming out.

Before we walked out the door, he stopped me. A firm hand on my shoulder, just like he'd done at the party.

"Swear to God, I'm done with her forever," Mike said. "You don't know what I've been through with that."

"No, I probably don't. But glad to hear it anyway." I clapped him on the back and we pushed out into the starry night air, leaving chicken wings and carpet mold and problematic girls behind.

Mike burped on the way to the Porsche. I stuffed him into the passenger's seat and walked to the driver's side.

That's when I sensed a presence at my back. It had beer breath.

❧ ❧ ❧

Someone pushed me in the back. My chest crashed against the car. He kicked my legs—they swung out from underneath me, and my chin struck the top of the car on my way down. My neck snapped back as my teeth sunk into my tongue. Fluid shot through my mouth like right before you puke.

A trickle of blood slid down my throat. The man who grabbed me had black hair fanning out from underneath a Tigers cap. When he spoke, I saw his chipped tooth.

"Hello," Snaggletooth Shales taunted.

He flattened me against his pickup and scraped for something on the flatbed. He came up with it quick, and I saw a brief flash of crowbar just before a metal sting lanced the base of my neck. My skull rang like a tuning fork.

In the brief second before I passed out, I sensed my body toppling and my right cheek thudding into pebbles and dirt. I caught a sideways view of Snaggletooth's weathered Adidas shoes.

I woke up in a recliner. I might have been out for three days, I didn't know. My tongue felt roughly the size of the Goodyear blimp and I couldn't move my limbs.

A waifish woman was balled up on a couch across the narrow room. Lines of shadow and light sliced her body. Her face fell into the light as she scooted away from me. Abby Shales.

I tried to bring my hands out from behind me, but my shoulders strained uselessly under the pressure. The sting of rope bit into my wrists.

"I'm tied up." It probably wasn't news to her, but I was just getting back to reality. My tongue was getting in the way of everything. "What's going on?"

Abby didn't reply. Snaggletooth had tied my feet, too; I wasn't going anywhere. The room had fake wood paneling and poles running down the middle. Drains spotted the linoleum floor. We were in somebody's basement, and my expert powers of deduction told me it was the Shaleses'.

Abby walked to a doorway.

"You need to let me go," I said.

She hesitated at the door, biting her lip. I think she wanted to help me.

It hit me then that this was really happening—I was in a basement, tied up, in some kind of serious danger.

"Just let me go. *Please.*"

But she didn't. She opened the door, revealing a flight of stairs, and shut it firmly behind her. The stairs creaked on her way up. I could barely turn my head to look around the room. Small windows up to the street. Seven steps to the door. A case of motor oil in the corner. I focused on details so I wouldn't hyperventilate. Maybe some of them would come in handy, like in a *Die Hard* movie. A minute later, the stairs creaked again and Abby reappeared, fear still written on her face. She put her back to the door.

"Listen, don't—"

The door jiggled and threw her aside. Snaggletooth walked in with a beer in one hand and a crowbar in the other. The crowbar that had knocked me out. He wore the same flannel shirt and Tigers cap he'd had on in the Hideaway parking lot. I hadn't been out that long after all.

"What do you want?" I said. Stand up to the bullies—that's what they used to tell us.

He laughed and tapped the end of the crowbar against my shoulder. It was still tender from breaking my fall in the parking lot. He leaned into my ear and spoke with stale, revolting breath. "I think you know."

"I really don't."

He jammed the bar into my shoulder. "You're scaring my wife, man."

He stepped back and threw his empty bottle at my face. I ducked, and it burst apart on the concrete wall. He pointed to Abby. "She ain't done nothing! She's a nervous wreck!"

"I swear I don't know what you're talking about." A sudden sweat chilled my back. I tried to piece it together as fast as I could. Somebody was harassing her, but I had no idea who or why Snaggletooth thought it was me.

The crowbar made a cold line under my Adam's apple. I swallowed saliva traced with blood. He pressed the bar harder into my neck, sending off starbursts behind my eyelids.

"She doesn't have anything. She doesn't know anything."

"Swear to God," I said before the sting in my throat got to be too much. My Adam's apple bobbed painfully with each word. "I don't know anything."

He was keeping the bar at my neck, making my eyes tear with pain and panic, when something clicked. *The silver car that followed me—could it have been tailing Abby, too?*

"Wade . . ." It was Abby's voice, small and scared like her face. He released the bar. I sucked air.

"Shut up. Get out of here."

"Wade, no."

He wasn't having any of it—he took a backswing, focused on my knees. I shut my eyes, ready for the worst, when Mike's voice broke across the room.

"Don't."

Something made Snaggletooth drop the crowbar. It clanged to the floor, horribly loud in the confined basement.

Mike was drawing slowly toward Snaggletooth. I saw him but I couldn't really believe it—he was carrying a silver gun, pointed right at Snaggletooth's chest. White light gleamed off the barrel. Mike took a split second to check me over.

"Okay, bro?"

"Yeah." I was still seconds behind everything, catching up from the shock of it all.

Mike motioned Snaggletooth into a corner with the gun.

"Easy, son," Snaggletooth said. He put his hands halfway in the air and retreated backward. Mike advanced, keeping a body length between himself and Snaggletooth, whose face had gone oily with sweat. He looked feebly to his wife as he passed her on his way to the corner.

"You, too," Mike said to Abby.

He shifted the gun to her for a brief second, getting her to comply.

The instant he did, Snaggletooth lunged.

Mike saw it. He swiveled, swinging his arm with his body like a backhand, and cracked Snaggletooth across the head with the gun barrel.

He fell to the floor like a sack. Silence rang through the basement.

"Oh, God," Mike said.

He swallowed hard and took a dazed step back from the body. I was across the room, but I knew why Mike had gone white. There was something instant and final about the way the guy's body had caved. Mike had caught him too perfectly.

"You couldn't have—" I cut myself off. I didn't know anything.

Abby stayed put in the corner as Mike tested for a pulse. He stayed there too long for good news. My throat closed up and I prayed for Mike—prayed that this wouldn't mark him forever. Finally his shoulders relaxed and he peeled his fingers away. I could see the relief in his eyes as he trained the gun on Abby again and ran over to me.

"He's only unconscious," Mike said as he hurried to untie my hands. It only took a second, and then he gave me the gun. "Hold it on her while I get the rest of this undone."

We didn't need to bother. She was cemented in the corner, defeated.

"What were you trying to tell me before he came down here?" I called to Abby. She picked her glazed eyes up from her husband but didn't say anything. "Look, have you been followed? Is that what this is about?"

Mike had almost finished with the knots. Finally Abby nodded. "They've been watching me, in a car. I think they've been in the house, too."

"It isn't us."

She didn't argue. "Wade thought it was. You had that silver car. He figured you came to the bar looking for me again."

We had come in the Maskes' Porsche. It did, in fact, look similar to the car that had followed me that night.

"Why are they after you?"

"I don't know." She was going at her lip again.

Mike threw the rope aside; I could stand now. "Let's get going," he said.

"Listen," I said to Abby, "I think it has something to do with Mitch Blay—"

And then it struck me. *She cleaned his room. They would have seen each other every day, they would have talked. Mitch had found a girl and taken her out to the Country Club . . .*

That look on her face as she barred the door, the plea in her voice—Abby wasn't afraid of me, she was afraid of what I might tell her husband.

"You were with him, weren't you?"

Her eyes shot away to the corners, glassy and lost. She didn't need to say it.

"You've got to tell me what's going on, quick. Somebody killed him. I'm trying to find out who."

Mike pulled at me. "C'mon. We don't know how long he'll be out."

"If you don't tell me what's going on, they're just going to keep after you," I said as firmly as I could.

"How are you going to stop it?"

"Just tell me what they're after, Abby."

Her hands fluttered at her side, nervous for a distraction. "I need to get him somewhere. You can die if you're hit in the head, even really light. I read that someplace." But she wasn't checking him over, comforting him, doing any of the things you'd do if you cared about the man knocked to the floor, out cold.

"Yeah, you should take him to the hospital. But tell me what happened the night he died. I know you were at the motel. Tell me quick, then go."

"I don't know anything."

"Yes, you do." I was sure of it. Mike was hopping toward the stairs, willing me to follow him, and I was almost ready to give up when Abby broke.

"I was just getting on work, night shift," she said in a rush. "Brian wasn't there—he's the manager—so I just went straight to Mitch's room because that's when we'd see each other and . . ." Her eyes welled. "I saw he was dead right away and called the police. The sheriff came real quick."

The sheriff. *Maybe he'd been there already,* I thought.

"Did anyone come with him? A policeman named Spencer, maybe?"

Abby shook her head, giving me a little relief. "No, nobody. The sheriff stopped an SUV on the road, probably making sure they had nothing to do with it. I saw that much from the office. Then he came in and got the master key from me."

If the sheriff had killed Mitch, and he knew that Abby had seen all the bullet wounds, she would have been a problem for him.

"He asked you what you saw, right?"

"Yeah, a bunch of times. I told him I just saw a guy in his room with blood on him, acted like I didn't know anything else."

"Because you didn't want anyone knowing about you and Mitch?"

"Yeah, that's right," Abby said. It made sense—she had probably played it with the sheriff just liked she'd played it with me in the Hideaway. If she had, he wouldn't have been too worried about her knowing anything.

So who was following her—and why?

"Why are they after you? What do they want?"

She was going to crack, I could feel it. She was going to tell us everything.

But then something rustled against the floor, and we all held our breath as Wade flopped over on his back and reached to his forehead. A welt had blossomed above his temple. He was deep in his own world, unaware of us, but it shattered the confessional mood to pieces.

"Get the hell out of here," Abby said. "I need to take care of this."

I wondered if she meant taking him to the hospital or smothering him with a pillow, but we couldn't stick around to see.

"Let's go," Mike said, and I didn't resist.

We were halfway up the stairs when Abby called to me.

"Hey, kid. What's your name?"

"Christopher Newell," I said, and she disappeared right back into the basement.

I trudged out of the house with Mike, heavy-legged and spent from adrenaline. By the time we got outside, I was consumed by the pain at the back of my head and the swelling of my tongue. I couldn't process what had happened yet. Getting abducted, seeing Mike with the gun—it was too much to absorb just then.

I could only think little thoughts, and one of them kept returning to me as we stumbled out to the car: *Why did Abby Shales ask my name?*

It would only take two days for me to find out.

16

Mike had parked the Porsche a few houses short of the Shaleses' place. He drove us away through a mist that speckled the windshield. It cast paint-splatter shadows on Mike's face as I slumped into the leather seat and watched the sad homes in the Shaleses' neighborhood pass by. They had tool sheds overflowing with scrap metal and hollowed-out cars sitting pointlessly on front lawns. Tire swings hung from a few trees, but that was about it in the way of fun.

We came to a road with a vaguely familiar name, and Mike turned left, shrugging. It didn't matter—the thrill of surviving the episode in the basement was too much to care about getting a little lost.

Mike reached across me and slid the gun inside the glove compartment.

"So, umm, where did you get a *gun*, anyway?"

"My dad bought it for protection. Then, of course, my mom

didn't like it in the house." They were always fighting. He used a hand to clear fog from the windshield. "She said it was freaking her out and put it in the glove box to return, but that was, like, a month ago. I don't even know how to use it. Guess it worked anyway."

"Yeah, thank God for that. So what happened in the parking lot?"

Mike smirked. "I was halfway passed out, but then I saw that guy peeling away with you in his passenger seat. I followed him all the way out here. Yeah, we came this way," he said, and took a sharp left turn onto Mercury Drive.

We weren't that far from the North Campus, much closer to home than I'd thought.

"Well, you did a stellar job," I said.

"I saw that guy tying you up through the basement window. Then he sat there and had a beer in the kitchen before he went back down. I had to wait for him so I could punch through the screen door and get inside."

"You punched through their screen door?"

"Well, on the fourth try." Mike held out his fist proudly—his knuckles had raspberry tears from the metal screen. "Not bad, eh?"

"One for the books," I said, remembering that we had to go back to Dana's to pick up the Escort. We crossed back over the city line (WELCOME TO PETOSKEY: WHERE NATURE SMILES FOR SEVEN MILES), but I still didn't want the ride to end.

"So you're done with all this now, right?" Mike said.

He said it normal, like it wasn't the most outrageous thing I'd heard all summer. "Done with this? Mike, something big is going on. She knows something—didn't you see? She was about to tell us."

He burned through a yellow light. "Dude, five minutes ago you were tied up in a basement with a madman and a crowbar. What's next?"

"Since when are you the careful one? You were telling me I was nuts to think the guy was murdered. Now I'm finally getting somewhere."

"Yeah, well—"

"They shot him in the chest *five times*. Nobody cares but me and Tina."

"Okay, okay. You're a man on a mission. Chill." In the uneasy silence, Mike made a fist and admired his wounds. "You should know, though, I'm only human. I can only save your ass so many times."

"Got it, Rambo," I said.

The mayor's neighborhood was funeral quiet, the houses ghostly boxes in the moonlight. I played at my swollen tongue as we pulled up to the Escort. We'd been going hard all night, and when the car came to a stop it felt like getting off a roller coaster.

"So really, thanks for saving my life," I said. "Seriously."

He barely opened his eyes. "No drippy shit, dude."

"Righto. I may send a fruit basket, though. Would you mind that?"

"Just make it tasteful," Mike said, and a laugh that had been bottled up inside me escaped from my chest.

"You gonna get home okay?" I said.

"I sobered up the second I saw that guy hit you."

"You didn't even move."

"See you tomorrow," Mike said, like it had been a normal day.

❦   ❦   ❦

Tina's cell phone number was on her business card, propped up against my clock radio, which read 2:30 a.m. She picked up after five rings and murmured something unintelligible.

The report from the bathroom mirror had not been encouraging. My scrape with the Hideaway's parking lot made the right side of my face puffy and allergic-looking. At least you couldn't see my tongue.

"Hey, it's Christopher."

"Yeah. And?"

"Yeah, sorry to call late, I just needed to talk to you about what happened tonight. You awake yet?"

A complicated rustling came through the line. "Sort of. Shoot."

I told her about getting abducted by Wade Shales and getting saved by Mike, and I threw in Abby's description of the scene at the Lighthouse Motel. I was a little geared up about the whole thing, and I realized I'd been going on for five minutes without a word from Tina.

"You still there?"

"Yeah, yeah," she said, alert. "My God, I'm so glad you're okay. You really think Abby knew something else?"

"Definitely. But we had to get out of there."

"Right, of course. But we'll have to go back to her for more."

"That's what I was thinking," I said. "Should we—?"

"You did awesome," Tina cut in, "but . . . let's talk about it more tomorrow." I sensed the slightest impatience in her voice. "You sure you're okay, Chris?"

"Yeah." I hopped into the safety of my bed. "I'm glad Mike was there. But maybe we should think about—"

"Do *not* tell me you're pussing out."

"I'm not pussing out."

"Swear."

"I swear." Still, Mike's warnings echoed in my head. "But you know, maybe there's some kind of state police or something we should get involved."

"No way. This story is my *break*. Who knows who'll get their hands on it if we tell the police? Now, listen, can we meet up tomorrow? This isn't really a great time."

"Wait a second," I said. "Where are you?"

I heard more rustling in the background, as Tina's voice became a whisper. "Lawrence's bathroom," she said. "*Score!*"

"Your girlfriend writes boring stuff." Daniel was munching on granola, reading an article by Tina about a ninety-year-old banjo player. He might have had a point.

"She's not his girlfriend," my mom said with a certain vigor as she spun about the kitchen. They were leaving the next day, and she now seemed obsessed with making sure all knobs, dials, and locks in the entire house were in proper position before her departure.

My face had looked slightly better that morning, but I didn't want to take the chance of my mom seeing the damage from the night before. I bid them adieu and headed for the morgue.

Not that I really needed to. I'd already put in enough hours that week, but somehow the morgue was feeling more like a place I *wanted* to be. That might sound gruesome, I realize, but it was the thing that connected me to Mitch.

Maybe Mike thought it was weird that I cared about finding his killer so much, and yeah, maybe hundreds of people get murdered every day and I hadn't taken up their cause or anything. But there are hundreds of homeless dogs, too, and it's different when you go to the shelter and a lonely beagle laps at your hand. Not that either of us was a dog—the point is, we'd picked each other somehow, and we'd done it at the morgue. I *saw* him there on that table, and I knew things about him that nobody else did, or cared about.

I was thinking these thoughts when I pranced into the office, wondering what new nooks and crannies I could search for clues. It was a Wednesday morning, when Dr. Mobley had his pediatric hours on the second floor. I hadn't even considered the possibility that he would be there until I saw him sitting on the sofa, weeping quietly.

His fingers glistened with tears as he pulled them from his face. He stared absently at me with red-rimmed eyes. Something about the whole scene scared the crap out of me.

"Are you okay, sir? I mean, Doctor?"

I don't think he even heard me.

He just said, "My wife died last night."

His voice stayed neutral, like he was giving me a half-interested opinion on the color of my shirt. He must have been up all night and cried himself empty.

"I'm so sorry, Dr. Mobley. Should I . . . would you like to be alone? Or if there's anything I can do—"

"She bought us this couch," he said, picking up like I hadn't spoken a word.

He spread his hands across the tattered, mangy fabric. It might have been blue years ago, but the color had leached out and left only the rumpled gray disaster that Dr. Mobley sat on.

"After I graduated from medical school—we'd been married six months. Our first proper piece of furniture." The couch was beaten by age like so many things in the office, but he ran his fingers deep into the cushions, clutching at memories.

He'd been a boogeyman to me all summer, and there he was, a frail and brittle old guy, wrecked by grief over his wife. It was so sad I wanted to puke.

The phone rang then and Dr. Mobley tried feebly to push himself up. It would take him an hour to get around to the desk. In that moment, I would have run a marathon if Dr. Mobley had asked me to—getting the phone was the least I could do.

"Medical examiner's office," I said.

"Is this . . . Christopher?"

"Uh, yeah." I recognized his voice right away, and it made me more uneasy than Dr. Mobley's news.

"Tim Spencer here." He sounded unduly flustered by the fact that he was speaking to me. Maybe he didn't know I was working in the morgue, but that seemed improbable. "Actually, I may have to—no, well, forget that for now. Is the doctor there?"

"Yeah, sure," I said, trying to keep the wariness out of my voice.

Dr. Mobley leaned against the desk, breathing with exertion. I handed him the phone as he made his way around.

"Yes?" Dr. Mobley said. "Yes, thanks for calling back. We need to talk. But hold on, hold on." The doctor settled behind the desk. A measure of life had returned to his eyes, now gazing at me firmly. It was pretty clear what he wanted.

"I'll just . . . leave you then," I said. I was probably supposed to add something about his wife being in my prayers or whatever the right catchphrase is, but it was all too much.

On my way out, Dr. Mobley spoke darkly across the line. "No, just a second . . . Yes, okay, now he's go—"

The door clicked shut and the rest of the conversation was lost to me.

I can't even say how much it disturbed me. I'd convinced myself that the sheriff was behind the whole thing. I'd been ignoring the signals pointing to Tim, hoping that he hadn't really eaten lunch with Dr. Mobley that day. But now I knew it wasn't a coincidence.

It wasn't like Dr. Mobley needed to talk to the police very much. He'd only done two other autopsies all summer, and neither had involved any foul play. The place wasn't exactly teeming with matters of forensic importance.

It was bad enough that Tim and Mobley were talking, but on top of it, Tim had been so awkward. Obviously, neither of them wanted me hearing the first word of their conversation. Yeah—Tim Spencer was knee-deep in this mess.

At home, my dad was reading an old leather book (as usual) in the kitchen, his feet splayed out in front of him and his head lost in some ancient world of Roman heroes. A tempting glass of lemonade dripped onto the table. I got one of my own and sat down with him, pressing the cool glass to my forehead. It didn't do much for my worries about Tim, but it took my temperature down a little.

The thrumming of the dryer pulsed through the kitchen as my mom bustled in from the laundry room. "I found those clothes of yours," she said, holding up the shirt I'd worn the night before. I'd tossed it in with the laundry when I got home—not noticing, until just now, the prominent tear across the shoulder. Thanks, Snaggletooth.

The slack my mom had cut me the day before was long gone. She was in a state. "Christopher, it's so dirty. And look at this." She pushed her hand through the hole, amazed at the destruction I had wrought. "What did you *do* last night? Gwen said you deserted Julia at the party."

"I wasn't really with her in the first place, Mom."

"Where'd you go?" my dad said idly, turning a page.

The dryer stopped and left us in silence. "I left with Mike. The party was kind of lame."

My mom held my shirt out again, like it was a sick baby. "And your *clothes?*"

"Oh, well, this guy sort of tried to beat us up."

"Oh, Christopher, you got into a fight?"

"Not really. It was just this weird guy. It's no big deal."

My mom peered at me, closer and closer, and then came around for a look at my cheek. Maybe it hadn't cleared up as well as I thought.

"Oh, dear," she said, and I almost expected her to reach for the Scotch. She stood there, arms crossed, eyebrows raised to my dad, when I got a reprieve from the doorbell. Just in time.

I was just getting back to the lemonade—placing more and more faith in its calming powers—when my mom returned from the door. Flushed face, bulging eyes. Something wasn't good.

My dad put his book down for the second time in two minutes. "Dear, what is it?"

"Well," my mom said, in a *funny-you-should-ask* kind of way. "Timothy Spencer is on our porch. On official business, he tells me. And he would very much like to talk to Christopher."

17

He was hunkered on our front steps, one foot up on the porch and his hat over his knee. In the driveway, the sun glared off his patrol car's windshield, obscuring a form in the passenger's seat. I hesitated at the screen door—I couldn't fathom what this was going to be about.

Tim gave me a subdued nod. "Heya."

"Hi, Tim."

He played with his hat, waiting for me to join him on the porch. Slowly, I walked the plank out to him; that's what it felt like anyway.

"So, Christopher. I'm here about Abigail Shales."

He said it in that flat cop voice. Icy and removed, portending doom. He wasn't fondly remembering the times we threw the football around in his backyard, that was for sure.

Abby? How does he know about her?

I shut the front door behind me, buying time, hoping that

our conversation wouldn't carry into the kitchen. "Yeah? Abigail Shales?"

"Look, don't be scared," Tim said, but I was not in a frame of mind to be assuaged. My mind did corkscrews, trying to connect Tim with Abby.

Is he the one driving the silver car? The one following her . . . the one who followed me, too? It was the only thing that really made sense.

"All I want is a little information, okay? Just tell me first: Were you at Abigail Shales's home last night with Mike?"

He knows. He knows we were there.

This interview felt like sinking in quicksand—or what sinking into quicksand looks like on cartoons and old Tarzan movies. Uncomfortable, at any rate. Sinews popped on Tim's forearm as his fingers played across the top of his hat. Whatever this visit was about, it couldn't be good that he knew about us being at Abby's house. Maybe he'd been staking it out or something—maybe he saw the whole thing. It was becoming impossible to believe that Tim didn't know every last thing about Mitch Blaylock's murder.

"Uh, what does it matter?"

"Don't worry, okay? This'll be over in a minute." A hint of annoyance—maybe more than a hint—threaded through his words. "I just need to ask you a couple questions about last night. So you were there, right?"

A trickle of sweat ran a slimy path down my ribs. *There's no denying it. You haven't done anything wrong—just tell the truth and keep yourself out of trouble.*

Then the door of the patrol car opened and a pair of legs swung to the pavement. Sheriff Harmon got out and rested his elbow on the roof, staring me down from the driveway.

"Christopher?" Tim insisted.

You can't lie to a police officer. You'll get caught in the lie and get arrested, because obviously he knows you were there.

"No."

Tim stopped fiddling with his hat. "No what?"

"No, I wasn't at Abigail Shales's house last night. Who is she, anyway?"

I thought I might black out from the nerves. Somewhere in Indiana, my galloping pulse was setting off a seismograph.

"Look, here's the deal," Tim said. "Abigail Shales has gone missing."

Gone missing! I was committing perjury or whatever to save our investigation, and now Tina and I would never find out what Abby knew.

"A neighbor saw you at her house last night."

"Hmmm." At that point, it was a struggle just to stay in control of myself. The sheriff caressed his stubble as he watched on from the driveway. The interview had turned into a full-on, out-of-body experience. "Sorry," I said, "but whoever it is, they're wrong."

Tim pinched his eyes. He didn't bother hiding his frustration anymore. "Christopher. C'mon. This is really serious."

We'd never had hard words before. I'd worshiped him for years, and part of me couldn't let it go—his disappointment hit me with a slap of shame.

"Are you saying she went missing last night?" I stalled. Tim nodded, but it didn't make sense. Everybody knows they don't look into these things until twenty-four hours have passed. "That was only a few hours ago. How do you know she's even really gone?"

Tim sighed. "There was an altercation at her house last night. Some people on her street heard it. But I'm sure that's not news to you because they saw two kids leaving in a Porsche around that time, and I know that could only be you and Mike. Her husband came to the hospital last night. He needs her, and she's gone."

I was trying to swallow the news—trying to force it down and figure out some way it didn't spell huge trouble for me, and Mike, and Mitch—when the sheriff pushed off the car and headed toward the porch. Tim saw him coming.

"So this is it, Christopher. We'll just forget what you said before. Now tell me what happened at that house last night."

He's giving you a last chance—take it.

"I wish I could," I said. "But I don't even know who that lady is."

Below us, the sheriff grasped the railing to the front steps.

"How we doin'?" he said in his cavernous voice.

"All done," Tim said, and glared at me as he retreated down the steps.

My mom was lying in wait for my return.

She'd stationed herself on the farthest edge of the living room sofa, while her foot tapped against the hardwood floor with the ferocity of a speed-metal drummer's. My dad gave her calming pats on the back while he spoke with an airline operator, confirming that they'd have vegetarian meals for their flight. I needed to get in touch with Mike fast—Tim and the sheriff were probably on the way to his house right then.

"Well . . . ?" my dad said as he hung up.

"It was nothing," I said quickly.

My mom was dubious at best. "Nothing?"

"Yeah, I guess somebody saw that guy picking the fight with us. They just wanted to be sure we were okay."

She inched back on the sofa, letting an ounce of tension ease from her hair-trigger nerves. My dad hummed, noncommittal. They looked almost as frustrated as Tim had, and it tempted me to ease their nerves further with another heap of lies about how totally fine and sunny my life was going.

"Christopher," my dad said, "you're getting into a lot of . . . situations here. That's what concerns your mother and me. We're leaving tomorrow, you know."

"I know. It was nothing, seriously. I'm gonna go read, okay?"

They were mumbling to each other as I raced up the stairs.

"You gotta do something for me."

"What?"

"Lie to the cops."

"That's my specialty," Mike said. "What about?"

I made sure my bedroom door was locked and spoke softly into my cell, even though I knew my parents were still downstairs, trying to decide how much of a delinquent their son had become and whether shipping me off to the Marines was the only option left. "Last night," I told Mike. "You gotta tell them we weren't at Abby's house."

A long silence darkened the connection. "Are you serious?" Mike said finally.

"Tim Spencer and the sheriff just grilled me about it. Somebody saw a car like yours at their house, but I told them I didn't even know who Abby Shales was. Can you back me up?"

"Why would you lie about *that*?" Now Mike was getting hysterical, too—the one person I could count on to stay calm no matter what. I wanted to stuff him and my parents in a car and send them to a day spa. They could take mud baths and stop worrying about me while Tina and I wrapped up the case and restored order to Petoskey. They'd get back just in time for the parade, where the mayor would give us the key to the city and proclaim our greatness.

"I had to," I said. "I told you, Tim and the sheriff are behind this somehow. They didn't come here to do their police duties—they're trying to make sure the murder stays covered up. If they know we're on to them, who knows what they'll do."

"But what if they *didn't* do it? No offense or anything, but it's just slightly possible that you're wrong. I mean, I do love screwing with the police and all, but this is kind of hard-core."

It took me a few seconds of deep disappointment to realize he was right. Mike had been unsupportive of my project from the start, but this was asking a lot. Tina was going to hate me for this, and maybe I'd get in a ton of trouble, but I didn't have it in me to press him anymore.

"Yeah, okay, do what you need to. But could you do me a favor? If they come to your house, could you just pretend you aren't there or something? I could use a few more days."

Right on cue, an electronic doorbell sounded across Mike's line.

"It's them," he said. "I'm looking out my window, and they can see me."

It was over. Maybe I'd be arrested, I didn't know. I could hear Mike's steps to the door as I sat there on the bed, eyes pinched shut, doom bearing down on me. My jaw ached from my grinding teeth.

"You still there, man?" Mike said. He'd stopped walking. He must have been standing right at the door, ready to let them inside.

"Yeah, I'm here."

Mike took a deep breath. "Don't sweat it, okay? I got your back."

The exhaustion took over—I lay back on my bed, clothes on, and fell into a deep sleep that did wonders for my overcooked nerves. Daniel woke me up for no good reason in the middle of the afternoon, but I was too relieved at getting through the morning in one piece to really care.

I picked up my room a little and took my spy novel downstairs. Keeping myself on lockdown for the day, I figured, would put my parents' fears to rest. I planted myself on the back porch for most of the afternoon, a fixture of conspicuous responsibility, until shadows crept over the garden and the backyard fell silent for the evening. The air had cooled a touch, and I was actually thinking of helping Daniel set the table (not that he would have let me), when I heard a familiar-sounding pair of boots clomping across our front porch.

Knuckles rapped loudly on the screen door, and I could hear my mom mutter from upstairs, "Oh good Lord, what now?"

At the door, Tina had a cigarette going. Smoke billowed into the house as she peered through the screen in a T-shirt that said PRIVATE

PROPERTY. My dad got there just ahead of me, and from the Botoxed expression on his face, I could tell that he didn't know quite what to think about the apparition before him.

"Hi there. Mr. N?" Most people called him Professor.

"Errr . . . that's one way to say it, yes."

"Tina McIntyre," she said. "Heard a lot about you."

The words went straight through my dad's ears. "Can I help you?"

"Dad, this is Tina. From the paper. Could you let her inside?"

"Errr, of course. Of course, of course, of course. Come in."

Tina flicked her smoke onto the porch and winked at me as she entered.

"Really good to meet you. I love this kid of yours." Tina gave my dad a close look as she shook his hand. "*Now* I see where Chris gets his good looks."

My dad snorted a variety of laugh that I'd never heard before, and if I wasn't mistaken, his cheeks colored a little.

"You aren't hiding any more Newell men around town are you?"

I really couldn't have imagined things going any better, until I heard my mom's rapturous voice call down, "Is that Julia I hear?"

"Errr," my dad said nervously.

My mom's feet pounded over the stairs.

"Errr," he said again.

I cringed.

"Now Ju—" My mom's lips froze as she rounded the corner. "Oh."

"Dear, this is Tina McIntyre, Christopher's friend."

My mom petrified halfway to the door. Her arms hung limp while Tina hugged her. "Great to meet you," Tina said.

My mom regarded Tina warily as they broke apart. Tina looked around at the historic map of Petoskey and the antique spinning-wheel. "Very nice. Chris says you're both professors. I can almost feel the brain power." She made accordion movements around my dad's head. "It's like, bzzzzzz."

My dad swung a chair behind her. "Sit down. Tell us about the work you're doing over there at the *Courier*. Christopher seems to be enjoying it."

And then Daniel appeared. "What stinks?"

"It's nothing," my dad said. "Come meet Tina McIntyre. She works at the *Courier*."

"Hello, stud man," Tina said, and I could feel my mom bristle.

"Your crossword puzzles suck."

My mom whispered a protest: "*Daniel.*" He never talked like that with my parents around, but I knew that somehow Tina would get blamed for his bad manners.

My dad shrugged an apology. "They're too easy for him, you see."

"Another cutie, *and* he's a brain?" Tina said.

Daniel beamed, and my dad's tongue was practically hanging out of his mouth at that point. My mom held stiff at the side of the room, deep in *concerned-parent* mode, but I figured two out of three was the best I could ever hope for and pulled Tina out on the porch to talk in private.

"My mom can be a little uptight," I said when we got there.

Tina shrugged. "She thinks I'm going to corrupt you. Moms are supposed to be protective. I'm serious, though, your dad's a hottie."

I ignored that and told her about the visit from Tim and the sheriff, and how I had denied even knowing Abby Shales. "I might be screwed, 'cause somebody saw Mike's car out there. They might have even gotten a look at us, I don't know."

"No," Tina said emphatically. "You're a rock star. You did the right thing. We're closing in on this—we just need to find out what Abby knows."

"Yeah, well, that's the other bad news."

"What?"

"She's gone. They said she disappeared last night, after she took Wade to the hospital."

Tina slapped a fist against her palm and swore too loudly. It must have carried into the house. On the sidewalk, a retired woman from down the street was taking her poodle for an evening walk—she looked up sharply and ambled away from us.

"Your friend Tim sounds like a dick," Tina said, burning off some disgust at the news about Abby.

I shrugged. "He didn't used to be. I still can't believe he did it, in a way."

"He's a dick, dude."

"Yeah, maybe." I plopped down next to her on the steps. The bad news bonded us as we sat there, moisture creeping into the air and the sky turning purple above us. Tina was the only one who cared about this case like I did. She was the one only who would've understood why I'd wanted to go to the morgue that morning.

"Crappy day, but you're a stud for hanging in there. We'll get them, Chris."

She pulled me up off the steps, and then something magnificent happened. I don't know if she thought about it beforehand. I didn't. All of a sudden my arms were going around her waist and hers were wrapping over my shoulders, and we were pulling toward each other. It wasn't sexual or anything. It was just a hug. But a wave of content crashed over me, and my worries about lying to the police leaked away into the night, as quickly as the far-off yipping of the poodle.

"We're gonna get them," Tina repeated in my ear.

Her lips were close, and my ear tingled with pleasure even as we drew apart.

18

"All set," my mom muttered to herself. "All set. All set."

My dad popped his head into the kitchen, his shoulders weighted down with suitcases. "We should have left ten minutes ago," he said, and rushed out to the car.

"We'll call you when we get settled, which should be pretty late tonight. Probably around—"

"Ten thirty or so. You've told me, Mom. We'll be waiting."

She hugged me tight. "Take care of him," she whispered. "And take care of yourself, okay?"

"I'll miss you, Mom." I meant it.

She enlisted me to carry a few of her bags, and eventually the whole production made it out to the driveway. "It's all yours now, partner," my dad said as he closed the trunk.

"Have a good time, Dad." I meant that, too.

"Keep the fights to a bare minimum, okay?"

"You got it. Three max."

He gave me his wry grin. "Let's not have any house calls from Tim Spencer, either, huh?"

"Yeah, sorry about that. That was just a . . . weird thing."

He wanted to touch me in some approving, fatherly way and settled on a sideways half hug. He said his good-byes to Daniel, took a drink of us with his eyes, and hopped into the car. My mom blew us kisses as they rolled down the street, hanging out the window like her sons were standing on a train platform and she was watching us as long as she could.

"Good-bye boys! Be safe! Good-bye! Good-bye. . . ."

Their departure was supposed to free me up to investigate Mitch's death, but mostly it was just a huge distraction. It was like having a missing tooth. It was hard to focus on anything but the hollowness in the den, where my mom would have been working on her research grant, or the empty-looking kitchen chair, where my dad would have been reading one of his old stories.

Daniel didn't seem to mind. He dove right into a pile of chemistry books he had checked out of the library—he was probably reinventing the periodic table of elements or something. Since I didn't have anything else going on, I figured I might as well check the list of household duties my parents had left for me.

Mow lawn. That could wait. *Take Daniel to pool.* Ugh. *Collect mail.* That I could handle.

The box had just three thin envelopes: the cable bill, a credit card offer, and a handwritten envelope addressed to me. It bore a postmark from Petoskey and no return address. I tossed the others on the kitchen table and went up to my room to open it. I didn't recognize the tiny, super-slanted handwriting, but somehow I already knew it was going to be about Mitch.

Fingertip-sized grease marks smudged the page inside, a half sheet of paper torn carelessly from a spiral notebook. Potato chip crumbs spilled to the floor when I unfolded it.

She hadn't signed the note or written my name at the top, but she didn't have to. I could practically see her looking my address up in the phone book that night, after she left Wade at the hospital. She probably dropped it in the mail slot at the bus station, her last act in Petoskey before throwing her chips away and hopping on a Greyhound.

You wanted to know, so here it is.
Mitch had pictures of the mayor with
a woman at the motel. (Her name was
Kate Something accoreding to Mitch—
some fancy bitch lawyer or something.)
Anyway, if you can't figure out what
he was doing with those pictures
you're not as smart as you seem.
   Mitch used to tell me he was
going to take his money and go to
Texas. It was just a stupid dream
like everything else he said. Well
I'm going. It's a big state and I

*plan on getting lost, so don't try
to find me. You actually seem like
a desert kid, so I hope your serious
about trying to find whoever killed
my Mitch. He might have been an idiot,
but he was good for a laugh and
that's more than I can say for any
other man.*

*Good luck kid. Do Mitch right—
somebody should.*

*P.S. He had a partner. They used
to meet at the pool, that's all I
really know. Mitch said he loved me,
but he didn't tell me much.*

I sat at my desk, rereading Abby's note with a strange exhilaration. If you're going to get invested in a dead criminal, it's nice to know that he was shooting for the stars. I couldn't help smiling at the thought of Mitch trying to blackmail the mayor. The uptight little man had been having an affair with Kate Warne, and Mitch had found out somehow.

It seemed reasonably certain to me that, admirable as his efforts at blackmailing may have been, they got Mitch killed. Abby's note had to be right. The blackmail scheme must have been what Mitch had been talking about at the country club bar the night he died, and the affair between the mayor and Kate Warne made a certain amount of sense.

Dana had told me how close her dad was to Kate Warne. It explained why the mayor had been giving her that weird look when she flirted with the bartender at the scholarship ceremony: he was jealous. It also fit perfectly with the sheriff's interest in the case— after all, his sister was being blackmailed by Mitch. Maybe the sheriff had decided to put a stop to it.

There was something else, too. As soon as I read about Mitch having pictures, my mind flashed to the Vista View case in Dr. Mobley's office. It had seemed like just another of Dr. Mobley's oddities, but now that I thought about it, the first time I'd ever seen it was the day Mitch arrived at the morgue. It could have all been a wild coincidence, but I doubted it. Somewhere out there was a Vista View memory card with Mitch's pictures on it.

I had no way of knowing where the card had gone—maybe Mobley had destroyed it, maybe the sheriff had taken it, or maybe it was gone before either of them got their hands on Mitch—but Abby had given me something else to look for that would be just as informative. We needed to find Mitch's partner.

I pounded on the wall between my room and Daniel's.

"Get your suit on! We're going swimming!"

PART III

CHAMPAGNE FOR TWO

or

UNSUPERVISED ADULTS

19

Tina came over in record time when I told her about the note. We sat on the porch so she could smoke while we waited for Daniel to peel himself away from his science books and get his swimming stuff together.

"So this is like the bachelor pad now, huh?" Tina said.

"I guess."

"Can I see your bedroom?"

I surveyed it in my mind. I didn't know what she would think of my *War of the Worlds* poster (the original) or my Green Hornet comforter from ten Christmases ago. I made a mental note to get a new one. Black, maybe. Or leopard print.

"Let's see if we can find this partner first," I said.

"Cool, I thought you might be thinking about puss—"

"Tina, I'm not pussing out." I took the note back from her and folded it carefully into my wallet.

Daniel was taking forever, but it was a great moment—sitting on the porch with the insanely hot Tina McIntyre, contemplating our break in the case, talking about going up to my bedroom. This was the good part of my parents being on vacation.

But something was bothering me about Mitch's blackmail scheme. "Do you think he really could have been doing that? He was only back in town a month."

"Have you been listening to anyone for the last week?" Tina said back. "The guy was a scam *artist*. That is what he did for a living. He gets out of prison, sets himself up in that dump of a motel. One day he's looking out the window and he sees the mayor and Kate Warne traipse into a room with a bottle of Dom and a box of Trojans. *Ding!* A big bright lightbulb, right over Mitch's head."

I wasn't sure. Just a few minutes ago it had felt like Abby's note had all the answers, but I was starting to realize how much remained a mystery. "Even if it's true," I said, "we still don't know who killed him. It could have been the sheriff, the mayor, or Kate Warne."

"Dude, don't focus on the negative. We'll find all that out when we talk to his partner." Tina seemed to think we'd spot him right away at the pool, wearing a sandwich board that said MITCH'S PARTNER. "You know, don't sweat these things so much. There's this theory that some philosopher came up with that says the simplest explanation for something is usually the right one. I'm sure you've heard of it."

I had no idea what she was talking about, but the answer was on its way. Daniel padded onto the porch in a pair of green flippers. He lifted his goggles off his face.

"It's called Ockham's razor. And he wasn't some guy—he was

William of Ockham, the fourteenth-century logician. Don't you guys know anything?"

"The male body isn't very attractive, if you think about it," Tina said.

We had set up on a pair of plastic-lounger things on the deck, giving us a full view of the small cross-section of Petoskey that had shown up to the pool that day: a gaggle of middle-school girls; three older women slathered in oil, arching their necks toward the sun; parents loaded down with beach bags and sippy-cups, unleashing spastic kids into the pool. Just about everybody was two square inches of lycra away from being stark naked. Unfortunately, Tina wasn't one of them. She also had a point—it wasn't a good look on most of the men, especially the one grilling hamburgers on the barbecue in nothing but a star-spangled Speedo job. I guess something about paying three dollars for a day pass to the Petoskey pool made people lose all sense of dignity.

Daniel's little flipper kicks splashed onto the deck. He had hopped in the water the moment we arrived, and now he was darting from one end of the pool to the next, industrious as ever. A lifeguard looked on from a seat raised above it all. His blond hair was tinged green from chlorine exposure. I was glad it wasn't the guy from Dana's party—I didn't like the idea of Daniel's life being in the hands of the guy who'd ruined Mike's summer.

It only took a minute to scan the crowd of thirty or so and discount all of them as possible partners in Mitch's blackmailing scheme.

"Do you have that picture of Mitch on you?" I asked Tina.

She went for her bag. "Yeah, why?"

"I know a girl who works here. I can ask her if she ever saw him here with anyone."

"Is she cute?"

"What?"

Tina held the picture out of my reach. "I'm just saying, we need to find you a girlfriend. Don't you think?"

"Not this girl—she used to go out with Mike."

Tina grudgingly handed over the picture. "Fine, but don't think I'm going to let this go." She took off her shoes and basked in the sun. Even her feet were pretty.

Three girls in GUARD shirts sat around behind the concession stand, slurping neon-colored ice pops. Sophie Hamilton was one of them. She was perched on an icebox, and she looked right through me when I walked up—like she didn't remember me from two nights ago at Dana's house, or three years of high school before that. It was pretty annoying.

"Hey. Is Dana here?" I said.

One of the girls was making a paint-pen sign about Bingo Night at the pool. "No," she said, taking her eyes off the sign briefly. "She just left."

"Oh, thanks. Do you know where she went?"

The third girl gave the others a creeped-out look. "Umm, home maybe?" she said, like I was a either a potential stalker or just an idiot. The others sniggered into their ice pops.

"Are you with *her*?" Sophie said sharply, giving a little point-out to Tina.

"Yeah, I am," I said proudly. "See you around, Sophie."

I turned, trying to feel triumphant about the exchange. But the girls started whispering at each other furiously as I left them, and I couldn't help wondering what they were saying about me. High school would never really end.

Tina refused to come with me to Dana's. "Chicks hate me," she said. "And a chick your age is going to hate me even more. You know what this sounds like? A solo mission."

Somebody needed to keep an eye on Daniel anyway, and Tina said she'd take him home from the pool when he finished his Olympic workout. Which left me all alone ten minutes later, standing on the Rubys' front porch, when Dana's mom answered the doorbell.

"Hi, Mrs. Ruby." A shorter, more delicate version of her daughter, Mrs. Ruby was trying to place me when Dana appeared in the foyer and squeezed past her as if she were a ghost.

"Hey, Newell," Dana said. "What're you doing here?"

"I just wanted to ask you about something real quick," I said.

I had the picture of Mitch in my back pocket. The investigation was starting to feel hopeless again—all our hopes rode on the off chance that she would remember Mitch and his partner from the pool.

She waved me in and led me upstairs like I was over all the time. The mayor's house always felt so lonely to me, except up in Dana's room, where she had all kinds of lights on and Petoskey's cheesy rock station playing on a pink boom box. The fifth caller was going ballistic over winning Weezer tickets. Dana didn't turn it down.

"You don't have to stand there at the edge of the room," she said, lying on the bed in a seductive way. It didn't mean anything— seductive was her default setting.

I pulled a chair out from the kid-size desk with a giant-size laptop on it. "Yeah, well, like I said, I'm doing this sort-of internship at the *Courier* this summer."

"Oh geez, it's Newell with his work again." She laid back on her bed like she was being tortured. "No, just kidding. What's up?"

"It's actually about this guy who died. His name is Mitch Blaylock." I pulled out the picture and handed it to her. "He used to hang out at the pool. Did you ever happen to see him there with anybody?"

Dana just stared at me—her eyes had gone dead at the details. The disc jockey was going on about their forty-five-minute rock block, and I wanted him to get on with it already so he wouldn't be yapping in our ears.

Dana wagged the picture. "So, you want to find this guy?"

"He's the dead one. I'm looking for the guy he hung out with at the pool."

Dana's laptop burped with a flurry of incoming IMs. The place was a sensory-overload chamber. I wondered if she would go insane if she had to be in a quiet place for fifteen minutes.

"What's the story about?"

"Oh, I don't even know. I'm just sort of a gopher. Every once in a while they ask me to do something like this—getting a phone number or whatever."

"Hmm. I might have seen him, but I don't know."

"You sure you don't recognize him?"

"Yeah."

She hadn't really looked that closely. "Just see if you can think about it for a minute. Try to, like, imagine that guy in sunglasses or a bathing suit or something. I mean, they say it's really important."

But Dana just flung the picture back to me. "I don't know the guy, Newell, I'm sorry." She was studying my face. "Is this even real? Is this, like . . . did Mike tell you to come over here or something?"

"No," I said quickly, but then I realized it wasn't an angry question.

A bunch of loose pictures were strewn over the desk—pictures of Dana out at parties, playing soccer, dressed up for Halloween with Sophie Hamilton. (Sexy nurses, of course.) Most of the pictures had Mike in them, and it hit me: she was *hoping* he'd sent me over here.

"You guys aren't talking?" I said.

"He's not talking to *me*, that's for sure." Dana's cell phone was lying on the desk, amidst the pictures and some beaded necklaces and a bunch of other junk. She checked the phone—making sure she hadn't missed any calls from Mike, I guess—and tossed it on the bed. I could feel her mood ping-ponging. The air in the room was turning cold.

She swept the pictures off the edge of the desk and into the trash. One of them missed, spinning wildly in the air on its way to the carpet.

"Screw him, right?" Dana said, more to herself than me. But he was my best friend; I couldn't let it go.

"He thinks you were cheating on him with that guy from the party."

"Yeah, well . . ."

She didn't finish the thought. It felt like an admission.

I picked the stray picture of her and Mike up from the carpet, not that it did much to unclutter the room. The bedroom had a walk-in closet but you wouldn't know it—stacks of jeans and sweaters lay around, some of them spilling from plastic crates. A pile of volleyball gear sat in a corner like it was being punished.

The dresser was the only clean part of the room, and it was immaculate. The mirror above it glistened, and the wood of the dresser-top gleamed from a fresh polish. It was bare except for a single framed photograph. It made sense—the one part of the room she looked after was the image of herself. I was curious about the picture she had chosen to place there, expecting it to be of her and Mike at the senior prom, but I couldn't see it from my angle.

"So you want to do something?" she said.

I was kind of shocked; we'd never hung out together before, just the two of us. I was thinking that I shouldn't, out of respect to Mike if nothing else, when the mayor's voice barked in from the hallway. "Dana! Where are you?!"

It jarred me—he was yelling at her, a hard edge of cruelty cutting through his voice. The door flew open and the doorknob hit the wall with a thud. It marked a spot indented from previous episodes. The mayor stopped short when he saw me.

"You've got company," he said, ratcheting himself back just a shade. It was for my benefit I guess, but he didn't seem nearly embarrassed enough. "You need to tell me when you have people over."

"I didn't ask him, he just came over," Dana said. "Hope that's okay."

The mayor reached over and turned down the radio. "I want to talk to you later," he said, and just like that he was gone.

Dana sulked. "He found out about the party," she said when he was safely downstairs.

If my parents found out I'd had a party like Dana's, we would have held hands in a circle or gone to therapy or spent a day in the woods playing trust games. But I never would have heard a demeaning voice like the mayor's. Something was off about it—something that made me think killing somebody might not be beyond him.

Dana was balling up her comforter like a stress toy. "So, like, what do you think?"

"Well, I mean, I think that was kind of harsh."

She laughed. "Not that, Newell. Do you want to hang out or what?"

"Oh. Yeah, well, I should probably get back to the paper."

She nodded. "Okay."

I had stepped back when the mayor came barging in, far enough to sneak a peek at the picture on her dresser before I left. When I did, it sort of killed me. There Dana was in her red prom dress— she had a spray tan and complicated braids, and she actually looked outrageously beautiful—but the guy on her arm wasn't Mike. It was her dad.

It was just a single picture at a dresser, but it said something unmistakable. The person she kept at her honored place before the mirror was the one who treated her the worst. I realized that I had misjudged her for ten years, and so had everybody else at Petoskey High. She didn't ask for attention because she was selfish. It had never been like that at all. The swim coach, Lawrence Lovell, the football players at the party—the whole lineup of older guys she attracted—they were substitutes. A psychologist could have had a field day.

I wanted to say something on my way out, something nice, but as soon as I crossed into the hall, the door shut behind me.

"Saved some fries for you," Mike said.

His eyes never left the television. The sleepy voices of two former Detroit Tigers were calling their game with the Chicago White Sox. Mike was stretched out on our sofa, his feet spilling off the far end. The french fries wilted on the cocktail table next to the ledger in which Mike recorded his bets.

He told me that he'd come over a little while ago and decided to babysit Daniel until I came home.

"Where have you *been*?" Daniel said. "I could have *died* or something."

His face glowed blue in the light of the television, which he sat about three inches away from. It was an odd picture; I had never seen Daniel actually watch a baseball game before. He prefers dissecting the box scores in the morning paper to the fun of actually watching the game.

I pushed Mike's legs aside and decided to give the fries a try. Soggy, cold. I pointed to Daniel. "What gives?"

Mike slid the ledger toward me. "I gave him a fifty-dollar credit to screw around with. Kid loves the action. Who knew?"

"He's betting with you?"

A run came home. Daniel raised his arms. "Yes!"

"Just fifty bucks, for fun. Just to make the night a little more exciting," Mike said.

I saw several bets by the initials DN. "I'm up two hundy already," Daniel said. I examined the page again in disbelief, and considered ripping it out for evidence to be used against him later. It could be the only thing standing between him and the presidency someday— it would be up to me to stop him.

"You're gonna lose it all, buddy," Mike said. A graphic came up on the screen, showing the score: Tigers 2, White Sox 10.

I made mac and cheese for dinner—Daniel, rubbing his temples and rocking back and forth in front of the television, told me he didn't want any—and by the time I finished, Mike had nodded off. I hadn't told him about my visit to Dana's yet; it made me feel guilty toward Mike, my best friend, snoozing away on the couch beside me. I wanted to ask him if he knew how the mayor treated her, but it seemed too personal. The least I could do for Dana was to keep my mouth shut and let her decide who knew about her home life.

The Tigers were down to their last out. Mike stirred upright, clapped his ledger closed, and gave Daniel a kick in the ribs. "Sorry bud, you lost it all. . . ."

Just then, a Tiger connected with a fastball. The bat hung loose from his arm and the ball traced an arc high above the outfield grass. The announcer said: "One of the greatest comebacks in Detroit Tigers *history*. Amazing. Unbelievable." The Tiger swept around third base, engulfed in a river of teammates.

Mike knelt down in amazement and broke up laughing. "I owe, let's see . . . let me find the lines here. Yeah, that makes it . . ."

"Thirteen hundred and fifty-two dollars," Daniel said.

"Whoa," I said, "I thought you said he only had two hundred dollars."

Daniel bounded onto the couch. "Yeah, but I had the Tigers on a parlay."

"Parlay?"

Mike finished a calculation and stared at Daniel in wonder. "Thirteen hundred and fifty-two dollars, that's right. Did you do that in your head?"

Daniel nodded.

"I could use somebody like you," he said.

Mike was laughing. Daniel had come out on top, as usual. For a brief moment, the world seemed right.

But it was a fantasy. It would all change the next day.

20

Things started out innocently enough.

Mike had crashed on the couch, and in the morning I found him pulling frozen boysenberries and other bounties from the fridge. He'd already found the blender, which could mean only one thing—another smoothie experiment. It turned out grainy. Plum colored. Bitter.

Daniel drained his whole glass in about two swallows and came up smiling.

"Thanks, Mike."

"No problem. I gotta remember this one—Purple Haze."

I swallowed something that might have been an acorn and gave up. I kept my opinions to myself and ruminated on Abby's note; I had read it about a hunded times before going to sleep, in hopes that it would reveal something new. At the kitchen table, I played the last part back to myself over from memory:

P.S. He had a partner. They used to meet at the pool,
that's all I really know. Mitch said he loved me, but he
didn't tell me much.

I still wasn't coming up with any fresh angles.

It was getting pretty frustrating, and I wasn't being very social, but Daniel and Mike hardly needed me for conversation. In the background of my musings, I heard Daniel asking Mike if they could go to the movies later.

"Yeah, pick one out of the paper," Mike said. "Just make sure there's lots of sex and violence."

They used to meet at the pool . . .

But Dana had never seen Mitch there, and I doubt she would have missed him if he'd been there regularly. Mitch didn't seem like a guy who would hang out at the pool, anyway. He liked to think of himself as a big shot, and the crowd at the pool wasn't exactly high society, not like at the—

Of course.

Mike was washing the glasses at the sink.

"Can you stay with Daniel this morning?" I asked him.

A banner fluttered across the second story of the Old Clubhouse: WELCOME TO THE FIRST-ANNUAL PETOSKEY CELEBRITY PRO-AM. We rolled up in Tina's Trans Am, the stereo blasting a profane Eminem song from her "Workout" playlist across the tranquil grounds of the resort.

"I really can't believe we didn't think of this before," Tina said.

"Yeah, I know."

It was pretty obvious: if Mitch had been hanging out at a pool, there was a good chance it would have been one at the New Petoskey Resort and Spa. He wasn't a member, of course, but he might have known an employee from his days working there and gotten in that way.

"Maybe the employee was even his partner," I had said to Tina when I'd raced over to the *Courier* from home. Two minutes later, we had piled in her car and started formulating our plan. Our best bet, we figured, was getting a list of current employees who were working at the club back when Mitch left.

Another tournament banner hung in the Old Clubhouse. Below it, men in pastel shirts and bright visors trafficked through, sipping coffee, checking watches, filling the room with a distinct energy. Some of them lined up at registration tables staffed by gray-haired volunteers. The tournament schedule tacked behind them showed that practice rounds started today.

I wanted to head straight up to Corbett's office, but Tina wasn't having any of it. She insisted on starting with one of Buddy the bartender's Bloody Marys instead. He beamed at her as he put down her drink.

"There you go, darlin'. I'd love to chat, but we're scrambling today."

"Well, don't be a stranger." Tina winked at him as he disappeared into the kitchen.

A leader board inside the bar listed all the tournament participants. The mayor and the sheriff, I noticed, made the "Celebrity" column, which seemed to render the term meaningless.

"Not to be a drag," I said, "but I don't see how this is getting us anywhere. Let's just go to the office and ask his secretary for the list."

Tina drained her glass and raised her hand for another. "Chris, you may not remember, but that's an ex-boyfriend of mine up in that office. It's awkward. Plus, his secretary's not going to just hand over that kind of info without asking the boss. Sometimes you've got to lurk around a little, wait for your chance to strike." She stopped and cocked her head. "Did I make that up? Lurk before you strike. Write that down for when you're older. It applies well for picking up chicks at the bar. You'll thank me."

It sounded like it applied well to stalking, but I didn't say anything. Instead, when Buddy came back with Tina's second drink, I flagged him. "Hey, do you know where somebody might run into Alexander Corbett, say, if they wanted a word but didn't have an appointment?"

Tina slapped my arm, and Buddy cut us with a sidelong glance. "You two are up to something."

"We might be," Tina said. "We might be."

Buddy sighed. "Well, not that my name would ever get mentioned, but somebody could probably just look out that big window over there and see the man out at the tenth tee. They could probably bump into him over there." He wiped his hands on his towel. "Now, I got work."

"See?" Tina said. "You lurk a little, you get your answers."

"I'm not sure it was the lurking. I think it was more the asking."

"Whatever. We're lurking till I finish this drink."

❦   ❦   ❦

The golf carts were lined up behind the clubhouse, all keyed up and ready for any of the tournament participants to take. Tina and I hijacked one and cruised past the practice tees toward the back nine. A hundred yards down the cart trail, just past the bunker-rimmed ninth green, Alexander Corbett was flashing his pearly whites around a large tent. Something about his eagerly projected confidence made him easy to pick up, even from just the painting and the photograph from the *Courier*.

I've heard that lots of movie stars have huge heads. I don't know about his acting skills, but Corbett was qualified in the head department. His giant helmet of black hair was gelled so thick I could almost see a reflection of the clouds in it. On his feet he wore tiny black loafers, equally shiny. In between, there was lots of tailored clothing.

"Let's lurk for a minute," I said.

Tina punched my shoulder. "Now you're getting it."

We pulled off the path and relaxed in the shade of the cart. The tent was a "Courtesy Station," established for the golfers to pick up a drink or a sandwich before making the turn to the tenth tee. We nestled behind a catering truck, unnoticed by the blue-coated officials, last-minute landscapers, and caterers servicing the area. Corbett was yukking it up with a group of pros collecting bananas and Gatorades. Standing a full foot shorter than them, he talked excitedly in their skyward direction, looking as though he'd be happy to feed them grapes if only they'd ask. When they left, he whirled and gave an earful to a man carrying food trays to the tent.

"Dude looks like an *ass*hole," Tina said. She leaned back in her seat, surveying the elegant tenth fairway that rolled out ahead of us like Heaven's front lawn. "So, what happened after they ruined the bluffs? Did this place even get into any trouble?"

"Not really." I remembered pretty well how it all ended. It had consumed my parents for three months—three long months in which they went off on passionate tirades about the power of corporations, inadequate laws, and how Mother Earth went unrepresented in our judicial system. Family dinners had never been so boring. Even Daniel got a little tired of it after a while.

"Some environmental agency brought a lawsuit against the developers," I said, remembering how my parents, after all their work to stop the construction that led to the disaster, had traded off days attending the trial. "If they'd lost, it would have bankrupted this place."

"But they won?"

"Yeah. Mayor Ruby was actually the judge on the case. He ruled that it happened because of all the rain, not because of all the tree-cutting or the cheap drain system, which, according to my parents, is the real reason it happened."

I could still see my dad's face when he came home from court. My mom and I were home when he stomped into the kitchen, pale and stricken. *Lies, dear. It's just a bunch of lies,* he had said, and I knew right away that the golf course had won.

"Mayor Ruby?" Tina said.

I nodded. "It was his last case before he ran for mayor."

"Didn't that make him kind of unpopular?"

"No. Businesses were depending on the tourism. They were all really happy the golf course survived. My parents think he ruled for the developers just so he'd win the election."

"Politicians," Tina said. "It figures."

Corbett was alone under the tent, lining up water bottles with obsessive care.

"I've had bosses like this guy," Tina muttered. "The insecure type. Probably wants to bone anything within a hundred feet."

"You might wanna stay back then," I said, and made for the president of the New Petoskey Resort and Spa.

Tina chanced it.

21

Corbett checked his watch as we approached. Wind rippled the tent but his hair didn't budge.

"Can I help you?" He looked Tina's body up and down but otherwise didn't bother to feign interest as we introduced ourselves.

"I know you're busy," Tina said. "We just need a quick word—"

"I'm sorry, but if you're not credentialed you can't be out on the course," Corbett said. "It's off-limits to anyone not participating in the tournament. Even under normal circumstances, it's members only. Now, if you could return the cart."

He fiddled with his gold bracelet, waiting for us to move along. Sweat glowed across his forehead, or maybe it was the hair gel melting down. A group of golfers came down the rise from the ninth green. I pegged a middle-aged man with a Hawaiian shirt as a local radio DJ, one of the "celebrity" players.

"It's just a quick administrative request," I said. "A list of your employees, from about two years ago."

"We're busy now," he huffed, and was off to play host again.

Tina was still steaming when we got back in the cart. She punched the accelerator, then stomped on the brake. I jerked forward.

"No, this is bullshit," she said.

"Tina, don't." Too late.

I couldn't bring myself to follow her. Tina's hair flowed behind her on her way over to ruin our chances of ever getting the list of employees. She stepped in front of the radio dude and said something to Corbett in a pointed way. Corbett gave the golfers a "one moment" gesture and barked something back. In no time they were into a full-on yelling match that I could hear bits and pieces of over the wind. Corbett's side of it was threatening, and Tina's side was vulgar. The golfers watched in stunned fascination, backpedaling away.

Corbett got on his walkie-talkie, and two seconds later a middle-aged security guy was leading her over to our cart, stashing her in the backseat. He drove us in silence toward the first tee, and Tina shot out of the cart before he even stopped in front of the clubhouse entrance.

The security guy smiled at me. "Spitfire, eh?"

"Give me two seconds," Tina said.

We were standing under a moose head. The crowd in the clubhouse had multiplied by three.

"Where are you going?" I said.

"Just stay here." She pointed to the bookshelves lining the walls. "Read a novel or something."

She headed toward the executive offices. I wanted to stop her from doing something stupid like breaking into Alexander Corbett's files, but something in Tina's tone told me I shouldn't mess with her at the moment. I found an empty chair by the magazine rack to wait her out.

"We playing skins?" a voice behind me said. It was Lawrence Lovell, in plaid knickers and pink stockings. Actual knickers. I couldn't tell if he was serious or making an ironic comment on bourgeoisie sport fashion. Not ironic, I decided. I turned away quickly and hid my face behind a magazine.

"You're on," said one of the guys with Lovell. From all the clinking and clunking, it sounded like they were taking inventory of their golf bags.

"Twenty bucks a hole?" Lovell said.

The clinking stopped. A third guy whistled.

"Watch out, boys, he must have fixed that slice. Either that or they gave you a fat pension."

They all chuckled, Lovell the hardest. "Yeah. Right before she put her foot in my ass." So Lovell wasn't hiding the fact that he was getting pushed out. Not to his golf chums, anyway. Somehow I doubted he'd told Tina about it when he got her into bed.

"Well, look who's here," Lovell said brightly, and I chanced a look.

Tina. She flashed me a thumbs-up signal before rushing over to give Lovell a distressingly intimate hug. I didn't know what her signal meant, since she didn't have any purloined files in her hands, and they probably would have squeezed out of her bag considering the force with which she and Lovell were rubbing up against each other.

"Hello to you," she said, and kissed him on the lips.

Lovell introduced her around to his mates, who had prurient

thoughts written all across their faces. He promised to catch up to them in a second.

"Great duds," Tina said, and pulled the magazine down from my face. "Chris, you remember Larry."

I shook his hand. "Christopher. Nice to see you."

"Yeah." He shook his wrist out. Maybe I had squeezed a little hard. "What brings you over here? Breaking news on the tournament?"

"Something like that," Tina said. "Are you playing in it?"

"No, I'm afraid I'm not celebrity material. But members get to go on the practice rounds early in the week. They've got the course in top shape, so why not?"

He looked at me like I'd understand this principle perfectly. "Righto," I said. "Why not, indeed?" I really wanted to slip in a comment about the knickers but I couldn't make it work.

"So, as long as we've got you here," Tina said, "could we ask you about Kate Warne?"

I didn't like the thought of Tina spilling all our secrets to anyone, much less Lawrence Lovell. I prepared myself to interrupt at any moment, encouraged slightly by the alcohol smell on Lovell. Maybe he was plastered and wouldn't remember this conversation in an hour.

"Is this about Mitch?" he said.

I gave Tina a nudge. "Not really."

"She's not married, right?" Tina said.

Lovell pulled a water bottle from his tank-sized golf bag and had a swig. "Nope."

"Is she seeing anyone?"

Lovell listed backward a little. "Not me, if that's where this is going."

"I know that," Tina said. Sex dripped from her words. She pulled a cigarette from her bag.

"I don't think you can do that here," Lovell said.

"Screw them. They hassled us."

Lovell kissed her impulsively. "You're priceless, babe."

It seemed to satisfy Tina for the moment. "So, how does Kate get along with the mayor?"

"He used to practice at our firm, so he came by the office sometimes. They used to have some cases together. They were friendly. Where are you going with this?"

It might have been too late, but I didn't want Lovell to get a firm idea that we suspected an affair between them. "Did you ever hear about Mitch having a partner?"

"Like a partner in crime?" Lovell laughed.

"Yeah. Like maybe somebody who used to work with him here?"

"Wouldn't shock me," Lovell said idly. "But I told you I don't know anything about that."

"Well, okay then," Tina said.

Lovell sensed her dejection. "Good luck with your story, whatever it is." He leaned in and nibbled her ear, at which point I turned away in horror. "Let me know if you figure out who shot JFK while you're at it."

A voice came from behind us—Bob the ex-boyfriend, walking over from the office area. "Hey, Larry, what's up?"

"Bob!" Lovell happily shook his hand. "I should get going," he said to us.

Tina pointed between them. "You guys know each other?" It had to be a little awkward for her, but her voice didn't betray it.

"An old client," Lovell said. He patted Bob on the shoulder and headed out to meet his friends.

"Uhh, Tina," Bob said, looking at the cigarette she still had in her hand. "Sorry, but you can't smoke in here."

She kissed him on the cheek and we left.

Tina and I sat on the hood of the Trans Am in the parking lot.

"Why do you hate him so much?"

She was talking about Lovell. "Tina, he's a loser. I wasn't going to say anything, but Dana told me he's, like, a gambling addict. Do you know that Kate Warne is kicking him out of the law firm?"

"Nobody wants a company man, Chris. They're dull."

"Fine, but did you see those clothes?"

"What can I say? Preppy guys turn me on, especially rich ones. It's always been that way—I can't explain it."

"Preppy's one thing. Pink socks are another."

She tucked her chin into her chest, playing coy. "Christopher's so hot when he's jealous. Oh, and now look at him blushing."

"So, uh, what happened up in the office, anyway? Did you get some good news?"

"You saw Bob?"

"Big Bob the ex-boyfriend?"

She got off the hood. "Yep. Guess I didn't burn that bridge too badly after all."

"Why?"

"Do you promise to be nice to Larry first?"

"I promise."

We got in the car. "Well, because Bob loves me dearly, tonight he's going to stay late, go through the records that are supposed to be off-limits to him, and get us a list of employees from two weeks before Mitch Blaylock left the country club."

Tina backed up and peeled out of the lot.

Mike had left me a note saying he'd taken Daniel over to his house. I did mail duty again (no more love letters from Abby) and headed over to join them. I hadn't been going full-tilt on the supervisory front since my parents left, so I figured a relaxing afternoon with Daniel and Mike was in order. Maybe we'd even catch that movie, I thought, when I found the two of them on the back deck.

They were lounging in deck chairs with sunglasses on and their pasty stomachs exposed, playing Las Vegas tycoons. From what I gathered, Daniel was lecturing Mike on how he should collude with other local bookies to jack up his profits.

"It's all in here," Daniel said. He leaned over and produced a library book from his backpack. It was about a thousand pages long and called *Anti-Trust Violations in Maturing Markets: A Case Study of the Petroleum Industry, 1873–1915.* "Those robber barons knew what they were doing," he said.

"Your little bro is an evil genius," Mike said as he hefted the book open. "Hey Daniel, go get my master spreadsheet in my room—I need some more of your advice."

"Thanks for watching him," I said to Mike as Daniel disappeared into the house.

"No problem. So how'd it go this morning?"

"Eh. It kind of turned into nothing. I thought Mitch's partner might have worked with him at the country club, but we didn't find out much."

"Can I help?" Mike asked.

I rubbed my ear. "Excuse me, but I could've sworn you just asked me if you could help out, after you've been telling me to give this up all summer."

"Yeah, yeah." Mike laid the book aside. "You know, I still haven't even seen Tina, and Daniel says she's smokin.'"

"Ahh, so that explains it."

"Can you blame me? I'm back on the market. Lock up your women, Petoskey." He spread his arms out, shouting it into the forest. A tiny echo was thrown right back at us, like nature didn't believe in Mike's talk any more than he did. When it faded away, Mike raised a single eyebrow at me. "Julia Spencer would be a pretty good catch, don't you think?"

"Is this your way of asking my permission to take her out?"

"No, this is my way of suggesting you do it yourself."

I was about to dismiss his comment when something crashed inside the house. Daniel. "I'll check on him."

"Don't worry about it. . . ." Mike said, but I was already walking inside.

I found Daniel in Mike's room, standing in a small puddle of pencils and paper clips and 3x5 cards. Lying on the floor beside them was the bottom drawer to Mike's desk. He'd accidentally pulled it all the way out, which was an easy thing to do. The drawer didn't catch at the end, so it slipped right out when you pulled. It had been broken like that forever, and as long as I'd known him Mike had stashed secret items in the well beneath the drawer.

"I barely touched it, I swear," Daniel said.

"Yeah, I know, it's okay. Did you find the spreadsheet?"

"No."

"Okay, go wait by the door."

"Why?"

"I'm going to check a secret spot."

"Why can't I see it?"

His questions could make your head hurt. "Just wait by the door," I said, and crouched to look into the well at the bottom of the desk.

Something tingled inside me as I did. I had been with Mike when he stashed a lot of stuff into that compartment (a prized note Dana passed him in sixth grade, some mini liquor bottles he'd swiped from a plane, a business plan we'd drawn up for a window-washing company that we'd never done anything about). The bottom of that desk was a time capsule of Mike. I smiled to myself, preparing for an onslaught of innocent memories.

But sometime in high school, Mike must have emptied it out. There was nothing there—well, almost nothing.

There, lying on the dusty pine board, was just a single item. It wasn't innocent at all.

The desk had been made of real wood, and the bottom of it used to smell like the needles that carpeted Duncan Woods. Maybe it still did, I couldn't tell. I'd stopped breathing.

My skin tingled in a different way now. My arm sizzled as I reached in for the Vista View memory card.

"What's wrong?" Daniel said.

"Go out to the car."

"Why?"

"*Go to the car!*"

I shouldn't have yelled at him like that, but I had my reasons.

The card was missing its plastic casing. A Vista View memory card without its plastic casing. I knew, of course, where the matching casing was: in Dr. Mobley's office. It would be way too much of a coincidence for them not to be a pair.

I shouldn't have been holding the memory card with my fingers. It was going to be evidence someday, because I knew what kind of pictures Mitch had been taking. I was holding the blackmail evidence in my hand, right on that card. And I'd just found it in Mike's desk.

It felt like a steel bolt sliding into place, locking me up alone. I wanted to scream.

22

I've been on this amusement park ride called the Demon Drop. You stand in a steel box with three other people, thick harnesses over your shoulders, and you zoom straight up in the air a few hundred feet. It's like an elevator ride to the clouds. Then the box inches forward from the elevator column, and it's just hanging there with nothing beneath it. The floor is made of wire mesh so you can see straight down to the ground. You can barely make out the details so far below you—the lines of people, the food carts, the gigantic tents like umbrellas in a drink. Little kids hold balloons that toss in the wind, and you get dizzy at the sight. And then the ride *click*s, and it releases you in a free fall to the ground.

That's what I was feeling like when Mike walked in.

"What's going on?" he said. And then he saw the card in my hand.

I couldn't think of anything to say. My head was full of air, whisking downward.

I was struggling to hold out hope that there was some crazy mistake here. If there wasn't . . .

Then the reason Dr. Mobley had only the casing, and not the card itself, was because Mike had gotten to it first.

Mike said, "You found it."

"Yeah." I waited for more, but nothing came. "Guess this is why you didn't want me bothering with the case, eh?"

He took off his sunglasses. White circles of flesh surrounded his eyes; the rest of his face was pink. It looked like he was embarrassed, but it was just the sun. Mike wasn't flinching.

"Is this what I think it is?"

"I didn't kill him, Christopher." It was supposed to be reassurance, but the words landed hard in my gut. Mike wasn't denying what I'd known—those were Mitch's pictures in my hand.

"Who did it, then?"

"I don't know." His voice was cold and clipped, with the emotion of a stone. He had shut something off inside himself. I'd seen him like this with his parents.

"Then how'd you get this?" I was holding up the card.

He didn't answer. I was searching his eyes for some kind of hint when a terrible thought struck me: *Mitch's partner . . . could it have been Mike?*

"I can't talk about it," he said. "I'm sorry, man, I really am, but it's complicated. You have to trust me."

"You've been lying to me all summer," I said. "That's going to be hard."

"I haven't lied to you."

"It's the same thing, Mike. Not telling me what you know, it's the same as lying. I got beat up over this. I was down in that basement—"

"*And I got you out!*" His face was red, veins showing on his neck. I shuddered, wondering if he was going to hurt me somehow. "*I lied to the cops for you! I've been doing everything I can!*"

"Except being honest."

"I can't, Christopher. I can't."

"Were you his partner? Were you blackmailing the mayor?"

It made sense, in some bizarre sort of way. Mike had always been eager to make money—he was a little bit like Mitch that way. Both of them were characters, funny guys that talked big and made people laugh. They probably would've gotten along well. I could see them meeting at the pool, sharing a joke. Maybe Mike had told Mitch about his bookie operation, and maybe Mitch recognized a fellow schemer. It wouldn't have been long before Mitch was bragging about his blackmail plan.

"I'm not telling you a thing," Mike said. He was beyond cold now—he was angry.

"Well, I'm not letting it go. I'm going to find out what happened."

I started for the door, and that's when Mike threw me against the wall.

He gripped my T-shirt tight. It pulled against my neck, and the fright of it had me hyperventilating.

"Christopher, I didn't do it."

"Tell me what you did, then."

"I can't."

"I'm going to figure it out anyway," I said.

He shoved me harder into the wall. I didn't resist. If it came to a fight, I'd be on the ground in seconds. My lungs throbbed beneath his fists. Everything was going cock-eyed in my vision.

I tried to slip out from his hands, thinking it was useless. But then he let me slide away. I stumbled toward the door and stuck the card in my pocket.

"Take it. I don't care about the pictures anyway," Mike said.

"Why do you have them, then?"

Mike just shook his head. "You should really stop this," he said.

There was nothing left to do but walk out of the house and go find the answers. But there was something final about leaving, and for a second my feet wouldn't move. I doubted that Mike and I could be best friends after this—whatever he'd done, this was too big not to change things in some irreversible way.

But I left.

I opened the front door, and I didn't say good-bye.

23

"You *what?*" Tina said.

"I got the pictures. Mitch's blackmail pictures."

"*How?*" Wind was blowing into her cell phone, crackling against my ear.

"It's a long story," I said. "Can you come over?"

"Not now, I'm tied up till tonight. What do they look like?"

"I'm still not sure, exactly."

I couldn't make myself put the card in my computer. Seeing the pictures would mean for certain that Mike was at the center of it all. Maybe he'd been Mitch's partner, maybe he'd killed him, maybe both. I didn't want it to be true. It was the Tim Spencer problem times ten.

"You sound like you're out on the lake or something," I said.

"Nice guess. Larry took me out on his boat." Another gust flapped across the line. "I'm calling you the second I get back. You need to give me the whole story tonight."

"Yeah, okay," I said, and clicked off.

I sat there for another few minutes, just me and the memory card. I forced myself to place it in the little slot on my computer, but couldn't push it in. It sat there teasing me, filling the whole world.

"What are you doing?" Daniel said.

It scared the lights out of me. He'd come far into the room, just a few feet from my computer, and I hadn't even noticed. If I'd stuck that card in, who knows what Daniel would have seen. Even without seeing the pictures, he sensed something—a wave of fear trembled through his voice. The fright in Daniel brought it home. My life was unraveling—all the things I trusted were spinning off in odd directions, unspooling, melting away from my grasp. I needed to get a grip. "Uh, nothing."

"What happened at Mike's? What did you find in that drawer?"

We'd been over this fifty times on the ride back already, but he never gave up. "Nothing, I told you," I said.

He was way too smart to believe me. Daniel looked down, brushed his foot against the carpet. Mike was just about his favorite person in the world; he was confused, afraid, and for once he seemed like a regular ten-year-old kid. "Look, sorry for yelling at you over there. Do you want to go to the museum?"

We both needed a break, and the Coast Guard Museum was Daniel's favorite place in the world. He was powerless to resist.

I dragged out the trip as long as I could. Daniel pressed his nose to the display windows and jabbered on about the finer points of maritime history. I was thankful for the background noise—it helped me set my mind blank. Eventually a security guy inched us toward the exit with some mumbled talk about the museum closing in fifteen minutes. We ate a long dinner in town after, but the whole trip had still passed in a blur. I didn't want to go back to those pictures.

My stomach was soggy with dread when we pulled back up to the house, and that was even before I saw Julia Spencer. She was knocking on the front door with a Netflix movie in her hand.

"Your other girlfriend," Daniel said in the car.

I told him to beat it inside and greeted Julia on the porch.

The sky above us was purple. The air was still and fragrant with the neighbors' flowers. Mother Nature cued the night sounds—the crickets, the rustling branches, the insect zappers. The moon was rising. A mood for romance, if you cared to see it that way. I didn't.

"Hey. So, what happened to you at Dana's?" Julia said.

"Oh, yeah, sorry I didn't get to talk to you. Mike wanted to leave."

"I figured. He didn't look too happy." She looked around aimlessly, smelling the flowered night. "So anyway, here I am again. Want to watch a movie?" She held it up: an old comedy called *The Break-Up*. "I figured it was kind of appropriate."

She forced a laugh, but I didn't join in.

Something had changed. Maybe the night at Dana's party had knocked some sense into me, or maybe I had too many other things on my mind, but I wasn't tempted anymore. Enough things had exploded in my face—another go-round with Julia wasn't high on my list.

She waved the movie at me again. "C'mon, you know. For us."

"For us?" I said.

Julia put her weight on one leg. "Because, you know, we kind of broke up. Sort of."

I didn't have the patience anymore. "Broke up?" I said. "We never went out."

Julia didn't care that my voice has raised a hair. She stepped closer, acting coy. "Technically, yeah. But Christopher, I think you could give me a break. I've been trying hard all summer, you know? I've basically been humiliating myself just to hang out with you again."

She reached out for my hand but I wasn't having it.

If I could have seen it from the outside I might have stopped myself, but things were getting tangled in my mind. I should have been mad at Mike, not Julia. I *was* mad at Mike—for having the pictures, for being involved in the mess. I'd been trying to ignore it all afternoon, holding back the feelings with a finger in the dam. It couldn't last forever, and there, on the porch, it all washed out over Julia.

"*You've* been humiliating yourself?

"Hold on. I mean I—"

"Think how it feels for me. Humiliation is when you get rejected. I've never done that to you."

"What . . . and I have?"

"*Of course you have.*" She looked a little stunned. I didn't care. I plowed on. "Remember Homecoming?"

She stumbled back a half step. Her eyes had grown large and bewildered against the sunset. A breeze pushed across the porch, smelling of hot dogs and lighter fluid.

"You think I rejected you?" she said. "You think that's what happened?"

"I know that's what happened."

I did. For over a year, I'd felt a physical pain of embarrassment every time I thought of her. I'd walked under that Homecoming banner a thousand times, confused and ashamed. A thousand times I'd wondered how I'd deluded myself into thinking she liked me.

It felt good to get it out. Or it should have felt good, anyway.

But Julia looked too wounded. She could get hurt like anybody else, but she didn't let it show, not until she was safe somewhere like the library, talking over her wounds with a trusted friend, smothering them in jokes.

"I waited for *months* for you to ask me out," she said. Julia looked around the empty street before she let loose. "I waited for you all summer. I called you all the time, I hung out with you all the time. If you didn't know I wanted you to . . ." She was speaking too fast to keep up with herself. She looked around again, stuffed the movie into her pocket, cleared her eyes.

I wanted to stop her from walking down the porch stairs but I couldn't move. Regret was weighing me down, sinking me into the porch. Suddenly, there were a thousand things I wanted to do differently.

"I didn't know."

Julia looked back from the bottom step. "Yes you did. You were just scared. I'm like that, too—maybe that's why we got along so well." She gave a sad little smile, the same one she had given me by her locker, under the Homecoming banner. I hadn't been able to figure the look out back then, but now I knew what it meant: *Sorry, I've given up on you.*

"No, but . . ." I couldn't find the words to go on. There's something unmistakable about the truth, and it was slapping me in the face. "I'm sorry," I said. It was the only thing I could manage, and it just seemed to make her more angry.

Julia shrugged. "It was a long time ago. But you know, if you want to ask somebody to a dance, you don't wait until a week before. It's actually kind of an insult." She brushed her watery face again. I could barely stand to look at her. She opened her mouth to tack something on and thought better of it.

"Forget it," she said, and got into her car.

Daniel handed me the phone when I got inside. "Tina," he said, waggling his eyebrows.

"Hey," I said into the receiver.

"You don't sound too good. What's wrong?"

"Nothing. Are you back?"

Tina responded with a sound effect. *POP! Fizz.*

"You like champagne?"

"Never had it, why?"

"You're about to. Lawrence just dumped me. Wanna get drunk?"

"Yes."

"Be over here in fifteen minutes." *Click.*

Daniel would be okay for a few hours. I made him get into bed and swear a blood oath that he'd stay put. And then I was off.

24

She answered the door in a white T-shirt with red lettering that spelled JUICY. She was clutching two champagne bottles. One of them was half-empty. She held out the other, wobbling.

"Here you go," she said. "Got a head start on you."

"Uh, thanks."

She stumbled to the living room and plunked down on the sofa. Her arm curled the bottle tightly to her chest, like it might go wandering.

"Cheers."

I clinked bottles with her. "Cheers, Tina."

She poured back a swallow like it was root beer. "Cheers."

"You got it. So why the champagne?"

"Little tradition of mine," she said. "Champagne always takes the edge off a breakup."

"Guess I can use it, too, then."

"What?"

"Nothing," I said, and had my first sip of champagne. I'm pretty sure you're supposed to drink the stuff from a tall, thin wineglass, but whatever. It tasted sweeter than one of Daniel's juice boxes. The red sticker on the side said $3.99. It went down easy. *Magnifique.*

A huge mound of newspapers sat on the carpet; Tina used them as a leg rest. Some kind of postmortem talk about Larry Lovell seemed appropriate, but I didn't know how to bring it up without sounding happy about it. I sat back and surveyed her apartment again: the tropical plant, the bass with the broken string, the worn-out carpet. A Twinkie wrapper on her coffee table reminded me, for some reason, of the body bag I'd seen in the morgue the day they brought Mitch in. Maybe the champagne was hitting me.

The smell of the lake mixed with scented candles that she'd lit all around the living room. The clutter in the room cast giant flickering shadows on the walls.

I shifted and felt the memory card dig into my leg. I'd stashed it in my pocket before leaving the house.

"You've got a computer, right? Let's look at these pictures."

"Computer? Umm, maybe you haven't heard, but reporters don't get paid crap. So no." She leaned in, almost touching her forehead to mine, like we were about to make out. "C'mon, let's go outside."

She lived at the peak of a hill that descended to Lake Michigan on one side and Duncan Woods on the other. We sat on the curb in the cool air, with the black lake floating beneath us. It was late and nobody walked on the little slice of beach. I told Tina about finding the pictures at Mike's place, and getting in a fight with him, and how

I thought it probably meant that he'd been Mitch's partner in the blackmail somehow.

"My God," Tina said. "Guess you need this worse than I do."

"Yeah, guess so."

I didn't mention Julia.

"Look," she said. "I don't want to think about anything tonight. Not Mitch Blaylock, not your friend Mike, not Larry. Is that cool?"

"Yeah."

It should've been a miserable night for the both of us, but being there calmed me. We sat on the curb and drank from our bottles, something loosening between us. The moonlight made delicate spiderweb patterns on the lake and Tina blew smoke that evaporated into the constellations.

She tossed her bottle on the lawn when she finished. "Come on," she said, "I'm going to teach you how to dance. And bring that bottle."

She ran up the street to the rickety wooden staircase that descended the other side of the hill into Duncan Woods. I found myself right behind her, energized, feeling strangely good about myself. The champagne sloshed as we wended our way down. Tina almost slipped but it didn't worry me—I could have saved her. I could have done anything just then. I was all-powerful.

At the bottom of the stairs, our feet hit the grass, and leaves of midnight blue waved in the wind above us. She ran under the sodium lights to a clearing with a lone picnic bench. The dew was coming early and Tina's feet made dark impressions on the grass as she twirled across it.

"C'mon, I wasn't joking," Tina said. She gripped my hand and brought me under the lights, like we were onstage. "Lower," she said. She pressed my arm, and my hand slid down. She had smooth muscles around her spine, little dimples low on her back. "There, presto."

She said the waltz was an easy dance; I could do it. We started slow and then she said I should make a quarter turn on the fifth count—then we'd really be dancing. I stepped on her. She laughed and told me it was okay, I was cute. My head spun.

We got a rhythm, our bodies turning in concert. I forgot what my feet were doing and felt my heart surge, and then we collapsed in a happy mess near the picnic table.

The bottle felt light in my hand. Tina peered at the remains, swished them, and finished off the champagne. She said good job because I had put most of it down and I must be pretty wasted.

"We need music," she said.

We raced up the stairs back to her house—I can't remember exactly, but we must have—and Tina pulled me inside. She dug through her CDs while I watched at her side. The world was at rest and not at rest, like getting off a carousel. The music had horns, it had a beat.

Her hand was slick with sweat when she put it in mine. We were ready to dance but she wasn't starting—she was staring at me. "Know what your problem is, Chris?"

"Uh, no."

"You're sort of on the sidelines. You're the opposite of me—too much thinking, not enough action. You can't just ponder stuff like some professor or something. You've got to make it happen."

My hand was low on her back. Our stomachs were touching. Our hips were touching. We'd started dancing again. "Make what happen?"

"Whatever you want."

I dry-swallowed and led her too close to the sofa. It wasn't on purpose. But still, she brushed the arm and lost her balance, tumbling down onto the cushions. She gripped my hand tight and then I was falling with her, landing softly at her side. A low, awkward laugh came from my throat.

Tina turned to me, her glistening eyes taking me in and her fingers moving strands of hair out of my face, staying longer than they needed to and curling against the back of my ear, teasing me. The room still moving but not moving, the music pushing through us like circulation. "One sec," she whispered. She slid underneath me to the armrest, arching her back, wriggling to turn off the lamp, her breasts pushing against her T-shirt until the blue light faded away and I could smell her strawberry shampoo and feel the coolness of her skin and my chest heavy against hers and we were all by ourselves and we could have kissed and no one would have known.

Somebody pounded on the door.

"Whoa," Tina said.

She slipped from underneath me, thumping against the carpet, laughing again and saying, "What the hell is this, wait here, Chris, I'll be right back." I watched the candlelight on the ceiling to keep the room from spinning. When I ventured a look at the door, I saw him there before I had to close my eyes to stop the world from whirring off its axis. Tim Spencer, outlined by the porch light.

"Hello, piglet. What brings you here?"

"You're lit."

"And what're you?"

"I'm the police. Try to stand up straight."

"What? Am I going to get a ticket for bad posture?"

"Is that Christopher Newell on your couch?"

"What if it is?"

"He's supposed to be with my sister tonight."

"What're you, keeping his schedule or something?"

"Keep it down. He's passed out, isn't he?"

"How 'bout you tell me why the hell you're on my porch."

"I like that kid."

"Well, we're even. I like him, too."

"A little too much, I'd say."

"What the fuck is that supposed to mean?"

"It means you better be careful with him."

"Screw you. You're on my porch and I still don't see a reason for it."

"I don't know what you and Christopher are up to—"

"*Let go of me!*"

"If you stop falling down, I will. I'm trying to tell you something."

"Spit it out, then."

"Whatever the two of you are doing, you'd better stop it. That's what I'm telling you."

"Is that a threat? Am I going to end up like Mitch Blaylock?"

"I don't know what you're talking about. Actually, you do whatever you want."

"Thanks a lot, dick."

"Just keep Christopher out of it. And don't mess with that kid's head, I mean it."

The door slammed.

"Jesus H."

The morning sun scalded my eyes. My head was throbbing, like an invisible vise was squeezing in on both sides of my brain. I stumbled to the kitchen and drank three glasses of water from an enormous plastic DALE EARNHARDT, R.I.P. cup lying in the sink. Tina was still on the sofa, and she wasn't going to be moving for a long time. I thought the water might clear my head up a bit, but no. The world was foggy and dull but intrusive at the same time. It was like walking around underwater with a flashlight in your eyes.

I didn't know what exactly had happened between Tina and me the night before—we hadn't kissed, I didn't think. Beyond that, it was too early to say what was real and what wasn't, like Tim Spencer showing up on the porch. Did I dream that?

And then the horrifying part came back—the memory of Julia, up on the porch, telling me that she'd wanted me to ask her to the dance all along. Yeah, that had really happened. Maybe Tina was right. Maybe I needed to do things instead of just thinking about them. I thought she'd been telling me to make a move, but now it just seemed like a piece of advice I should have taken long ago.

Suddenly I needed to get moving—to get out of Tina's dark and stuffy house. Daniel had been alone for ten hours by then. He might have set the town on fire, or won a Nobel Prize. Nobel Prize, probably. I wrote Tina a note to call me and reached my hand into my pocket. The memory card was still there.

Time to look at the pictures. Time to act.

25

Daniel was still asleep.

My computer was on.

The memory card was in the slot.

My heart was in my throat.

I pressed Transfer on my Picture Project software and listened to the whirring of the hard drive as the pictures made their way onto my computer. I didn't have the energy to be scared of what they would tell me about Mike anymore.

According to Abby Shales, Mike wouldn't be in them anyway. If she was right, they were the pictures that Mitch (with Mike's help, somehow) had used to blackmail the mayor and Kate Warne: pictures of them in some kind of compromising position. I scrolled through the images, displaying them one by one on the screen.

In the first, Kate Warne strode toward a room at the Lighthouse Motel in a blazer and one of her short-short skirts. Grime streaks darkened the door's turquoise paint. You could see something like its original color only where the numerals 103 had fallen off it.

In the second one, Kate Warne had disappeared, presumably into the now-open doorway. A man in a three-piece suit was heading for the room now—the mayor.

In the third picture, the mayor appeared to be leaving. He was headed away from room 103. The doorway was partially open, and you could make out Kate Warne inside the room. It looked as though she might have been putting her heels back on. Yellow numbers ran at the bottom of each picture, marking the date and time.

Abby wasn't lying. The history of Mitch Blaylock was coming into view; I was seeing how it had happened now. Mitch had gotten his room at the Lighthouse Motel, and had seen the mayor and Kate Warne using it for a tryst. He was a natural schemer and realized he could squeeze them for money if he got evidence of it. Somewhere along the line, Mike had entered the equation, but I was too charged up to worry about that now. I'd been chasing his trail all summer and now I was right there. I wanted to know every little thing about Mitch Blaylock.

But then I opened the rest of the pictures and it all fell apart. I'd misread the situation rather dramatically.

Picture Project hadn't put the JPEG files in chronological order. When I got through the whole set of pictures, I could see the sequence. The picture of the mayor and Kate Warne entering the hotel room were the first two, but the one of the mayor leaving the hotel room was actually the second-to-last. After Kate Warne and the mayor entered, the following pictures showed a third person entering the room. Most of the photos were taken in a two-minute span in which all three of them were talking in the hotel room. The mayor pulled the curtains shut, and that was it, until the final pictures, in which the mayor, Kate Warne, and the third guy all left the hotel room five minutes apart.

The third man was short, squat, and wearing a necklace. His black hair glistened in the streetlight. I knew that hair—it was Alexander Corbett, president of the New Petoskey Resort and Spa.

That was weird enough, but when I looked closer, I noticed that the time stamp was from two years ago. Mitch hadn't even taken them. Or if he had, it was before he went to prison.

I spent another half hour staring dumbly at the thirty-one pictures, with no idea what they meant. The screen was making my retinas burn by the time I got up out of my chair.

My hesitant legs took me to the bathroom, where I stood under the hot water, full blast, for a week and a half. The steam clouds cleared the champagne from my brain. Well, enough to perform simple arithmetic anyway. I wrapped myself in two layers of towels and ventured out of the misty bathroom. The cool air of the house refreshed me as I dressed and went downstairs to find Daniel demolishing a bowl of tofu pasta salad.

"Really? You eat that for breakfast?"

"What?" Daniel said. "It's got protein!"

"Just . . . keep it down a little, okay?"

"Where *were* you last night? I could have *died*."

"Yeah, I remember, you said that last time. But look, still here." I gave him a little pinch on the arm. He didn't like it—it took his focus off the Business section of the *Courier*.

"So, did you make out with Tina last night?"

"No, Daniel."

"You made out with her. You guys made out all night."

"Mmm-hmm, you're right, it was awesome." I was making myself some cereal, staring absently at another front-page story about the judge who had taken bribes from petty criminals, clearing them of criminal charges in exchange for thousand-dollar bribes.

"So are you and Mike enemies now?"

"No. We had a fight, don't worry about it."

"What did you fight over? You never tell me *anything*!"

I tried to tune him out by actually reading the story about the judge. My eyes ran over the print, not really taking it in. I flipped to page fourteen to finish it anyway, just hoping Daniel would get the point and leave me in silence for a bit.

. . . grand jury expected to convene later this month to consider charges against the once-distinguished jurist . . . bluh blah blah . . . vacation property in the Upper Peninsula may have been paid for in part with takings from the illegal . . . blah blah blah . . .

Daniel was putting his plate in the dishwasher. It wasn't until I put the paper down that a line from the story came back to me. I snatched it up and rifled back to the front page.

"What's wrong?" Daniel said.

Right there. "*. . . sources at the district attorney's office refused to comment on previous indications that the bribery scheme was not an* *isolated instance, and that a pattern of bribe-taking at the Petoskey courthouse may lead to a wider investigation implicating other past and present judges. . . .*

I picked up the phone. Tina answered on the fourth ring, sounding like someone had taken sandpaper to her vocal chords. "Dude, what are you doing calling—"

"Tina, get over here. I know what happened."

26

I was watching out the front window when her Trans Am rumbled up the driveway. Tina dragged herself up the porch steps in a plain white T-shirt and dark sunglasses; she stepped inside and checked me over.

"How you feeling, stud?"

"Actually, not that bad."

"That makes one of us." She took her sunglasses off, squinted harshly, and put them back on. "So, whaddaya got?"

"If I'm right, the biggest story of your life."

"Spill it, genius," she said.

"This way." I turned to head upstairs and found Daniel watching us from the corner of the room. "Don't even think about going up there," I said.

We had topped the stairs when I heard him call, "Are you guys going to make out some more?"

✤　✤　✤

Tina took a seat before my monitor and clicked through the JPEG files with rising bafflement.

I had reordered the pictures so she'd see how it had happened: the mayor and Kate Warne entering; the short, dark figure right behind them; the three of them talking in the room; and then all of them leaving.

Tina tilted back in my chair. *"Corbett?"*

"Yeah," I said.

"What the hell is this? A threesome?"

That was for laughs, I think. When you saw the whole set together, it didn't look like anything sexual. Corbett wore a crisp and tailored suit on his stocky frame, and his face was all business. He looked preoccupied, harried. At first I'd thought one of them showed Kate Warne putting her heels on, but after my in-depth inspection, I decided the grainy image actually showed her grasping a small briefcase.

"Notice the time stamp?" I said.

Tina checked the little yellow numbers running along the bottom of each picture.

"Two years ago," she said, realizing it just then. "So . . . Mitch didn't even take these?"

"I don't think so. Not when he got back from prison anyway. They're from before he even went inside." I couldn't imagine Mitch sitting on blackmail evidence for more than five minutes, let alone two years.

"I'm not getting this," Tina said.

"I didn't either, not at first."

"You better spell it out for me. I'm a little slow today."

"Okay, but I need to check something first. Does the *Courier* have copies of all its old papers? The Web site doesn't have an archive."

"Yeah, they've got them all," Tina said. "In the morgue."

"The morgue?"

"Not *that* morgue. That's what newspapers call the place where they keep old copies."

"Oh, all right. We need to go there."

She gave me a sideways look. "Look dude, I don't have the energy today. I need to know what I'm getting into before we head over there."

I exhaled. "Okay, you know about the judge taking the bribes in those criminal cases?" Tina nodded. "Yeah, well, those stories keep saying that there could have been more than one judge doing it. There could be others taking bribes, too."

"So?"

"So, what's the biggest case in Petoskey in the last five years?"

"I dunno. Is there a point here, mysterioso?" But then I saw it dawn on her. Tina took off her sunglasses. "The golf course case."

"Yeah, the one clearing the New Petoskey Resort for letting the bluffs slide into Lake Michigan. And who was the judge on that case?"

She turned to the computer screen and back. "No, you don't think—"

"Yeah, I do. That's exactly what I think." I pointed to the picture of the mayor leaving the hotel room. "It was two years ago—he wasn't the mayor then. He would have still been a judge."

"We're looking at a man taking a bribe," I said, ejecting the memory card and sticking it back in my pocket—I wasn't going to be separated from that thing until the mayor was in handcuffs. "We can confirm it at the paper."

"Let's do it," Tina said.

When I told him we were leaving, Daniel was puttering around the living room, making his plans for world domination. Well, okay, he was just repeating French phrases from a Rosetta Stone video.

"*Partez-vous?*" he said. "I mean, you're leaving?"

"Yeah, you can go to the library if you want, but stay out of trouble."

"Where are you *going*?"

"We have to do some work at the paper."

"Can I go with you?"

I blinked. It was kind of touching, actually. "Look, I'm sorry. I guess I haven't been the best babysitter—"

"You aren't *babysitting*. Forget it, I'm gonna call Mike."

"No," I said quickly. "Don't bother him today."

"I won't keep him long, little man," Tina said. "We'll be right back."

"Will you come back with him?"

"If I can," Tina said. "You can teach me some French, okay?"

"Okay," Daniel said, and plopped happily on the couch. We gave him high fives on our way out, and I thought to myself, *He's not such a bad kid after all.*

Tina floored it to the *Courier*. We were flying past MacGruder's Market when she shot me a look. "So . . . do we need to talk about this?"

"Uh, talk about what?" Actually, I was pretty sure I knew what she was talking about, and it wasn't Mitch Blaylock. I didn't know if I wanted to broach the topic just yet, if ever.

"Last night was a good time, right?" she said.

"Yeah."

"Yeah, and well, I may have acted in the moment for . . . a moment, and . . . Look, I don't know what the hell I'm even saying. This is a stupid conversation."

"Ummm, we don't necessarily have to—"

"All right, here it is. I don't remember it too clearly, but I might have sort of led you on there, and I just don't want you going soft on me. Are you going to go soft on me?"

"Uh, no."

"I don't know why I'm even needing to say this. You know your prick of a hero, Tim Spencer? He came to the house last night, after you passed out. Basically called me a pedophile."

"I heard it."

"So you heard him give me the big 'hands off Christopher Newell' speech."

"Yeah, sorry 'bout that."

"Not your fault." Tina blew smoke out the window. "Jerk. What is he doing, keeping a watch on my house or something?"

"Let's just forget the whole thing," I said.

Tina pulled down her visor, slumping back in her seat at a red light. "Screw him. Are we cool about this?"

I had no idea what just got negotiated, except that we weren't going to be stopping for edible undergarments on the way back to my place. "Sure, we're cool," I said, feeling stupid for the sunken feeling in my chest.

The "morgue," as it turned out, was an orphaned room down the hall from a guy sitting at the biggest computer monitor I had ever seen, arranging the placement of stories in tomorrow's edition. Tina whisked me past a set of restrooms, a fire exit, and a water fountain to an industrial gray room with a metal door.

She flipped the light switch, and the bulbs struggled to life at one-quarter strength. They provided enough light to make out a micro-fiche machine, a cabinet of film drawers, and leather-bound books of the *Courier*'s past volumes, stacked in a bookshelf made for a giant.

"Okay, what are we looking for?" Tina said.

"All we really need is the date that the mayor dismissed the case against the golf-course developers." He wasn't the mayor yet when it happened, but Tina knew who I meant—Dana's dad. "Also, I want to know who the golf course's attorneys were."

"Hmmm. Stay here a sec, okay?"

"Where are you going?"

"It could take forever to go through all these." Tina waved a hand at the tomes lining the walls. "We've got a search function on our internal network. Just give me a minute."

"Okay," I said. I didn't know if I could wait even five minutes anymore—I wanted to dive into those things and start looking.

But Tina came back in record time, a huge smile on her face. She shut the door, leaving us alone in the little room with the microfiche files and the wavering buzz of the fluorescent lights. "I could kiss you right now," she said.

"Well, uh . . ."

"Sorry, shouldn't have said that. Here, gaze upon your genius."

She walked around the metal table in the middle of the room, pulled one of the giant volumes off the bookshelf, and flipped it open on the table. It was one of the later volumes, a little more than two years old. She turned gray pages crisping with age until she came to a front page with a blazing headline: RESORT CLEARED IN DECISION. The article had a large picture of Corbett standing on the courthouse steps with his arms raised, fists clenched. A subheading over the first column of the article (written by Art Bradford, natch) read, RULING SETTLES LEGAL QUESTIONS AROUND BLUFF DISASTER.

Tina pointed to the date. "How about that?"

"How about that." It was seven days after Kate Warne, the mayor, and Alexander Corbett had met in the hotel room.

"Now, check this out," Tina said. "Third graf, right here."

She pointed to a quote from none other than Kate Warne, identified in the article as "counsel to the New Petoskey Resort and Spa." Her statement was a BS-sounding line about how nobody had wanted the damage to happen less than the golf-course owners had. "The state wanted a scapegoat for this natural disaster, but in his well-reasoned opinion, Judge Ruby wisely declined their invitation."

I turned to Tina, who actually kissed my cheek. "They did it, Tina. Corbett and Kate Warne—they bribed him for that opinion. It was one of the last things he did before he became mayor."

"I know."

If people knew, the scandal would set Petoskey on its ear. "It's not enough to print a story, though, is it?"

"Not yet, but now we *know* it. I'm out of my gourd right now."

The pictures didn't really prove anything, expect that Kate Warne, Corbett, and the mayor had met at a hotel one night. Even if that was prohibited by the court rules, which I suspected it was, it didn't necessarily mean that any bribery had occurred. But Tina was right: we knew it.

I gobbled up the rest of the article while Tina flipped to others that her search pulled up. They detailed how Mayor Ruby's ruling had prevented a trial that "would have torn the community apart, for no good reason," according to Kate Warne, who was quoted liberally in the reports. My parents appeared a few times, too. They were featured in one sidebar story about citizens who had protested the development. Somebody had shot a photo of a meeting of the Ad Hoc Committee to Preserve Petoskey's Beautiful Spaces, which had moved out of our house by that time to accommodate their "increasing popularity among environmentally minded citizens from Petoskey and beyond."

Julia Spencer showed up in the background, wearing a button that said DON'T BLIGHT THE BLUFFS. I wanted to reach in there and apologize to her.

Tina wrapped her arms around me from behind. "Do you realize how huge this is?"

"Yeah."

"What's wrong?"

"I'm okay," I said. "But does this really get us any closer to who killed Mitch?"

It was unlikely that the mayor, Kate Warne, or Corbett had killed Mitch for the pictures. If they had, they would have destroyed them.

But we knew that hadn't happened—they'd ended up with Mike.

"Maybe not," Tina said. "But we know a big part of the picture, Chris. We just have to give a little push, and it's going to tumble right over into our laps."

"Yeah," I heard myself say.

"I'm going to ask Larry about this," she said.

"No, Tina."

It wasn't that I worried about them getting back together. It wasn't that I saw her going back to him, retreating to his bed of silk sheets with a bucket of ice and a champagne bottle at the ready. Well maybe, but there was more, too. "He could be loyal to Warne. He might . . . ummm . . . warn her."

"Kate Warne? You said she pushed him out of the firm."

"Yeah, but Tina, don't bring it up without me there, at least. Please."

"Dude, I'd do anything for you right now," she said. "Almost anything."

"Thanks," I said.

"No prob. But I've got to do some work now. Call you later?"

"Sure." I stood up, ten feet tall and ready to conquer nations.

27

I didn't have my car, but I didn't care—I had brought my camera along with me, and I had this idea that I would take some pictures on the walk home. It wasn't like I didn't have some things to sort through.

Daniel didn't pick up when I called from the sidewalk on the way back to Main Street. I kept walking down to the Rialto Cinema, called home again, and left a message for him that he should be ready to go to a 7:05 show or he'd miss out on his chance to see Angelina Jolie naked. Then I called my parents' hotel room and left a message that everything back home was going swell.

At the house, I yelled inside for Daniel. He didn't answer, like I knew he wouldn't, and I headed out to the Escort. I tried the library first, but his favorite chair was empty. It was in the reference section, where a small collection of wispy, fragile-boned men whiled away the summer entombed in silent, air-conditioned comfort. They gave me mistrustful looks of the kind I imagined their wives had to be familiar with.

"Is Daniel here?" I figured they were regulars and would know him.

"The whippersnapper?" one of them said.

"Yeah."

"Nope, ain't been round."

I nodded in defeat and headed out to the Escort. It wasn't a surprise, really. I'd known where to find him all along; I just didn't want to deal with it.

I started up the engine and headed for Mike's.

It had always seemed cold to me, Mike's parents' house. A box of glass on stilts that could look pretty in a magazine, if you had an extremely expensive camera and caught the light just right. But it was late afternoon by then and the sun was hiding behind the clouds, as it did most of the year. When I swooshed through the S curve on the way to Mike's house and caught a glimpse of it through the forest, it looked like it always did to me: blank, fake, reeking of money and nothing else.

Maybe that's why Mike's parents had chosen it—the description of their house fit their marriage pretty well. I'd never thought it could fit Mike, too, but my world had turned upside down.

Something was amiss in the driveway. Mike's mom's Porsche—the car he used all the time—wasn't there. In its spot was a red Jetta with a girl sitting on the hood. Her back was to me, shaking from tears. Dana Ruby was crying, all alone under the trees.

She'd more or less gathered herself by the time I parked and came up to her.

"Hey, Newell," she said with a sniff, not really hiding the fact that she'd been losing it a minute ago. I felt like her friend for the first time ever.

"Hi. You okay?"

She shrugged. "Yeah, sure. Well no, I'm not. Eventually maybe. Look, do you mind . . ."

"What do you need?"

"He's not answering the door, but I think he's just avoiding me."

"Do you have a key?" I figured she might—when they were together she was over all the time, sometimes spending the night.

She shook her head. "Not since we broke up. Look, do you mind, like, going up there?"

"Yeah, sure. Stay here."

I walked the woodchip path to the front door. I heard the doorbell chime inside, but the only response was a long silence broken by one of the crows that liked the woods behind the house. "Hey, Mike, it's me!" I called. "I'm here for Daniel!"

Nothing. I motioned Dana to wait and checked around back, but the deck was bare; Mike and Daniel weren't playing moguls today.

"The Porsche isn't here," I said to Dana on my way back. "He must be out somewhere."

"Yeah, and he's not taking my calls," Dana said.

"Let me try him, but he might not take mine either, to be honest."

My cell got only a couple of bars in the woods, but it was enough to place the call and hear Mike's voice-mail message. "Nope, not answering."

"Why wouldn't he answer for you?" she said.

"Uh, it's a long story. We sort of had it out yesterday."

"Was it anything about me?" That was the Dana I remembered—a little self-important, a little pathetic—but it didn't bother me. We weren't so different. I'd been pretty self-important, and pathetic, about Julia.

"No, it didn't have anything to do with you. Are you sure you're going to be okay?"

"Yeah. Thanks, you know, for doing that." She waved in exasperation at the house.

"No problem. I hope it works out for you, Dana. With Mike, or whatever. You should be happy." I was thinking about her dad and the way he treated her, but I couldn't say it. I think she knew that's what I was talking about anyway.

She slid down from the hood, hopping to her feet athletically. "Jesus, Newell, get all serious why don't you? Are you gonna start crying now, too, or something?"

"No, no. I just mean—"

"Whatever," she said, and hugged me like a guy—rough enough to show it didn't mean anything. "Thanks. I'm taking off."

She put the Jetta in reverse and backed around the Escort. And then I was alone under the trees with the distraction of Dana gone. I was missing a brother, and I didn't like the feel of it.

✹   ✹   ✹

Daniel didn't have a cell phone; my parents had been adamant on the point. I think they believed, somehow, that having a cell phone was going to corrupt him in ways that reading Nietzsche, Machiavelli, and *The Art of War*—all of which I'd seen on his bookstand at various points—wouldn't. It was kind of a silly stance to take, and I cursed their decision as I sped toward home, dialing our number over and over to no effect.

Everything was heightened when I got to the house. Eager for signs of Daniel, I saw things I'd stopped seeing long ago: the parted curtains in the upstairs windows, the lock around the front tire of his bike in our driveway. I heard familiar sounds like they were fresh and new. The scuff of my shoes on the walkway. The squeak of the screen door. The texture of the lock as the key fit in the door.

I put one foot in the living room and stopped. They jumped out at me like ghosts, the askew details spread throughout the room. The sofa was pushed too close to the wall. Something was off with my dad's rolltop desk, which sat decoratively at the side of the room. He'd brought it home from a yard sale, strapped to the top of the Escort, and my mom had stashed it in the corner because there was nowhere else to put it.

It had sat there, undisturbed, for years. And now somebody had pulled the rolltop up and left it. Daniel wouldn't do that. The dark, S-shaped rolls of wood had been such a fixed reference in my world that seeing its interior exposed felt like a gross violation.

"Daniel!"

I walked into the kitchen. My stomach fell when I saw the catchall drawer, the one only my mom used, sitting open.

They'd left the note on the whiteboard.

It was written with Daniel's special red pen—he never let anyone else use it. The note was in his handwriting. I guess they made him write it so I'd know they really had him:

They want the pictures. Wait for their call. No police if you want me back.

PART IV

THE MORGUE AND ME, AGAIN

or

DEATH IN DUNCAN WOODS

28

For an hour I sat in the kitchen, head pulsating, phone at my side, unable to move.

I can't remember those minutes passing, really—it's just a dark crevice in my memory, an hour-long coma I passed through before reengaging, horrified, with the world. I've heard the mind does that. It knows when something is too much to handle and shuts off. It might happen once in your life, if you're unlucky—and when it does, your brain just takes an eraser to the whole thing.

The darkness brought me out of it. The sun had dipped below the kitchen window, and I realized I was just sitting there in the murky night like some kind of deranged person. Which I was, in a way. I turned on the light, carrying the portable phone with me, triple checking the battery to make sure Daniel's call—it would come, I told myself, it *would* come—got through.

I avoided looking at the whiteboard. I didn't want to think of him picking up that pen, writing out the letters in a shaky red hand that couldn't quite master his fear. I put my head in my hands and felt my body pound.

My parents had left me alone with a single responsibility—Daniel—and now he'd been kidnapped.

Who? The mayor? Kate Warne? Alexander Corbett? How could any of them possibly know that Tina and I had discovered the bribery scheme? Would those people really do something like this?

They wanted the pictures. Mike was the only one who knew I had them. Mike? No way. He's my best friend, he couldn't do this. . . .

I grabbed the portable phone and stalked around the house, but it didn't do much to fight the feeling that I was drowning in my own uselessness. I had to keep the house line clear for the call from whoever had taken Daniel. My cell was lying on the kitchen table—I used it to dial Tina.

"Yo," she answered, and I heard my voice come out in a rush. When I got to the fact that Daniel had been taken, she told me to hang tight and clicked off. The call had lasted about seven seconds.

I called Mike next, almost without thinking about it.

"Hey." His voice was guarded.

"Hey, do you have Daniel with you?"

"No." Awkward pause. "What do you mean?"

"You have no idea where he is?" I insisted. "Really?"

"No, no clue. What's going on?"

"Somebody took him, Mike. It's because of those pictures, and you're the only one who even knew I had them."

Tina knew, too, of course. I'd called her out on the boat to tell her I'd found the pictures, and then I spent the night at her place right after. But she didn't count; she wasn't the one who'd taken my brother.

"Hold on," Mike said. "Are you saying he's been, like, kidnapped?"

"Yeah. You have to tell me everything you know about those pictures. It could help me get Daniel back."

"I can't tell you how I got them. I just can't."

"They've got my brother, Mike."

"I'm sorry, I know, but I can't. But look, I didn't tell anybody you had them. Whoever is asking about those pictures, they didn't find out you had them from me."

"But you're the only one who could have," I said.

I was milling through the house as we talked, obsessively turning on all the lights, as if it would help. They hadn't bothered to cover up the fact that they'd searched my room. The bed had been stripped. My books were splashed all over, spines broken and pages creased awkwardly against the floor. They'd taken apart my bookshelf, now just a mess of wooden planks on the floor.

"It wasn't me, Christopher," Mike was saying. "I swear to God it wasn't me. I'm coming over there to help you."

I was barely listening. The destruction in my room was making me sick. I had just noticed the empty spot on my desk—they'd taken my computer—when a knock came from the front door. The thought of Tina's company gave me a surge of relief.

"Christopher? Christopher?" It was Mike, still talking on the line.

"Don't come over. I've got to figure out what's going on here."

"But Chris—"

I clicked off and raced downstairs, not bothering to look before I swung open the door.

A police cruiser sat big and bulky in the driveway, closer to the house than we ever parked. It was shadowed by the porch and the top of it glowed with the reflection of a far-off streetlight. Looking sideways, I saw Tim Spencer peering through our living-room window. He had one of those cowboy/police hats on, pressing it up against the glass as he looked in. The night was turning black behind him.

"Christopher, hi."

He pulled open the screen door—it was like a toy in his hand—and trod past me inside. In the living room, he stalked around, forehead wrinkled as he made a quick inspection.

"Why are you here?" I said.

"Some neighbors called. They saw somebody they didn't recognize enter through the back door earlier."

"The Gradys?"

"Yeah."

They lived behind us. I used to cut through their lawn on the way to school until I realized Mr. Grady spent his days looking out their windows, never missing a thing. Daniel never took that route because it was trespassing.

"Mr. Grady, he said it was probably nothing, but he knows your parents are away and decided to report it. Actually, he calls every week about something or other." Tim glanced around the room again. "So . . . everything okay? Did you have a visitor?"

I shouldn't have trusted him. He worked with the sheriff, he'd been staking out Tina's place, and he'd met with Dr. Mobley. And there he was now in the living room, just happening to show up when my little brother got kidnapped. No, I really shouldn't have trusted him—but I was desperate and he'd been my hero once.

"They took Daniel," I said.

"What?"

"Daniel's gone, somebody took him." I led him into kitchen and showed him the note.

Tim read it over with a blank expression. "This isn't a joke?"

"No."

He scrutinized Daniel's message some more. "They want the pictures," Tim said softly, to himself. "Christopher, are these pictures—"

The screen door banged. A second later Tina was there in the kitchen, stopping cold when she saw Tim. "What's he doing here?"

"Take it easy," Tim said.

"Not likely," she said.

The whiteboard was right between them. She read the note, then pulled me over to her for a kind of sideways hug thing. I felt weak but stayed put, soaking up her warm, protective energy.

"Really, what *are* you doing here?" Tina said. "Stalking Christopher's house now?"

"I came on a call," Tim shot back. "But I think—"

"It says no police. You're putting Daniel in jeopardy."

"Shut up for a second," Tim barked, then tried to calm himself. "Let's just step back, okay. I think I know something about what you're involved in here."

"I wouldn't be surprised," Tina said dryly.

He stepped forward, into her personal space. "Hey, I'm here to help. His brother's been kidnapped, and arguing isn't going to help us get him back." Tim turned to me. "Now tell me, what pictures are they talking about in that note?"

He was looking me square in the eye, holding my shoulders in his hands. Tina gripped my arm. It was like being asked to choose between parents. I was still holding the phone for dear life. Half my mind was focused on it, willing it to ring.

"I want to tell you," I said, "but we don't know who to trust. We think the police could be involved."

"We think *you* could be involved," Tina said. "What were you doing out at my house, for one thing? Explain that, at least."

Tim ignored her, waiting for me to give in, but I didn't. "It's a fair question," I said.

"Yeah, okay," he said bitterly, pulling a chair out from the kitchen table. "Sit down for a second." We did, and then Tim leaned across at us. "I'm only saying this because your brother needs help, and I'll probably deny that I ever said it later."

"Go ahead," I said.

And then he started in.

"Stop me if this sounds familiar," Tim said, "but what if I told you that somebody was murdered, and the medical examiner helped cover it up by calling it a suicide? And what if I told you that he did it because powerful people told him to?"

He knew about Dr. Mobley. Tina propped her elbows on the table. "What people?"

"Maybe the mayor," Tim said. "Maybe Kate Warne and Alexander Corbett, too."

"And what's this supposed to tell us other than the fact that you're involved somehow?"

"I'm *not* involved. If you have those pictures, you know a lot more about this than I do. I only know what I do because of Dr. Mobley. He faked Mitch Blaylock's death certificate—he's told me that much—under pressure from the mayor."

"It wasn't just pressure. The mayor paid him to do it," I said.

Tina slapped my arm, but I ignored it.

Tim did, too. "Yeah, he's admitted that. But then his conscience starting working on him, and he asked me to lunch one day."

"At Dino's," I said.

Mike must have had the pictures even back then—when I sat in the car with him in the parking lot, imagining us like cops on a stake-out. I wondered how scared he must have been that day that I'd find out the truth. I was pretty close to it now, I knew that.

"What has Mobley told you?" Tina said to Tim.

"Not much more. He was feeling me out over lunch. He kept it all very vague. Then his wife died and he really cracked up. He said he wanted to clear his conscience. He told me the mayor was the one who had paid him off, and that Kate Warne and Alexander Corbett were behind it, too."

"You don't know how they're involved?" Tina said.

"No. The mayor told Mobley that they'd all been harassed by the dead guy, Blaylock. Other than that, I have no idea."

Tina and I shared a look. We'd discovered the blackmail scheme quicker than Tim had. "What about the sheriff?" I said. The sheriff had to know about the cover-up, too—he'd seen Mitch's body at the hotel, brought it in to the morgue. There was no way he was oblivious.

"He's Kate Warne's brother," Tim said. "If she was in on the murder, the sheriff would have been willing to look the other way."

"And that's why Mobley came to you," I said. "Because the sheriff was in on it."

"Right. See, I'm investigating my own boss here, in a way. My own police department. I've been trying to build a case that I can refer to a State Police task force, but Mobley hasn't given me anything solid. Meanwhile, you two are popping up everywhere."

"What do you mean?" Tina said.

Tim sighed, annoyed. "Like when Christopher showed up at the maid's house the night before she disappeared." I wondered if I should stick to my story that I wasn't there, but Tim said, "I know you were out there, so don't bother denying it. Anyway, that's why I've started keeping an eye on you. That's why I showed up at your house," he said to Tina, "trying to warn you off—so something like this wouldn't happen."

Tina still looked pretty pissed, but I believed him.

"So now," he finished at the table, spreading his hands, "tell me what these pictures are all about."

I made a snap decision and grabbed both phones—my cell and the portable for our home line—off the table. "Can you keep it from the rest of the police?"

"If there's any good reason to, yeah."

I turned to Tina. "Tell him everything."

I didn't want to do it, but I had to. Parents have the right to know when their son has been kidnapped.

I pressed Send, and a shudder of fear went through me when my dad answered the phone. He started right in with a chipper tone that clawed at my heart, going on about a hike they'd just taken. A brown bear had been climbing up the side of the mountain, maybe— *"What do you think, dear? Five hundred yards?"*—about five hundred yards away from them. He was glad that I had gotten him those binoculars for Christmas, they really came in handy. The guide said it was a female. You could see the muscles rolling across her back when she stepped over the rocks. Oh, Christopher, it is absolutely gorgeous out here.

"Dad, stop for a second."

Then I gave him the worst news he could imagine.

He started asking questions, and a lot of stuff poured out from me—about Dr. Mobley and the sheriff and the mayor and Kate Warne. My dad cut me off because he said I wasn't making sense. I hadn't said a word to them about Mitch Blaylock all summer and my story must have sounded looney. In the background, my mom was already making reservations for the next flight home. My dad asked if anyone was with me, and then he asked to talk to Tim Spencer.

I told him I was sorry.

"Put Tim on the phone, Christopher."

We got the call twenty minutes later.

Tim had already gotten off the cell with my parents. They couldn't get a flight out of Idaho that night, and they had to make two connections after that. They wouldn't be back in town before the next evening at the earliest.

Tina had finished filling Tim in on the details. How the mayor took the bribe to fix the case in favor of the golf course, Mitch's blackmail scheme, the bullet wounds in Mitch's body, everything. Neither of them had tried to claw each other's eyes out during the discussion, so obviously relations between them had improved.

We wanted to show Tim the pictures—I had the memory card in my pocket—but they'd taken my laptop away so we couldn't.

He and Tina were sitting together on the sofa when the call came. I was pacing the living room in front of them. The portable was on the coffee table.

Tina handed it to me gingerly when it rang. "Just find out where he is. It's going to be all right."

I pushed the talk button.

"Hello."

"Christopher?" Daniel's voice. My heart swelled.

"Yeah." Now he would tell me how it had been a trick. Or how he had escaped his kidnappers using a ballpoint pen and advanced principles of physics. But he didn't.

"Just bring the pictures and yourself." His voice had a robotic quality—he was reading something. "You do that, you'll get me back."

"Daniel, are you okay? Are you hurt?"

Some rustling on the other end, and then Daniel's detached voice again. The reading voice.

"There's a fence at the edge of the golf-course property. Follow it to the bluffs. Bring the pictures and you'll get me back."

"Daniel, are you okay? Cough or something to let me know."

He didn't cough.

"Be here in thirty minutes," Daniel said, and then the line clicked off.

❀ ❀ ❀

I ran out the front door. Tina didn't catch up to me until I was already at the Escort.

She barred the door when I went for my keys. "What's going on, Chris?"

"He told me to meet them alone. I just want Daniel back."

Tina sighed and looked to Tim, who had bounded out right behind her.

"You've got to let us come," he said.

"I don't want to chance it. I just want Daniel back. Sorry, Tina, but I don't care about the pictures anymore."

"Of course not," she said. "But . . ."

They were struggling for a way to help me. In the moment they hesitated, I forced the door open and took off.

29

I made it out to the New Petoskey Resort on a single shot of adrenaline. The drive gave me something to do, something to occupy the nervous energy that had been crawling through me. It hadn't been easy to leave Tina back at the house, but I didn't second-guess myself. Whoever had done this was acting rationally—they wanted the pictures back. Either to destroy them or to blackmail the mayor and the others. They had put Daniel at risk to get the pictures—and maybe they would pay for it somehow—but they were doing it for a reason, not because they were crazy, and they had no motive to hurt him. That's what I kept telling myself.

The hollow quiet of the golf course stilled my mind. I drove the thin road along the resort property, windows down, watching for the fence that would take me to Daniel. The fairways sat empty, strangely peaceful, spotted with curved pockets of sand. I passed one of the putting greens, where the yellow flag hung limp on the pole like a nightcap. Then a stand of bushes that obscured my view for hundreds of yards. They stopped abruptly, and I saw a long, metallic flash running away from me. The fence.

I crossed to the shoulder and parked. The far side of the course was a flat field of trees. I set off along the edge of it, along the fence to the bluffs. Clouds obscured the starlight. I couldn't see the bluffs yet—ahead of me was only a deep blackness and the whisper of the lake, growing slowly as I walked. I was too shot with fear to feel anything or to think about what lay ahead. A small breaking sound pricked the air and I stopped, terrified. Sweat ran down my temples. It could have been a squirrel. A bird, maybe. I turned back around, barely making out the Escort behind me.

I walked another quarter mile before I saw him. Daniel stood at a gnarled tree with twisted roots popping from the earth. A hulkish black form stood shuffling awkwardly at his side. The form froze when it saw me, fifty yards away. I had no game plan, no weapons. You could say I was stupid, but I needed to get Daniel back, so I walked straight ahead.

The giant silhouette next to Daniel slowly took shape. It was Bob. Big Bob the ex-boyfriend, of the tiny desk and humble manner, from the New Petoskey Country Club. It didn't make sense to me then.

Could this all have been the doing of Bob, the guy who stumbled over his words to Tina? Was he Mitch's partner in the blackmail scheme? Could he have killed Mitch Blaylock himself?

I tried to remember our conversations at the country club. My image of him was a vague blob of hesitant warmth—disappointing, in terms of clues. He worked at the country club, which meant he could have been partners with Mitch. Of course, he also worked in the office—close to Alexander Corbett. Maybe he was Corbett's muscle, hunting down the blackmail evidence on his behalf.

He was shifting his weight nervously from one foot to another, holding a fistful of Daniel's green Izod shirt by the back. The collar was pinched up to his neck, keeping him in place. A tight grimace had nested on Bob's features.

I stopped twenty feet away. "Daniel, you okay?"

He nodded. His eyes were clear and he didn't look injured. I wondered if he was as scared as I was—it didn't look like it.

"You better have those pictures," Bob said. False bravado rang through his voice.

"I've got them right here."

"Okay, then." Bob shifted some more, eyes darting around. "Y-y-y-you didn't bring anyone, right?"

"Right."

"'Cause I, like, saw some lights behind yours." He peered into the distance, and I could see the sweat creasing his face. His nerves calmed me.

"It's just me—I came alone like you said." I walked toward them, able to discern details now—the bark on the tree, the folds in Daniel's shirt. I didn't see any marks on his arms or legs.

"Stop there," Bob said, semifrantically.

The guy was losing it—I figured a direct approach might get through to him. "What are you doing here, Bob? Who put you up to this?"

"Who says anyone put me up to this?"

"Tina says you're a nice guy. Call me crazy, but it doesn't seem like your style."

"Yeah, well, Tina—"

He heard something and turned sharply to the left, into the trees. They were thick out by the bluffs, the final slice of forest that hadn't been chopped clean for the golfers. "Did you—?"

"It's just forest sounds, Bob. No one's there."

He gripped Daniel's shirt harder. "B-b-better not be. I've got a knife on me, you know." He swallowed hard when he said it; he was horrible at playing tough. "Let's just get this over with."

"Fine with me." I reached into my pocket, pulled out the Vista View memory card. "I've got the pictures right here."

Bob pulled a camera out of his pocket—it had a large display on it. Somebody had thought ahead. "Okay, throw it over," Bob said. "If they're r-r-really the pictures, I'll let him go."

"Bob, there's no way I'm giving these up before you let my brother go. Throw me the camera, and I'll show you the pictures from here."

He fidgeted on his feet some more, looking like he needed to go to the bathroom. "Yeah, fine," he said finally, and tossed me the camera. "Just hurry—I want to get out of here."

"Yeah, I don't exactly want to hang out here with you all night either, you know." It only took a second for me to get the pictures in the camera and hold the screen for him to look at. I scrolled through as Bob squinted at the pictures. He nodded. "Those look right."

"Okay, then," I said, trying to keep control. "Now I'm going to toss the camera back toward the street, and you're going to leave Daniel there and go get it."

"Yeah, okay."

I heard something for real then—a twig breaking in the trees.

"Who's there?" Bob said.

This wasn't what I needed, not when I was so close to getting Daniel back. He was standing there at Bob's side, staring into the forest with wide-open eyes, taking in everything. When he turned back, he gave me the tiniest nod. I didn't know what it meant, but I trusted the kid.

"It's nothing—let's just get this over with."

I tossed the camera back toward the street, far enough to get some distance between us but not far enough to break the thing. I held my breath and watched Bob take his hand away from Daniel's back, leave him at the gnarled tree, and walk toward the camera.

I ran to Daniel. *It's over,* I thought. *It's over and I got him back.*

But it wasn't over.

When I hugged him, Daniel whispered in my ear: "Tina's here."

I thought it was some kind of reaction to the shock. "What do you mean, bud?"

"In there," he said, pointing into the forest, where the sound had come from

And ⬛n, a bright yellow beam split across the grass, shining hot on l⬛e had just picked up the camera, ambling back to the road.

"Hold it!" Tim barked the command as he edged out of the forest, the flashlight in his hand. Tina trailed right behind him. "Lay it down, Bob, and put your hands in the air."

Tim was in his street clothes—I wondered if he had his gun or even his handcuffs on him—but Bob dropped the camera right away. He gave me a stung look, and in the brief second before Tim made it over to him, I actually felt sorry for the guy.

"Okay, okay, okay," he said, as Tim and Tina advanced on him. "I never would've hurt the kid. I didn't even want to do it." He was blubbering, slightly pathetic.

Tim handed Tina the flashlight and spun Bob around. "Hands on the fence," Tim said, preparing to pat him down.

"Yeah, okay," Bob rambled. "I'm not going to do anything, you got the kid back."

Tina had the light in his eyes, and you could see them freaking out. He wriggled at the fence, turning to plead his case.

"Just be quiet a second and stay still," Tim said, and that's when it happened.

Tim was patting his shoulders, under his arms, making his way down to the pockets of Bob's hoodie. Before he could get there, one of Bob's hands reached down.

"Hey," Tina yelled, but it was too late.

Bob had been surprisingly quick about it. Before Tim could stop it, Bob's hand had dipped into his pocket. It came out holding a thin piece of metal. I heard the *flick*, a short and sharp and sickening sound. The switchblade gleamed in the yellow light.

Tim danced back but it was over already—Bob was already plunging the blade into his side.

Tim fell to the grass, going fetal and clutching his side.

Bob staggered backward, amazed at what he had done. He looked at Tim's pain like a drunk contemplating his own puke. The switchblade fell from his hand as Tina rushed to Tim. Daniel and I did, too, in time to see a patch of red blossoming across Tim's shirt.

"Oh, God. S-s-sorry," Bob said behind us, tripping backward onto the ground.

"Tim—" I said.

"Yeah . . . fine," he said. He looked pale in the yellow light that Tina flashed against his side.

"Don't move," I said, and took my T-shirt off. I folded it in thirds lengthwise and slipped it around his torso, cinching it tight around him. My hands were slick with a slime of blood by the time I finished knotting it.

"That's good, Chris," Tina said over my shoulder. "That'll keep it." I don't know if she believed it or not. "Now let's get him to the hospital."

Bob made a lumbering path through the trees, looking in horror over his shoulder, slipping away from us. While I watched him, Tina and Daniel got Tim standing, his arms around their shoulders.

"Daniel, you okay?" I said. He nodded eagerly as he and Tina and Tim got their steps in rhythm, trudging toward the road. I walked alongside them for a few paces before stopping. Bob was almost out of sight. It was stupid to even think of it—I had no weapon, no help, no plan.

"Hold on," Tina said to the others as she turned back to me. "Go. Do it. I'll take care of Daniel."

Bob twisted through the maze of trees. He plowed forward, slump shouldered, a cloud of dust rising under his tennis shoes. He wasn't fast but he'd gotten a long head start on me, and when he heard me chasing him down he picked it up, sides jiggling as he ran. He knew the grounds out here much better than I did and made it through the thin forest before I could catch him.

I broke a sweat getting through the trees and then into a small clearing on the other side of the forest. The dense branches, the leaves, the tree trunks gave way to a view of the lake, stretching out to the horizon, three hundred feet below us. The tide churned against the walls of the bluffs, making it hard to distinguish my own heaving breath from the crashing water. The clearing was close to the road. He'd driven his car right across the flat expanse and parked here, ready for a quick getaway.

He was putting his key in the door when I reached him. I didn't have time to think, I just rushed up and tackled him against the car. His body was stiff and heavy and more powerful than mine, but I caught him well enough. I ducked my head and launched myself into his stomach, pinning him against the car before I heard an *oof,* and then he fell over me onto the ground. He scrambled back, crab walking to the edge of the bluff.

"I didn't have anything to do with it!" he shouted. "I promise. I was just here to make sure you got your brother back safe."

I pinned my knee over his chest, knowing I was out of my league—knowing he could throw me off in a second if he wanted to. But playing tough had worked so far.

"I know your car, Bob," I said. It was an old Honda thing with a sagging bumper. It probably had more miles on it than the Escort. But there was no mistaking the silver paint job. "I know you followed me that night. I know you followed Abby Shales, too."

"I didn't hurt anyone."

I pressed my knee harder into his chest. "Start at the beginning," I said.

"I . . . don't . . . know anything, really." He could barely breathe.

"Why did you follow me that night? Why did you have Daniel out here?"

"I was just trying to get those pictures back."

"Why?"

"Somebody told me to. They made me, I didn't have a choice. Look, I don't want to hurt you, either. . . ." He pushed my knee off him, and I spun a half circle to the ground. "Just take it easy," he said, holding out his hands. "I'm telling you, somebody made me."

"Do you know Mike Maske?"

"Who?"

"Never mind. Who made you do it, Bob?"

"I can't say. I did some bad things, okay? Back before I went out with Tina. This guy, he could have had me arrested if I didn't help him find those pictures." His jellyroll stomach jostled as he stayed clear of me, moving to his car. "I didn't even know you that night I followed you, or that you and Tina were . . . working together, or whatever you're doing."

He tapped his fingers on the roof of the car, staring out helplessly at the lake. "I'm really sorry about your brother—there's no way I would have hurt him."

I believed him—I believed he was a weak guy, a guy who'd been manipulated. But who was controlling him?

You've got to act. Make it happen.

I walked over calmly, projecting confidence as best I could. "Bob,"

I said, "someone's been murdered, and whether you know it or not, you've been helping to cover it up. You just stabbed a policeman tonight. There's no way we're leaving here before you tell me who made you do these things. So tell me, who made you take Daniel— who are you supposed to get the pictures for?"

I could read the torment on Bob's face. He looked out at the lake while he talked. "I can tell you this. The guy I'm giving the pictures to, you can find him tomorrow night at Duncan Woods, ten o'clock."

"You're not giving him the pictures. You're giving them back to me."

"I'm sorry for this," he said.

"For what?"

That's when he punched me in the face.

I didn't even hear his car drive off.

30

Daniel was sucking down a Coke, looking at Tina with the kind of interest that I thought he reserved only for chemistry textbooks. He swished his legs in one of the waiting area's plastic chairs. I saw them through the glass as I approached the emergency entrance at the side of the hospital.

The automatic doors swooshed open. My work at the morgue never took me to the emergency room, so it was foreign territory. I marched in, probably looking a little sketchy—shirtless, bedraggled, a ripening shiner on my left eye.

Daniel ran to me, little splashes of Coke jostling loose from his bottle. "Tim's gonna be okay," he said. "Why's your eye green? And purple? And yellow?"

"It's fine," I said, and Daniel went with it.

"The doctor says the knife didn't go in very deep. It didn't hit any organs or anything."

"I thought you only drank carrot juice and stuff," I said, pointing to his soda.

"Tina bought it for me. We're celebrating."

I knelt down to get a good look at Daniel. He mistook my intention and came around behind me to get on my back, the way he used to do when he was little. My arms hooked under his knees reflexively. Daniel hadn't wanted to do this for years. Odd behavior. Perhaps a sign of post-traumatic stress disorder.

"Tina told me what you're doing," Daniel said in my ear.

"Yeah?"

"Yeah. Solving a murder." His voice rang with strange tones—they took a moment to identify—of admiration and respect. I guess his getting kidnapped was the best thing that could have happened to our relationship. If Tina had told him even the barest details, he would have the case cracked in minutes.

"Hey there," Tina said, inspecting my eye. "That's pretty impressive. I guess Bob got away?"

"Yeah," I said, saving the details. "Which way to Tim's room?"

Daniel pointed, and we bounded down the hall. Through the narrow window looking into Tim's room, a doctor tended to his wounds. I set the little guy down and got on his eye level. "Daniel, I'm really sorry about what happened to you. We should talk about it—it must have been scary."

"Kinda." Daniel shrugged. "But I can't believe you're solving a murder." I decided to let it go—I suspected he was immune to attempts at therapy, and I probably wasn't the best one to administer it.

The hall smelled of antiseptic; the walls had been slathered in white paint. Plastic fixtures were set against each door, stuffed with patient charts. In a hospital, everything is pale. Some day a feng shui master will get a crack at one of them and start a revolution.

"Let's call Mom and Dad," I said, and got out my cell phone. FIVE MISSED CALLS, the screen said—all of them from Mike. I pressed Ignore and dialed my parents' cell, leaving them a rambling message that Daniel was okay. At the end, I passed him the phone so they could hear his voice.

The doctor emerged and blankly surveyed the three of us waiting in the hallway. After a moment, he pushed his glasses up on his nose and said he didn't see any reason why Tim couldn't see a few visitors, but that I would have to put on a shirt first. It was hardly an unreasonable request.

I sent Daniel inside and held Tina back to give her the lowdown.

"So Bob got away with the pictures?" Tina asked when the doctor turned the corner, leaving us alone in the hall.

"Yeah, but he told me some stuff. He said he was only doing it because somebody basically made him. He said the person knew about something he did that could have gotten him arrested."

Tina nodded. "I think he sold drugs for a while, but he never really talked about it. He would have been terrible at that—he's too nice."

The guy had just kidnapped my brother, but I didn't argue the point. Instead, I told her about Bob's comment that whoever wanted the pictures back was going to show up at Duncan Woods the next night at ten o'clock.

While I told her, my mind flashed back to memories of Bob—the first time we saw him, sitting there at the tiny desk. And then again at the golf tournament.

The day he came down into the lobby and saw us talking there, Tina with a cigarette in her hand . . .

Oh, God.

". . . go there tomorrow night, we have to. Christopher? Christopher?"

I hadn't heard a word she said.

"Tina, how could you?"

"What?" She was baffled. "Don't look at me like that—what's going on?"

"You told Lovell," I said. "How could you?"

"I told Lovell what? Christopher, you're not making sense." But I saw it already. A slight hesitation. The truth just peeking out at her.

"What do Mitch Blaylock and Bob have in common, Tina? Think about it."

An old client, Lovell had said . . .

She looked up and down the hall. "Where are you going with this? Both of them worked at the country club, but that doesn't make them partners."

"No, not that."

Her mind spun, trying to catch up. "Oh, well, yeah . . . both of them were Larry's clients."

I nodded. "Tina, the day I found those pictures at Mike's, you were the first person I called. You're the only person I told."

She was starting to get it—I could see the guilt in her eyes.

"You were out on the boat with Lovell when I called," I said. "You told him, didn't you? You had to."

"Oh, God . . . Christopher, I'm . . . I'm so sorry. . . I never thought . . ."

He was the only one who knew I had the pictures—the only one besides me, Tina, and Mike. He had to be the one trying to get the pictures back. Suddenly, it was obvious: Lovell had been leading the blackmail scheme all along. He was the "partner" that Abby had talked about in her note. He must have been using Mitch as the contact point, the bag man.

It made sense of everything. For one thing, it explained the two-year gap between the pictures being taken and the scheme coming into effect. Lovell would have been in a good position to know about Kate Warne participating in the bribery, and it wasn't hard to imagine him documenting her involvement as a kind of insurance policy. Maybe he never would have collected on it if he hadn't been pushed out of the firm by Kate Warne. I suspected that's what triggered his decision to go through with it.

But somebody had killed Mitch before they could go through with the blackmail, and so Lovell had used another one of his old clients—Bob—to get the pictures back.

"I didn't even tell him that much," Tina said helplessly from the floor of the hallway. "I guess I told him we'd had a big break, that you found some pictures."

"It would have been easy for him to put it together," I said. "He already knew we were looking into Mitch's death."

"Christopher, I'm so sorry. I thought I really liked the guy—maybe I wanted to impress him, I don't know. I never thought he had anything to do with this. I never thought he'd be dangerous. . . ."

I offered her a hand up. "I know you never wanted anything to happen to Daniel."

She stared into the hospital room. "God, this is all my fault."

"We're going to get Lovell tomorrow—for now, let's talk to the patient."

Tina stared at my chest. "Here, let's keep you out of trouble," she said, and stripped off one of her T-shirts.

I walked in wearing something that said MAYBE IF YOU LOSE A FEW.

Tim's cheeks had gained some color, and despite the gargantuan bandaging around his stomach area, he looked a lot better than I thought he would. Daniel was engaging him in a discussion about the history of the Pinkerton Detective Agency for some reason, but I didn't care. I could have listened to Daniel pontificate on the wonders of isosceles triangles with a smile on my face.

We all stood around him while Tim made jokes about how he screwed things up out at the golf course. When it was time for me to take Daniel home, Tina stayed to give Tim the details on what I'd found out from Bob. We agreed to huddle up at Tina's the next morning to strategize.

"Dude isn't as much of a pain in the ass as I thought," Tina whispered when she hugged me good-bye for the night. As Daniel and I walked out, I took a final look back through the window and saw her resting her hand on Tim's head. He was looking up at her, and there was something in his eyes that—even if I tried—I couldn't mistake.

My cell phone rang when we got back in the car. My dad, weak from stress and lack of sleep, told me he'd gotten my message—they were thrilled that Daniel was safe, but getting home would take a while. He and my mom had missed their connection in Denver. The next plane to Detroit wasn't leaving until morning. It meant they wouldn't be back until tomorrow night.

I had one more day, and it was just enough time.

31

Something was off about Tina's house. She had scrubbed the kitchen counter to a bright white and cleared most of the debris from her living room. She'd even put out a plate of glazed doughnuts from the bakery. She was scarfing down one of them when I got there at noon, Daniel in tow. I wasn't about to leave him unsupervised for a second.

Tim sat next to Tina on the couch, with a smaller bandage bulging out from his hip. The night before had put a different stamp on each of us. Tim sat there with a firm jaw, dressed in his police uniform, determined to get something done. Tina was angry, still steaming from Lovell's betrayal. I was jumpy. Daniel, he was happy as a clam. Tim and Tina gave him a war hero's greeting before Tina sent him to her spare room so we could talk.

Tim got right down to it.

"So you're sure it's Lovell that was blackmailing the mayor and the others?" he said.

"As sure as I can be," I said. "It's the only thing that makes sense."

He nodded and checked with Tina, who was finishing the last of her doughnut. "He's right. I wouldn't bet against the kid," she said.

"Okay," Tim said. "What about the thing tonight, in Duncan Woods?"

I'd thought about that. "He's going through with the blackmail. Tonight's the exchange—he gives them the pictures, they give him the money."

I knew I was right. Lovell wouldn't have gone to all that trouble to get the pictures back if he wasn't planning on getting something in exchange for them.

"I think Mitch was supposed to do it originally," I said, explaining my theory. "Lovell probably wanted to use Mitch because the mayor, Kate Warne, and Corbett didn't know him. It would have kept Lovell out of things."

Tina nodded. "Right. And he was going to give Mitch part of the action. That's why Mitch was bragging to the girl at the country club the night he died. That was the score he was about to get rich from."

I'd almost forgotten Buddy the bartender telling us about that, it seemed so long ago now: *She was young, too, like the man said. But that's all I know.* I wondered if Abby Shales had really gone to Texas. I hoped she had—I hoped she'd gotten lost in the big state like she said she would.

"Yeah, it makes sense," Tim said, "but it's still mostly hunches—we don't have much evidence. I called my contact at the State Police this morning, and they're giving me a meeting, even though it's Saturday and they're not too happy about coming in. If I can get them here for the exchange tonight, we can get them involved in the case. But I might need something more."

"I've got something," I said, and turned on my camera. Bob had stolen my computer, and he'd gotten the blackmail pictures back, but he hadn't taken my camera. I'd been carrying it around with me as usual that day, so I still had my pictures of Mitch's body. Tim and Tina winced when I showed them. I'd almost forgotten how gory they were.

"That's no suicide," I said, and handed the memory card over to Tim.

"That's good. Okay, I should get going if I'm going to get back here with them."

"How far are you going?" Tina said.

"Traverse City."

Her eyes blazed. "That's an hour's drive."

"I know—I told you, I had to go to the state with this. They don't have offices in every city. I had to go through a Michigan Bureau of Investigation task force—"

"Well, get the hell out of here instead of explaining it all day," Tina said. "We need them here tonight."

Tim laughed. "Is she for real?"

"Welcome to my world," I said, and Tina kicked him to the door before we could gang up on her any more. On his way out to the driveway, he stopped.

"I don't know how long it's going to take to get them up here. But whatever happens, promise me you won't go to Duncan Woods tonight."

"Of course," Tina said.

Right. Of course.

Tina and I watched from the front window as Tim's police cruiser rolled down the street. Maybe it was like watching your kid go off to college or something, I can't really say, but it felt like the whole thing was out of our hands now, and it was making me queasy. We were about to gather Daniel up when my pocket buzzed with an incoming call.

Mike again.

Tina looked over my shoulder at the display before I sent it to voice mail.

"He's got to fit into this somehow," Tina said. She was going gentle—she knew how close we were. Or how close we'd been.

She was right, though. Now that we knew that Lovell had been Mitch's partner, it made even less sense that Mike would have the pictures. And it made even less sense why he wouldn't tell me where he'd gotten them. Those pictures were the reason why Mitch had been killed—so how had they ended up in his hands, if he hadn't killed Mitch himself?

"I'm going over there," I said.

The trees in Mike's neighborhood grew tall, their leaves meeting high above the twisting road, throwing cooling shade onto the asphalt. The night before was catching up to Daniel; he was crashed out in the passenger's seat, head bobbing against the window at each tiny bump in the road. I wanted to go home, tuck him in, watch over him.

He stirred when I stopped in the driveway. "I'm just gonna see if he's home. You okay here?"

He slapped my hand away when I brushed his head on the way out. Good old Daniel.

I heard it from the front door—the blender, churning out another dubious smoothie creation. His quirks used to seem funny, but Mike didn't make me laugh anymore.

I banged on the door. It took a while for him to hear me, but he came, slowing up when he saw me. He opened the door reluctantly.

"Hey," he said.

"Hey. Can we talk out here, so I can watch Daniel?"

"You got him back?" A thin smile creased Mike's cheeks when he spied Daniel in the car. He raised an arm but Daniel was oblivious, asleep again.

I nodded. "Is that what you were calling about?"

"Yeah, of course. I wanted to make sure he was okay."

"Anything else?" I said.

"Anything else what?"

"That you want to talk about. Like how you fit into this whole thing." It was strange talking to him now. My voice was different, even—I was using tones that I used with strangers, teachers, guys from the Petoskey High soccer team who I didn't particularly like.

Mike shook his head and said it softly: "I can never tell you, Christopher. I just can't."

"We've got most of it figured out already." Mike didn't bite, so I asked him, "Do you know Lawrence Lovell?"

And then Mike said, "I had nothing to do with that guy getting killed, but my advice is to just stay away from the whole thing. Not that you're going to take it."

"No, probably not."

He nodded. "I'm glad you got Daniel back."

It sounded like a good-bye, so I left.

We pulled into the driveway at one thirty. An afternoon of waiting stretched out in front of me. Time was funny that day, the way it didn't budge. I played chess with Daniel, I tried to read, I cleaned up the mess in my bedroom from Bob's search for the pictures. It felt like I had fit three afternoons into one, but the clocks held back, drawing each minute out torturously.

Every forty-five minutes or so, Tina called with an update. A non-update, I should say—she hadn't heard from Tim all day.

The calls got more hysterical until six o'clock, when she broached the topic: "If he's not back, we're going to Duncan Woods. You know that, right?"

"Tina—"

"Yeah, yeah, I know what he said. But you remember what I asked you at the start of this thing?"

"I wouldn't call it pussing out at this point."

"Oh, I would," she said. "Big time."

At seven thirty she called again, this time with news. "They wouldn't meet with him till five o'clock, but he says he's bringing two agents up with him."

"Agents?"

"Whatever the hell they're called, I don't know. Tim said they're from the Michigan FBI, but he's waiting there for one of them still.

He's going to be cutting it way too close, so get your ass ready."

"Umm, for what?"

"We're doing this, Christopher. We're going to get pictures of the exchange. Bring your camera, and don't even think about backing out."

I wanted to. I wanted to back out in the worst way, but Tina clicked off before I could tell her.

I put down the phone and listened to a tinkering sound coming from the porch. Daniel was playing with an abacus out there; I looked in on him for a second before retreating to my room, sweeping up the last of my books that Bob had knocked to the ground. Sir Arthur Conan Doyle, Edgar Allan Poe, and a copy of *The Spy Who Came in from the Cold*. I placed them on the desk and sat down heavily on my bed.

You feel like a fraud when your dreams come true and it turns out you don't want them. I guess I never really wanted to be a spy, not if going to Duncan Woods that night had me scared out of my mind. All that stuff I told myself—wanting to work in the NSA and everything—it was just an excuse to read stories and watch movies. Mike was right all along: I should have gotten out of my head a long time ago.

I texted Tina: BE THERE SOON.

I brought Daniel to Julia's at eight thirty. She was the only one I trusted to watch him, and when I told her it was an emergency, she didn't ask questions. I paused on the front lawn, charging myself up. This was the start of it—the new me.

The front curtains were pulled back. They gave me an angle to the sofa, where Julia had nestled in the corner with her face glowing in the flickering blue light. Julia: high-school nerd, wallflower, best friend, missed chance. Maybe I could make it happen.

Daniel had bounded ahead of me up to the door. Julia heard him knocking and collected herself.

I shot up to the front door and gave Daniel a hug good-bye before he rushed inside like her place was Disneyland.

Julia looked at me for the first time. "Has he eaten dinner?" she said.

"Yeah. Thanks a lot for doing this, really. I wouldn't ask but—"

"Don't worry about it. When will you pick him up?"

"Before midnight. It shouldn't be too long."

She nodded. It couldn't have been clearer that she didn't care where I was going or whom I was doing it with.

"So, you know, I've been thinking about what you said the other night. A lot, really."

Julia saw it coming a mile away. She was already shaking her head. "I think we've just had bad luck. It's probably best to leave it at that."

"Oh, okay," I said. "Yeah, for now."

"No. Forever, I think."

She had thought about it, too—she was done with me. I would have left it at that, but tonight I was going to be different.

When she grabbed the doorknob, I held it fast from the other side. "I sort of woke up to some stuff in the last couple of days. Maybe the last hour, actually." It was like she'd heard me for the first time all night. Her eyes narrowed a shade; she released the door, intrigued enough to listen. "Anyway, umm, I really wanna try. I want to make it real this time—me and you. Not just something to obsess over."

Her face softened, opening a crack. "Obsess over? I don't remember that part."

"My mistake. I'm certified obsessed. In a healthy way."

She grabbed the doorknob again, her pink fingernails curling against it. "You've always known where I am, Christopher," she said with a hint of invitation in her voice. "You've always been able to call."

Then the door closed, and I called it a victory.

32

W e walked up the hill from Tina's house, stopping short of the long wooden stairway down to Duncan Woods. "That thing all charged up?" Tina said, pointing to my camera.

"Yeah." I threw the strap over my shoulder and led the way to the top of the hill. Crouching at the wooden landing, we had a bird's-eye view of the clearing at the edge of Duncan Woods. The overhead sodium lights shone off the paint-lacquered picnic benches, where I had watched Tina twirl in the night before she pulled me down to waltz with her. The same picnic benches that the sheriff had scoured that day. He'd known the exchange would take place here—that's why he'd been casing it.

We were early, a half hour till showtime. The park was empty, and the visible notch of Lakeside Drive in the left distance was bare of traffic. "What's the latest from Tim?" I said.

"He called me when he finally left, maybe forty minutes ago. He'll have to hurry to make it."

"You wanna stay up here?" We were far from where the action would be and a little exposed, but if we lay flat on the landing, no one would see us.

"Not much time before they get here," Tina said, " but let's go down." We hurried down the stairs, surveying the grounds for a spot to set up.

It was obvious. At the edge of the park sat a clump of leafy bushes, tall enough to settle under. "Stay here a sec," I said, and crawled low into the bushes, lying between their thin trunks. I could see Tina plainly enough through the leaves. A pair of headlights flashed across Lakeside Drive behind her, then disappeared again.

I wouldn't be able to use my flash and had to pray they stood close enough to the light over the picnic table to get a decent exposure. I took a test picture of Tina, checked the lighting on the screen. Good enough. "Did you hear that?"

"Nope."

"Can you see me?" I asked.

"Just the glow from your camera."

I shut off the display and snapped another one. "Anything?"

"No."

"C'mon then, we're good."

Tina scurried under the bush with me, hunkering on the opposite side of a trunk. "You're a genius, brainy," she said. "Goddamn. It's like a friggin' apartment in here."

She pulled her cell phone out and punched at the settings. Silencing it, I figured, so nobody would hear if a call came in. "Okay, we're officially flying blind here."

It almost didn't matter if Tim showed up anymore—Tina and I

were in this for good. We wriggled against the earth, finding comfortable positions.

"Christ, I could really use a smoke right now," Tina said after a
minute. And then, getting serious, "Hey, thanks for sticking with me."

"Sure."

Her hand reached out and clasped mine in solidarity. She released
it with a nod, and we understood without saying it that it was time
to stay quiet. It was getting close to ten, and they could show up any
minute. It felt like we had taken large breaths and dipped under
water.

I adjusted my leg a final time, triple checked the camera settings,
and scoped the grounds through the telephoto lens. The sodium
light over the park hummed white noise that I hoped would cover
the clicks from the Nikon. My elbows were aching from digging into
the ground, when we heard the crackle of brush on our right.

They hadn't come from Lakeside Drive, the way you would if
you came for a Sunday picnic. They advanced from the woods, two
shadows making for the cleared park area with light steps and swivel-
ing heads. I poised the camera.

Kate Warne came first, a thin briefcase in her right hand. The
money. She had dressed in a dark jogging suit with white piping
that picked up the light. Tina grabbed my arm as the second figure
emerged: Sheriff Harmon. Her older brother, there to protect her. I
wondered if he planned on arresting the blackmailer when he showed
up, and if so, how they would explain the pictures of the golf-course
bribery. Surely they'd come out if he tried to press charges.

They stayed at the edge, close to the trees. I turned a dial, slowing the shutter speed—with some luck the pictures would be bright enough. I nodded at Tina and reeled off some shots of them standing together.

The sheriff gripped Kate by the elbow, said some last words, and retreated into the darkness of the trees. I clicked a last picture of him and then he was gone, sucked in by the black forest. He was going to take Lovell by surprise.

Kate Warne stood alone for a good five minutes, rolling her neck every once in a while, switching the briefcase from hand to hand. Then a soft crunch of gravel sounded through the park. A car door shut. A sturdy, satisfying *shhhuck*—an expensive car.

Thirty seconds later, Lawrence Lovell walked up to her. They stood, stiffly facing each other and there was no question—this was it. Lovell was the one blackmailing her, and they'd come to make the exchange.

Tina stared out at Lovell with a brittle, hard-eyed look of accusation.

"So, it's you," Kate Warne said to Lovell. "Why am I not surprised?"

She wasn't talking loudly, but their voices carried in the night. Lovell must have been using Mitch as his contact, like we thought. With Mitch dead and the money in reach, he was revealing himself to her for the first time.

Lovell wore cargo pants, looking like he'd stepped out of one of those adventure pictures in his office. I got Kate in the viewfinder with him and snapped off more shots.

"Let's get this done," Lovell said.

"Why are you doing this, Larry? Your gambling problem's that bad?"

Lovell shrugged. "We all have debts. You should have never kicked me out of the firm, Kate. That was your mistake."

Then his head jerked right, hearing something. He looked to the picnic bench, the stairs up to Tina's street, into the woods. Lovell didn't seem to catch any sign of the sheriff—or us.

"The money, Kate." Lovell fished in his pocket and pulled out the Vista View memory card. "And this is yours."

She kept the briefcase at her side. "They're digital pictures. You could've sent copies anywhere."

"You can copy film, too." He stepped a foot closer. "This is a trust relationship we've got. You trust these are the only pictures and hand over the money, or you don't and I send them everywhere. Your call."

"Show them to me," Kate said.

Lovell reached into another pocket and pulled out the camera that Bob had used, inserting the card and flicking through the images. "That's it," he said at the end. "Now let's get this done."

After a moment Kate resigned herself, turning dials on the case. I wondered if the sheriff would wait until Lovell had the briefcase before he showed himself.

Kate opened the case. I don't know how much was there, but it was more than $15,000. Lovell smiled—the same smug grin that had annoyed me about him from the start.

"Easy now," he said, offering the memory card to Kate. She handed over the briefcase and it was done, their bodies relaxing just a hair. I had caught the whole thing on camera.

"Happy trails," Lovell said, keeping his eyes on Kate as he walked away. She nodded into the woods, a signal to the sheriff. The three of them stood on our right. At the same time a single fiery burst came from the left.

I looked, and by the time my eyes turned back to Lovell, he was on the ground. Tina's hand dug into my bicep. I shot pictures, trying to stay detached and aware.

Kate Warne scrambled back in horror, shrieking. The sheriff lumbered to her, crouching with his gun drawn, eyes madly searching the field to the left of us. He pulled Kate behind a tree. She covered her mouth, hyperventilating.

The sky had opened in a summer rain and metallic slivers fell softly through the lights.

Lovell didn't move. I zoomed the lens over his body and swallowed. His eyes were frozen, his cheek shattered by the bullet. We'd just watched somebody die.

The rest followed in a blur.

When I turned back to the left, Mayor Ruby was striding in toward Lovell's body. The gun hung limply in his hand. I kept taking pictures while Sheriff Harmon marched over to meet the mayor. Kate Warne staggered behind the sheriff.

"Jesus, Julian. I said I'd take care of it."

"I knew you wouldn't, though. It was my problem anyway." Mayor Ruby was standing over the body like it wasn't even there.

The sheriff leaned in to the mayor. "There's more than you involved here," he said. He held an arm out behind him, holding Kate back. "Get out of here, now." She hesitated, unable to keep her eyes off the body.

"*Get,*" he said again, and she snapped to the present. She tore an awkward line back into the forest, back from where she'd come.

"We couldn't risk it," the mayor said to the sheriff.

"You can't do this, either. I could have scared him off."

"No, you couldn't have. It never would have ended." He was running overtime, on a manic spell. "It's good for all of us. Kate doesn't have to worry anymore. Blaylock's gone; now he's gone, too." The mayor peered down at Lovell, a cold fixture on the grass. "It's over."

"Blaylock was different," the sheriff said. I didn't know what he meant but his voice was hard as a wall.

"I'm getting the wagon here," the mayor said, and pulled out his cell phone. I knew it then: He was calling Dr. Mobley.

The mayor wandered across the grass, waiting for an answer, while the sheriff held his head in frustration. For a moment the night took a breath, slowing down. But it was just starting.

The next seconds happened like this. A car took the bend on Lakeshore Drive, brights on, sweeping a flash of light across the woods. The sheriff's body jerked upright, eyes holding on the bushes we huddled under. It could have been the strength of the headlights or a stroke of bad luck, maybe a reflection from the camera lens meeting his eye. I don't know, but we were done. The sheriff played it cool, looking off but not too far. Tina and I reached out to each other at the same time—she'd seen it, too.

I skirted inches forward, knowing what we had to do. I grabbed

Tina's arm and pulled her with me. The sheriff was closer to the stairs than we were, but getting to Tina's house was our best shot.

I pointed to the stairs, and Tina nodded. The mayor had connected—he talked sternly into his cell. The sheriff sauntered away from the stairs now, walking easily, preparing to take us by surprise. Now.

I yanked Tina's arm with me and broke through the leaves. We ran wildly for the stairs, knowing we couldn't make it unseen and hoping for the best. The sheriff had an angle on us, but he was slow. We made it farther than I thought before hearing a burble of confusion at our backs. I grabbed the railing and felt Tina pushing me forward from behind. The wooden steps had been put in years ago—the thin boards hammocked in the center. I charged up them two at a time. The sheriff was yards behind us getting to the stairs. We were going to be okay.

Tina charged behind me, her hand on my back. I felt it slip away as Tina yelled in pain. I checked back and saw her huddled, clutching the ankle she'd twisted on the stairs.

The sheriff closed in instantly.

It would be no matter for him to slap cuffs on Tina now. He was reaching for them already. Without thinking, I descended two steps and kicked out at him. My foot landed squarely on his chest, and when I pushed off, he tumbled down the quarter flight. His body stopped just short of the ground, jammed across the stairway.

"Can you move?" I said to Tina.

She winced tightly as soon as she got to her feet. With her arm around my shoulder, we made it up the stairs, Tina hopping for balance on her good foot. From the top we looked down and saw the sheriff just getting up.

"They don't know your house," I said.

We hobbled down the hill, getting a little pace going by the time we made it to her front door. The sheriff hadn't made it to the top when we shut ourselves in. I locked the door and twirled the blinds closed and found Tina on the couch, head down, elbows on her knees, sucking air, spent.

"Call Tim," I said, peeking through the blinds. The sheriff hadn't appeared—maybe he'd given up on us. Tina pulled her cell phone out. "You can't even walk, can you?" I asked.

She shook her head. "That hurt like hell."

She pressed Tim's number on her phone and held it to her ear.

"Tell him to meet me," I said.

"Where are you going?"

"The morgue."

33

"Chris, no."

"They're going to do it again—just what they did to Mitch." I had to stop it if they were going to try to cover up another murder.

"Don't," she said. "We're lucky we got away; we've got to stay out of it now. You know what we just saw."

"I'm going."

I was heading to the door when she gave in. "Go into my bedroom then," Tina said, "in the drawer of the nightstand. Just do it."

She wasn't trying to stop me anymore, so I went. The house got darker down the hallway to her bedroom. I flicked the light and found a rumpled bed with scarlet sheets and a jungle of curiosities that I couldn't bother to investigate. A Dalí print hung over a black laminate nightstand. Stepping through a week's worth of laundry, I pulled the tiny drawer open.

The handgun sat alone inside the drawer. Metallic and small, cold to the touch. I heard Tina's muffled voice, talking to Tim, telling him she couldn't stop me, he had to get over there now. I picked up the gun and carried it back.

Tina waved me over to the sofa. "Turn your phone on. Tim's on his way there." I nodded, distracted by the thing in my hand. I didn't know the first thing about guns. Tina ejected a clip from the handle, checked it, and put it back in.

"This is the safety," she said, showing me. "You pull this back, and then all you do is pull the trigger."

"Hopefully not."

"Yeah. But take it."

The Escort rattled to a stop a block from the hospital. I didn't want them seeing it if I'd beaten them there. I ran through the soggy air to the hospital.

Sweat was rimming the neckline of my shirt within thirty seconds. Mobley's Oldsmobile wasn't in the parking lot yet; I hoped that meant I had a few minutes to get down there ahead of him. I bent at the waist by the front doors and let a few sharp breaths pull through me, until I got control.

The doors were open and the lights on, but they didn't staff the volunteer information booth this late. The morgue would be locked—I had to get the key from Dr. Sutter's office. A candy striper walked through the lobby, carrying charts in her hand. I ducked down to a water fountain, waiting for her to pass.

"Can I help you?" she said when I pulled up.

"Which . . . uh . . . way is the emergency room?"

The question satisfied her. "Out the doors, around the building to your right."

"Ah, thanks." I hung there, waiting for her to pass down the hall, when an EMT van pulled up outside. Lovell's body, probably. There was no more time to wait—I jogged back to Dr. Sutter's office.

His door was open, but the desk drawer with the keys to the morgue was locked. I banged on it uselessly, with a sinking feeling that I wouldn't be able to prevent another cover-up. My camera strap weighed on my shoulder—I shouldn't have brought it with me. I had enough evidence in there to at least show that the mayor had killed Lovell, and I was putting it at risk by carrying it around with me.

It was a metal desk, an old one from the fifties or something. Dr. Sutter had a paperweight of an Irish clover on his desk. It weighed a ton, much heavier than the gun. The lip of the desk hung out over the drawer. I checked out in the hall and saw no one, then rammed the paperweight up into the lip of the desk. After a few more hits, the lip raised enough to show the small metal bar that locked the drawer in place. Dr. Sutter had a letter opener in his pen holder, a mug shaped like a brain. I slid it through the opening and the metal bar turned down easily. I had seen Dr. Sutter open that drawer plenty of times and knew right where the key to the morgue would be sitting. I took it out and headed downstairs.

I set up on Mobley's sofa. I'd been waiting there five long minutes, the cold air freezing my T-shirt to my chest. Every once in a while I snuck a peek at the empty autopsy room through the large window looking out from Mobley's office. It was pointless—I'd know if anybody entered. I'd be able to hear them. The gun sat on the cushion next to me. I didn't want to touch it. I doubted if I could use it.

My cell phone rang loudly, the electronic noise banging against the hard walls of Mobley's office. I didn't recognize the number.

"Yeah," I said.

"Christopher. Are you at the hospital?" Tim.

"I'm down in the morgue." I figured Tina had told him everything. "It sounded like they were calling Mobley before."

"You're out of sight, right?"

"Yeah, in the office."

"Okay, good. I'm almost there. Don't come out. Don't make yourself known. Just stay put, okay?"

"Yeah, okay, Tim," I said. It was his deal now. A wash of relief came over me, and I closed my eyes.

I had just closed my phone and lain back on the sofa when I heard something at the morgue entrance. Somebody had opened the door. A second door opened and brought another wave of relief—whoever came in had gone straight into the autopsy room instead of heading back to the office.

I heard a different, harder clack of shoes. Two people.

The door to the autopsy room closed, muffling their sounds. I leaned closer to the window when their voices picked up in anger. Concentrating, I could distinguish their words.

"It's not gonna happen again." And then a cough. It was Dr. Mobley. I could see him in my mind, dabbing at his mouth with the handkerchief.

"Whatever you want. I'll give you more." The mayor. Like I thought—he'd bribed Dr. Mobley the first time, and he wanted to do it again.

"This is different," Dr. Mobley said. He'd already come to Tim about Mitch Blaylock—he wasn't about to fake another death certificate. I figured he was stalling, but it was funny how he'd chosen the same words as the sheriff had: *Blaylock was different.* I still didn't know what that meant.

"Whatever you want," the mayor said. He was almost shouting.

Mobley didn't answer. Finally, he said, "I'm going to talk to the sheriff. You should be gone when I get back."

I heard Dr. Mobley leave and waited for the mayor to follow him.

After a minute the door opened, and I thought he was gone. But when I looked into the autopsy room, I saw that it was Tim, entering with a severe look on his face. His eyes focused downward, against the wall; the mayor must have been sitting there. I should have ducked back down, but I couldn't peel my eyes away.

Tim pulled a pair of handcuffs from his belt. "Mr. Mayor, I have to arrest you."

I raised up another few inches, far enough to see the Mayor slumped against the wall. He had placed his gun on the floor. It lay alongside his leg, and I wondered if Tim could even see it there.

"No," he said to Tim. "The sheriff'll talk to you. We'll work this out."

Tim shook his head. "I'm arresting you for murder. The sheriff can't help with that."

I don't know if I saw anything snap in the mayor's face or not, but afterward I thought I did. His hand flashed to the gun as he pushed up off the wall. Tim didn't have time to react. He hadn't realized how far gone the mayor was; he hadn't prepared himself for this.

In a split second, the mayor had risen to his feet, his back turned to me. I could see Tim's face, watching helplessly as the mayor raised the gun. I was going to watch Tim Spencer die right there in the morgue. Another fraction of a second.

The shot I fired blew a chunk of the window apart. The shards sprayed like confetti, and the mayor's left knee buckled. I had hit him just below the shoulder. He held the gun in his right hand, not giving up, struggling to forge on. His right arm made a wide, arcing motion as he turned himself around. His eyes latched onto me as the gun traveled up to my chest.

I pulled the trigger again. Glass clinked to the floor as the Mayor clutched his ribs. Blood ran across his fingers, spilling over his knuckles. I must have hit his heart.

"C'mon, Christopher."

It was the third or fourth time Tim had said it. Calmly, softly, trying to pull me away with gentle words. I had come into the autopsy room to see what I had done, and now the mayor's blood was pooling around my feet. My mind was stranded in a vast nowhere.

Nurses rushed in from somewhere, and then the mayor was being lifted to a table. White coats swept past me and closed around his body, huddling over his chest, frantic with activity.

Tim's hand closed around my arm, and I let him take me away.

He sat me on the plastic bench at the front of the hospital lobby by a dying fern. Everything turned to background noise—Tim making calls on his radio, police funneling in, red and blue lights from squad cars swirling pointlessly around the lobby. I don't know what Tim told them, but it was enough to convince them not to arrest me.

My cell phone rang. Home. Daniel.

"Hey," he said.

"Hey, Daniel."

"What's wrong?" It took him two words to sense it, and I wondered if, for the rest of my life, people would know something was off about me with my first introductory sentence.

"Nothing."

"Mom and Dad are home. They picked me up from Julia's. Where are you?"

"The hospital."

"Where'd you go tonight?"

"Nowhere. I can't talk about it. . . . Daniel?"

"Yeah."

"Tell them I'm not coming home tonight. Tell them I'm sleeping at Tina's."

Tim was standing by me when I hung up the phone. "I'll drive you," he said.

"I'll go to your parents' place next and tell them everything," Tim said as we parked at Tina's. I nodded, though I wasn't understanding much of anything.

Tina met us at the front door. I don't know what we looked like, but she took a sharp breath of surprise before smoothing out, smiling weakly.

"He saved my life," Tim said, before Tina could ask any questions.

He drew her aside, whispering the bare details to her while I stood numb at the door. On his way out Tim clapped me on the back. "I might come over later, when I've finished for the night."

Tina nodded. "Sure."

"It might be real late."

"Whenever," she said.

PART V

SUSPENDED ANIMATION

34

We limped together into the living room. Her ankle wasn't any better, but it felt like she was the one holding me up.

"Tell me," she said when we sat on the couch.

I wanted to, but I couldn't speak.

She stroked my arm, doing what she could. "Take your time."

I'd slumped into her house like this before, after getting tailed coming back from the Hideaway. A little thing like that had seemed dangerous back then. For some reason, I remembered Tina badgering me for details then, demanding the scoop while she made us hot chocolate. A small, deep part of me smiled at the memory, and it was enough to bring me back, lurching slowly to the world.

"I got to the morgue first," I told her. "The mayor, he tried to convince Dr. Mobley to do it again, with Lovell this time. He said he'd give him anything."

"Mobley was there?"

"Yeah, but he left quick. I thought that might be it, but the mayor stayed in the morgue. That's when Tim came. The mayor, he still had his gun, but Tim didn't see it. He stood up with it and I thought . . . I could see it happening . . . I didn't even think. . . ."

"You saved him." Tina was hugging me. I let my head fall on her shoulder, pressing into her wiry black hair. "You saved him," she kept saying, over and over.

We stayed like that for a while, and then without a word Tina pulled me up. "C'mon, keep me company," she said, and brought me to the kitchen.

I sat on the counter as she made grilled cheese sandwiches. The pan crackled against the bread and the smell filled her house. She made two plates up and handed me one. "Comfort food," she said. "When all else fails."

I managed a bite, and then my hunger kicked in and I finished the whole thing. Tina put on some music while we ate, so low I could hardly hear it. A woman, singing softly to us. Tina didn't try to make me feel better. She didn't give me any lines to soothe me. She didn't pretend that my life hadn't just changed. She was perfect.

Tim dragged himself in around three. Tina was changing the CD— we hadn't even thought about sleeping.

"It's a mess over there," Tim said.

Tina shut off the stereo. "What do you mean?"

"I did what I could tonight, getting Christopher out of there and giving the whole story to the Bureau guys. I had to wait for one of them forever in Traverse City, that's what took me so long getting here."

"So, they know Christopher did it to protect you, right?" Tina said.

"Yeah. But now the sheriff's over there, and he's trying to stay in control. It's going to be a struggle before this gets worked out. Christopher, you're going to have to do a lot of police interviews before this is through."

I really only cared about one thing. "Is he alive?"

Tim shook his head. "They're still working, but it isn't looking good. Not at all."

"They can't arrest Christopher or anything, right?" Tina said.

"I'm trying to keep that from happening. But whatever happens, even if the Sheriff tries to make this look like something different, the truth is going to come out. You're going to be okay."

I hadn't even thought about it—getting arrested. I drew into myself again, and only heard Tim and Tina's conversation as background noise. They were putting together the pieces, analyzing the jigsaw puzzle that it seemed we'd put together.

The piece in the center was Mitch Blaylock, and if people ever really did find out what happened that night, it'd be easy for them to think the mayor had killed him. He'd paid Dr. Mobley off to fake his death certificate—that was clear from what the mayor had said.

But something was off. I could think now, more clearly than I had in the last few hours. If the mayor killed Mitch, he would have done it to get the pictures back. But he never got them; Mike did.

I couldn't guess why Mike wanted them, but I could try to think of connections. Who knew about the pictures? Lovell, Mitch, and anybody Mitch told. Abby Shales, at the least.

And then my mind leaped across a chasm and I knew.

I knew, and it was terrible.

❦　❦　❦

Tim drove me back early. It was part of the deal, he said—he'd promised to keep a police watch on me instead of making me come to the station. He said that was why he stayed at Tina's with us, but he'd slept in her room. It failed to inspire even a hint of jealousy in me—which is to say, I was dangerously unwell.

We'd barely gotten any sleep, and it was more night than morning on the ride home. Yellow-blue light veiled the darkness, but the world stayed still, looking empty and hollow around us in the quiet. A policeman was posted on our front porch; Tim waved to him from the car.

"I'll call you later," Tim said. "We're gonna work it out."

"Yeah."

My parents were sitting vigil at the kitchen table. In an act of heroic restraint, they let me go to my room without delivering any message except the love in their tired eyes. I didn't know it then, but they'd spent the night finding me a lawyer, and by four o'clock in the morning, they had secured the services of one of the best criminal defense attorneys in Detroit. They let me go to bed without a question, and I'll always love them for it.

35

My parents hired the other guy—the shrink, I mean—by ten o'clock in the morning. He had an exalted reputation, but I had the sense that the primary thought on his mind throughout our sessions was his liability insurance rate. His big advice was that I shouldn't joke around.

I didn't leave the house for a week, but I never felt more cooped up than during our sessions out on the porch, talking pointlessly over lemonade and cookies. Pointlessly, I say, because there was one big thing on my mind, but it was something I'd never tell him. I was the only one who knew who'd killed Mitch Blaylock, and I hadn't decided what to do about it. I hadn't even told Tina.

The week passed quickly considering I was holed up in the house, penned in by the cameras outside and my parents' strict instruction to stay put. It felt like being in a spaceship—suspended there in my cabin on Admiral Street while important information trafficked back and forth from outside. Most of it came from Tim and Tina, and most of it was good.

The mayor was still alive, for one thing. Maybe not for long— hooked up to tubes, still unresponsive—but alive.

The state authorities had opened an investigation into the events at Duncan Woods, and Tim was working closely with them. Some guy from a "task force" came out to our house and questioned me for hours about what had happened. I sat there with my lawyer at my side and only lied once during the whole thing, when I told the guy I didn't know who killed Mitch Blaylock.

The district attorney decided not to charge me with shooting the mayor. He said it in a big press conference that Tina covered. I saw clips of it on television, too. The district attorney was being a little cagey; he wouldn't promise that I wouldn't be charged with some other crimes, like breaking into the morgue. The events of that night were still being investigated, he said, and there was a lot that his office still wanted to know before they would make further announcements. But I figure I'm in the clear.

They buried Lawrence Lovell that week. Tina told me about the funeral. My parents didn't like her coming over, but they allowed it for brief visits; I overheard my dad one night, telling my mom that talking to Tina was the only thing that lifted my spirits, and I guess he was right. We sat in the living room, and she gave me the details— the small crowd that turned out for him, the way his glossy white coffin with a dozen roses on it fit him perfectly.

"Here's the best part," she said, and handed me an envelope.

"What is it?"

"A gift from Larry."

I opened it and saw two things: a letter and a memory card. I pulled out the card.

"Is this what I think?"

Tina nodded, biting her lip in excitement. "He put it in a safe-deposit box the day before he died. The instructions were to send it to me if anything happened to him. A last bit of insurance. I guess he liked me after all, eh?"

She smirked and told me to read the letter, which fleshed out the things we already knew.

He said he got the blackmail idea when he sensed that his position in the firm was precarious. Kate had cut him out of a lot of projects, including the representation of the New Petoskey Resort and Spa. He knew the mayor had taken payments before, like some other judges, and started to wonder if Kate planned to fix the big case. He started tracking her and pretty soon found her at the Lighthouse Motel. He took the incriminating pictures, saving them for a rainy day. When she edged him out of the firm, he decided it was time to collect on his lottery ticket. Mitch was just the front man, a disposable guy Lovell could use to keep himself anonymous.

Between the letter and the pictures she had gotten from Lovell, Tina had more than enough to write story upon story about the scandal. They started coming the next day.

Kate Warne and Corbett denied it all. They said it was a bunch of made-up lies, but within a day after Tina's first story, it was already unraveling for them. Kate Warne is on her way to getting disbarred. The sheriff is clinging to his post, but he might have to resign, too, because Tina has written about him being in Duncan Woods when Lovell was shot. I had the proof of that on my camera, but my lawyer made me turn the pictures over to the police. When Tim releases them to Tina, it'll really be over for the sheriff and Kate Warne.

A bunch of papers from downstate picked up Tina's stories, but the *Detroit News* and *Free Press* didn't come calling like she thought they might. When they talk about it on television, most of the commentators say there's something weird about a reporter trying to figure out a murder on her own, especially with an eighteen-year-old kid. There's always a hint of sexual activity in their comments. I saw the *Eyewitness News at Seven* the other day, and it was pretty blatant. A psychology professor from Michigan State University was comparing Tina to one of those female teachers who seduces her sixth-grade student.

My mom snapped the television off and said that I shouldn't listen to any more garbage like that.

The only thing she hasn't written about is Mitch Blaylock's murder. For that, she needs me to go on the record, but I'm not ready yet. I wish I didn't know, but I do.

It keeps me up at night.

36

"You know the Hippocratic Oath, right?"

My dad was reading Emerson in his study. His leather bookmark was sitting on the desk, glossy in the lamplight. He slid it inside the Emerson and rested it slowly on his lap. It was two thirty in the morning. Nobody in the house was getting a lot of sleep these days.

"Not the actual text, but I know what it is."

"Dr. Mobley had it up in his office. In a frame."

My dad hummed, biting his top lip, like he sensed dangerous territory. "Have a seat. Relax."

The cushion wheezed as I sat. "You know the start of it: 'Do no harm'?"

"Sure. 'First, do no harm,'" he repeated.

"I know something, Dad. Something about what happened. I can't figure out what to do."

He set his book aside. "Because you think it'll do more harm than good?"

"Yeah. It could ruin somebody's life."

"This isn't something you want to share with me, is it?"

"Not really."

My dad sighed. He pulled two cigars from his drawer and told me to follow him out to the backyard. I think it was supposed to be a man ritual of some kind, but I told him I'd pass on the cigar. "Don't blame you," he said. "These things aren't that great."

"So, what do you think?"

"I think you probably know what the best thing to do is. And if you don't, find someone you're comfortable talking to about it. It always makes things easier. Maybe Tina."

"Mom would kill you for saying that."

He laughed. "Maybe. Ah, no. I think she likes her, actually. You just have to give your mother a little time."

"Yeah."

We let it go at that, and I waited out there with him until he stubbed his cigar out and put it in the trash can. "It's three o'clock in the morning," he said. "Do you think you're going to be able to sleep?"

"Maybe."

He opened the screen door, hinges creaking, and stopped to let me in first. "So, do you have a plan to get out of your quandary?"

"I'm working on it."

The next day was my first time out of the house since the shooting and before I left, my mom hugged me tight and told me to be safe, don't be too long, bring a friend back here if you want to. I kissed her on the cheek and walked out the front door. The camera crews had pretty much given up by that point, so that wasn't a problem.

Tina met me in the parking lot of the New Petoskey Resort and Spa. I was just going to show a picture to Buddy, that's all, but I wanted her there with me. Maybe I was still feeling a little shy toward the world—my face had been plastered on the *Courier* for days before Tina started writing up her own stories. But I hadn't asked her just to have some company out in public. If I was right, Buddy was going to tell us who did it.

She parked alongside me and gave me a hug when we got out of our cars.

"So?" she said.

I pulled a piece of paper from my pocket. I'd gotten Daniel to print it out from the Petoskey High Web site. When I handed it to Tina, she just stared. "Really?"

"Yeah."

Dana's Jetta sat in the driveway, the only car there. I prayed that her mom, the mayor's wife, was at the hospital—this would be hard enough without facing her. I walked up the path to the thick double doors.

Dana answered with a mask of sleep over her eyes. I'd shot her father, and there I was. I thought she might just close the door back in my face. "Yes?"

Her stereo was on. You could hear it in the foyer, a tinny hip-hop song lost in the elegant space.

"Dana . . . I . . . I wanted to talk to you, if I could."

304 ♣ JOHN C. FORD

"I'm leaving for the hospital in ten minutes." She said it coolly and then retreated inside to the stairway, where she'd left a pair of shoes. She watched me as she put them on—I think it was her way of telling me I could come inside.

I stepped in, remembering that evening at the scholarship ceremony. The painted walls in the foyer were hospital clean, like they had been assaulted for days with Formula 409.

"Why are you here?" Dana said. I couldn't have blamed her for being resentful at my presence, but she seemed more curious than anything else.

I could have danced around it, but there was no point. "I know you killed Mitch Blaylock."

"What?" Only a slight uptick in interest registered in her voice. She rested her elbows on the stairs and looked at me full on.

"I know you killed Mitch Blaylock. It's what I've been doing this summer, figuring out who killed him."

"Wha—" She tried to gather herself. "What do you mean?"

"I saw his body in the morgue, and I found out that Dr. Mobley had been paid to cover up his murder and rule it a suicide. By your dad."

She listened to me calmly. "And you're saying I killed him?"

"I know you did. Mike's been trying his best to protect you, but I found the blackmail pictures at his place. It didn't make sense to me—Mike had no reason to kill Mitch Blaylock. But your dad couldn't have done it, either. If he had, he would have recovered the pictures."

"So . . . this leads to me somehow?"

I was a little thrown—she was staying even, not fighting me on it. It was like she just wanted to hear a story.

"Yeah. You're the girl that Mitch was with at the Country Club the night he died, weren't you?"

She just stared at me, betraying nothing. I already knew it was the truth—Buddy had confirmed it when Tina and I showed him the picture.

"I thought it was this other woman, who's actually in Texas now. She said it wasn't her, but I never really thought it was important," I said.

"Just tell me why you think I killed him," Dana said a little more sharply. Her jaw was jutting out protectively.

"It was Mike. I kept wondering how he'd be involved in this thing with your dad." I should have seen the link back when I found the pictures, really. It was obvious. "You're the only connection between them, Dana. You killed Mitch, took the pictures, and went to Mike's place that night. That's where you go when things are bad for you, I know."

She wasn't responding, but once I'd started, I wanted to get it all out there.

"The sheriff stopped your car on way out of the Lighthouse—somebody saw that, but I never connected it to you before. You told him what you'd done, didn't you?"

She folded her arms across her chest. "Just go on," she said.

"The sheriff's sister was being blackmailed by Mitch, so he would have wanted Mitch's death kept quiet just as much as your dad. So they organized the fake autopsy with Dr. Mobley. I thought they'd done it all to cover up the bribery that your dad and Kate Warne were involved in. But they did it to protect you."

That's what the sheriff and Mobley had been talking about when they called Lovell's death *different*. Dana was just a girl—they were willing to protect her. But the mayor shooting Lovell was a different order of things.

I kept talking. "That's how the pictures got to Mike's, right? You left them there that night—you probably never wanted to see them again."

"He was supposed to destroy them," Dana said. Her head was down—she was talking like I wasn't even present. When she picked her head up, I saw that she'd given up entirely. She almost looked relieved.

"Did you even know Mitch before that night, Dana?"

She closed her eyes, shutting out her pain. "Barely," she said in a small voice. "I'd see him around, that was it."

"He started talking big to you, right? Telling you about his scheme." She must have realized in the bar that Mitch was blackmailing her own father. "Why'd you go back to the Lighthouse with him, Dana? To protect your dad, right? To get the pictures and get rid of the evidence."

It was so sad, and strangely hopeful, how she and her dad had done these terrible things for each other.

"You didn't plan to kill him, did you, Dana?"

"Of course not," she said quickly, and looked back up at me. "I convinced him to show me the pictures, and then I tried to take them and get out of there." She left it hanging.

"But he fought you," I said. "And he had a gun in his room. You got to it first, I guess."

"Stop." Dana was staring upward, biting her thumb. "Just tell me, what are you going to do?"

"I really don't know. I've been trying to figure that out," I said.

She nodded. "Well, let me know when you do."

When I left, her eyes were wide, fixed on the bright white paint of her ceiling.

37

We sat out on the Maskes' porch and drank smoothies. Strawberry Fields again—it was getting better. Mike had listened to the whole story. His face grew heavier and heavier as I told him about Dana. I asked him if he'd known all along.

"Maybe, in a way. She never said so, but she was crazy that night. She's right, she told me to throw that card away. It was such a weird thing to ask that I had to look at them." He shrugged. "I know, I shouldn't have. And then when Abby told you about Mitch having the pictures of the mayor and Kate Warne, I knew. I knew what she'd done."

I spent the rest of the afternoon there, wanting to feel the comfort of our friendship. I waited for our old patterns to peek through the awkward haze left by Dana Ruby's crime, but it was too much to get past. It was going to take more than a few hours—it might take years.

When we finished our smoothies, Mike asked if I wanted a beer. I didn't. He got one for himself, cracking it loud, foam dripping down over his fingers and onto the ground below us. The sound of the can opening echoed in the woods.

He was halfway through when I called my parents to tell them I was at Mike's and would be home in an hour. I'd just hung up when my cell rang, a number I didn't recognize.

"Hello?"

"Christopher?" It was Dana, and she'd been crying.

"Yeah, it's me."

"Look, could you do me a favor and come to the hospital? I'll meet you at my dad's room, okay?"

It was the last place I wanted to go, but Dana was barely hanging on. "Yeah, sure, I'll leave right now."

"It was her, wasn't it?" Mike said.

I nodded. We never hugged good-bye, but we did it that day, strong and fierce.

She stood in the hall outside his room, and even from there you could hear the bleeping of machinery keeping him alive. He was under a blue sheet, his body lumpy and lying awkwardly on his side while a nurse tended to him. Dana's red eyes watched sympathetically.

Seeing her cry, you'd never know how mean that man had been to her. And still the two of them had ruined themselves for each other.

"If I don't tell what happened, people will think he killed Mitch, too, won't they?"

"Maybe," I said after a time. She still wanted to protect him. There was hardly anything left to protect—he already had been disgraced by taking the bribe in the golf-course case. Everyone knew that he killed Lawrence Lovell. He had no honor to speak of, but Dana wanted to save it. "To tell you the truth," I said, "I'm not sure people will care much about who killed Mitch. Nobody seemed to, this summer."

"You did."

I nodded. "I did."

The nurse exited the mayor's room, her rubber soles squeaking down the long hall. Dana waited for her to disappear around a corner.

"I want to look in on him," she said. "After that, if I wanted to go to the police station, would you go with me? I don't think I can do it by myself."

"Yeah. I'll go with you."

She asked for fifteen minutes, and I didn't want to sit there hovering. Or maybe it wasn't that—maybe I knew what I was doing. I drifted down the hall, then down the dark stairwell, and I was looking at the yellow light against the frosted glass of the morgue entrance.

A shadow bobbed down the hallway, growing larger as it approached the door. I held my breath as it creaked open, and there he was. Dr. Mobley, laboring forward, his cane in one hand and his brown briefcase in the other. He stopped at the sight of me, paused, and turned to lock the door.

He slipped the key off his chain with a slight tremble in his hands. His cane wavered uncertainly in the air while he did it.

He steadied himself and gave me a respectful nod. "You should know," he said, "that I've worked my last day." It sounded like an apology.

"I'm sorry," I said.

"Don't be sorry," he said, and teetered past me up the stairs.

After a moment I followed, and found Dana outside her dad's room.

"Let's go," she said.

38

I never tried again to get the black-and-white picture I had wanted so much at the beginning of the summer. The one out by the lighthouse, with the waves swimming in the moonlight.

I go out to the bluffs, the place where I got Daniel back. There's a rocky beach underneath, with smooth stones and good quiet for thinking. The best part of the bluffs slid into the lake, but it's still impressive out there—on a good night the cliff wall will catch the sunset, sparkling orange and red and pink. It's a good break from the sessions with the shrink.

Sometimes I think about Dana. She's under eighteen and it looks like whatever happens, she's going to have a life.

There's lots of other stuff to think about, too, like what the dorms are going to be like. I've decided to live on campus after all, even though my parents may hire a SWAT team to follow me around, protecting me from the world and vice versa. Or I think about Tina and hope she doesn't take another job. She's been getting a lot more calls about jobs since her stories broke. I overheard Tim telling her about this position with the Detroit police force one day. Tina had her cell on speakerphone, and she shut him up real quick, trying not to look at me. I give it about a month before they end up down there together.

Sometimes I don't think at all. I bring my camera with me and just take a lot of pictures. Daniel still hates most of them.

It's a good place to let your mind go. I can sit on those rocks on the beach for a whole afternoon, just feeling the big presence of the cliff above me. The air is still, because the cliff shoulders the breeze. I wait there until the sun goes down, and then I pick up my camera and go back into the world. There's stuff to do out there, like getting Julia back.

ACKNOWLEDGMENTS

Thanks to my sage editor, Catherine Frank, whose large reserves of insight, care, and red ink improved this book beyond measure. Thanks also to Kendra Levin at Viking for astute reading and much-appreciated good cheer.

I could not dream of a better tour guide to the world of publishing than the wonderfully supportive Sara Crowe, literary agent par excellence.

I began writing *The Morgue and Me* in a workshop at The Writer's Center in Bethesda, Maryland. I am grateful for that remarkable institution, the instruction of Daniel Steven, and especially the friendship of writers-in-arms Barb Goffman, Tim Jungr, Mary Nelson, Carolyn Mulford, Laura Durham, and Elizabeth Frengel. Elsewhere, Laura Caldwell and Mindi Scott gave keen-eyed readings to early drafts that had no business being inflicted on them. Many thanks.